LIFELINE

A novel

Dave Borland

Ideas into Books®
W E S T V I E W
Kingston Springs, TN

Ideas into Books®
W E S T V I E W
P.O. Box 605
Kingston Springs, TN 37082
www.publishedbywestview.com

ISBN 978-1-62880-218-4

First edition, May 2021

Cover design by: Raven OKeefe

Printed in the United States of America on acid free paper.

CHAPTER ONE

It had taken quite a long time for Jamie Sloan, a retired architect, to come out of a shell after Louise, his wife died ten years ago. Louise had been the most important person in his life and when she went her way quietly one Sunday morning, Jamie was devastated. For the next few years, Jamie struggled to begin a new life, minus Louise, by continuing to work, but picking jobs close to Pittsburgh by assisting the primary architects. It took his mind off how drastically his life had changed. Over the last nine years he kept working off and on, until he realized he was tired of working on projects which he had always loved. Fortunately, as he tried to figure out what he could do of value for himself he found two great part-time volunteer jobs at the Carnegie Library because of his love of books and at the Transplant Center at the University of Pittsburgh Medical Center Hospital because he admired how they had saved a college friend with a liver transplant. Gradually over the past months his life became full again as his volunteer work became important to him and he knew he was contributing to both important elements of life at the library and the hospital.

It was a new day for Jamie, and he spent a three-hour session at the transplant center entering patient medical information into the data system. It always gave him a good feeling because he knew he was helping the center, but more importantly for people who were going through a life-threatening experience. When he finished his work, he left the hospital and began to walk down to the Carnegie Library, not to work his volunteer job, but to do one of his favorite things, which was to peruse books. Over the weekend he decided to pick out some books on travel to the British Isles and especially Scotland, something he had been toying with for years. As he walked down the steep hill towards 5th Avenue, he thought of his work at the transplant office, he realized how much he enjoyed the mental challenge at his age, because it tested his brain capabilities which he knew he needed. He wasn't ready to hang it up, to use an old expression of years gone by. As he reached Fifth Avenue, he thought of his other volunteer work at the

1

library. Both jobs made him continue his methodology of when he was working, which was he was always well organized. His weekends over the past years were just times of walking or reading, plus an occasional movie if there was something palatable to his narrow, grownup, old fogey tastes. As he got closer to the library, he thought back to his recent urge to travel to Scotland, where his ancestors resided many centuries ago. His also noted how his walking was steady today, not bothered by his arthritis in his knees and he actually jogged up the wide stone steps of the library's entrance way.

He was soon immersed in books he picked out, one a pictorial of the islands off the coast of Scotland. Another had been of interest to him because he remembered a letter his grandfather had given his Dad who had passed it on to Jamie. It was about their ancestral habitat on an island, a name he couldn't remember, after moving in the early 1800's from Ayr in southern Scotland near the English border. They lived on the island in almost seclusion. His grandfather had been born there but had been sent back to Ayr to go to school and then off to Edinburgh for his university training, as he called it. He came to Pittsburgh in 1887 and worked for an uncle in the steel industry who worked in the offices of Andrew Carnegie a fellow Scotsman. Pittsburgh in the late 1800's was the melting pot of melting pots, as thousands from Eastern European countries and Ireland, joined the already entrenched Scotch, Scotch-Irish, and Germans in Western Pennsylvania. His grandfather eventually worked for a new company, U.S. Steel, formed when Mr. Carnegie sold out to begin his philanthropic enterprises at the end of his life. When his father was thirty-six, the year World War Two ended, Jamie was born and spent his entire life in in the City of Three Rivers, except time spent overseas doing architectural projects. The City was literally in his genes and he loved this small town of a city. But, for the last few months, he was taking a fresh look at his life and for some reason, Scotland seemed to be calling him. He had spent time in London as an architect but had never been in Scotland. He had started reading through books about the islands off the coast of Scotland and just the other day, he'd found family references to Ayr, Scotland. So, between, possibly going to the islands and Ayr, he was seriously beginning to plan for a trip.

As he sat there turning pages in a book with colored maps of Ayrshire, he felt like someone was watching him and he looked up to see the smiling face of Rachel, a new bartender from his favorite bar, McDonough's, looking down at him.

"My God, for a second, I thought I hadn't paid my tab or something," he said, sitting back and looking at her bright face.

"Oh, Mr. Sloan, I just wasn't sure if it was you. Things are different behind the bar and in this well-lit library."

"Jamie, for god sakes. Have a seat or are you off to somewhere?"

"Sorta in a rush. You know I just saw your badge, so you must know the Library pretty well."

"I do," Jamie replied and laughed, fingering his badge, "I volunteer here and always wear my badge because it gets me discounts at the coffee shop," he paused and added, "So, can I help you find something?"

She came over and sat down next to him. Jamie moved the books he had in front of him and turned to Rachel.

"Well, I'll make a very long story, short as I can. I'm looking for the section in the Library that covers how you find someone."

Jamie didn't respond, but straightened up in the chair and said, "Well, there are several areas that you could begin with, one probably not here in this room but upstairs and the other in that iPad you probably have."

"I have tried and so far, all I got was White Pages and other sites, but I needed an exact date of birth, spelling of the whole name and some address, none of which I have."

Jamie said, "Well, yes, that is the basic stuff for people who have records available. That's the usual information. So, you have none of that?"

Rachel's soft face changed to a serious look now; the brightness and pure beauty of her facial structure were tight and then Jamie could see tears forming in her eyes. She reached up and slowly wiped them from under eyes. Her head lowered and he knew she was quietly sobbing as her body tightened.

Jamie reached over and patted her shoulder. Then he said, "Hey it's okay, Rachel. It's okay.

Rachel sat back up and took a handkerchief out of her purse, slowly wiped her cheeks and said, "Oh, God, I'm so sorry. You have only known me for a couple days and here I am blubbering away"

"Blubber young lady, blubber away. I have blubbered in places worse than this, believe me. If you want to know, next time at the bar ask me and I'll give you time and place of when and where I blubbered."

She laughed a good hearty laugh that made Jamie feel good.

"That's the way, just laugh a bit. Much better than blubbering," he said.

Rachel reached over and gently took hold of his left hand. "Thanks, it's just that I am at a loss about something and I think it has finally gotten to me."

"Well, how much time do you have?"

She laughed again, the same hearty laugh as before and said, "Well, not much time today, but maybe, some time, some day we can sit down, and I'll explain what I am trying to figure out. Even right here would be perfect."

Jamie replied, "That's a deal. I am here during the week as a volunteer, so any other time that is good for you, just let me know." He reached into his wallet and pulled out a small business card. "My email and cell phone number are on this card, so if there is some time you want to meet here, I can show you upstairs where you can get information that might help you to find history of someone locally. If not here, I have other sources."

Rachel slid her chair back and stood up, then looked down at him with a querulous look on her face, "Out of curiosity, Jamie, how old are you?"

"Why are you proposing?" he said quickly with a smile.

Her same laugh erupted. "Well, maybe. I have always liked older men."

"Well, honey, you might break your record with me."

She leaned over and kissed him on his cheek, "I think I have. Now back to business. How about tomorrow afternoon, right here?"

"Well, that will work. Any change, just email or call me. I'll just be here whenever you say."

"Two o'clock?"

"Perfect, with bells on."

"My God, I can't believe you are going to help me. I just feel I…we will find him."

"Him?" Jamie asked.

"My Father."

"Your Father?"

"Yup."

"You don't know where he is?"

"Nope, I have never seen the man."

Jamie sat there a bit stunned. "Oh, wow. That is really something, Rachel," as he paused, then added, "Well, Inspector Clouseau, at your service."

She laughed that laugh again which made Jamie laugh.

CHAPTER TWO

Jamie got around town on buses using his Senior Citizen free pass. He could get anywhere. When he went to the Pirate games, he'd take a bus into town and then get on the "T" subway system. He had a ten-year old Ford which sat behind his apartment house in a parking space. Rarely did he drive anywhere. He'd left the library after talking with Rachel and taken a bus out to his neighborhood. Up ahead was the Café Latte, his favorite haunt for just sitting and pondering the world, his, in particular. He loved the ebb and flow of customers, mostly ones just beginning their lives at the universities or a few old codgers like himself, just filling time, or people meandering outside on the sidewalk. As he walked along today, he suddenly laughed to himself as he thought of the word codger, he had just thought of. Jamie was an aficionado of the derivation of words in the English language. To him, following how a word was created over the years, centuries in many cases, by people speaking, changing and updating meaning and pronunciations, was a science he was fascinated by. 'Codger', he thought, where in hell did that word come from and decided as he walked along, that when he was at the library next time, he would find out. Ahead he saw the sign of the Café Latte and he hustled up to the front door. As he reached for the handle, the door swung open and a swirling bunch of students poured out, jabbering away and laughing, all in the same boisterous explosion. Jamie stood back as they bustled out onto the sidewalk without even noticing that he was holding the door for them. 'So much on their minds," he thought as he went into the coziness of the coffee house.

He waved to Denise and Betty, the usual waitresses, as he headed to his favorite table next to the window. As he pulled back the chair and sat down, he knew he was a voyeur who loved to watch the world pass by and let his mind weave around whatever it decided to bring to his attention. He ran his hand threw his gray, but still bushy hair, as he settled into his position that gave him both a view of the shop and with a slight turn of his head, the sidewalk. Across the way at the counter Betty, who had become his favorite waitress gave him a wave and lifted her hand in a sign of "you want a cup?". Jamie waved back. He leaned back in the chair and turned to look onto the sidewalk which was usually a busy stretch. This coffee shop was not far from Jamie's apartment and in a busy section between Shadyside and the East Liberty part of town. It was a changing neighborhood, a mixture of the long time African American community of East Liberty right next to the historic, upscale Shadyside neighborhood. He loved the urban mix that was full of excitement of races and religions now blended with new restaurants and bars that was making his old hometown of Pittsburgh a hot spot for young entrepreneurial types. He thought of his younger days of running amok in the Shadyside bars of the late sixties listening to the great Harold Bettors at the Encore. He grew out of that quickly when one night, he met the most beautiful woman in the world, his Louise. She stopped him literally in his tracks and he didn't waver from then until the day she died.

"Here you go, big shot," came the deep vocal thrust of Betty as she put the coffee down on the table. "Anything else?"

"No, my dear. That will do it for now and thanks so much," he smiled at the big woman who had become his chatting friend.

On the table, next to him he saw a folded New York Times. Jamie reached over and picked it up and spread it in front of him. The headlines were the usual dire status of our country and the world with a couple exceptions that seemed to be the papers topical flavor of the month, which was anti the current President, who was obviously not to their liking. He always read opposing viewpoints so as to either confirm his own beliefs or garner some insightful information that might make him change his opinion. He had always been like that; ready to listen or read opposite views because there were times when he found information that proved his position wrong. Not often, but he always was open. The usual, China, North Korea, Iran and Russia, topics had no counter viewpoints, but the role of government in solving all the ills of our country was the consuming thrust of the Times. They believed that was governments' role, while Jamie did not. He felt our country was losing individualism which created the vibrancy of America. Help people who needed help, no question, but they needed to also aspire to helping themselves. Dependency, as in drugs, created the inability for people to be able to decide for themselves, positively, how to lead their lives and ones that were dependent on them. Of course, deep down, he knew there were so many that never had a chance and it seemed like a problem that would never get solved, democracy or no democracy. 'It is the dilemma of these times and all times', he thought as he turned to the Arts Section.

"Hey, you old seducer," came a familiar voice.

Jamie looked up as his glasses dropped on his cheeks and saw a nurse from the hospital where he volunteered. "Why Sandra McDermott, what are you doing in my coffee shop?"

"Didn't know you owned Café Latte, Jamie?"

"Well so to speak. Sit down, got time for a cuppa, as they say in the old country?"

"I do. A quick one, so to speak," she said a quick smile crossing her face as she pulled out a chair and sat down.

Jamie looked over at the counter. Betty was on the phone, but the barista working, a new guy with a humongous beard, waved back.

"So, what is all this sexual innuendo I'm hearing."

"What the hell do you mean?"

"Seducer, a quick one so to speak."

"Jamie, your mind is in the gutter," Sandra quickly replied then added, "That's okay, you are the macho guy in our lab. All the ladies want a piece of you, Jamie."

"That's about all they would ever get, is a piece," he said laughing at the innuendo, then he went on, "So, my dear, what are you doing in this neck of the woods?"

"I am looking for an apartment."

"Why's that?"

"Bert moved out on me. In fact, he moved out of the 'Burgh. Went to Florida. I think he got a babe in the bargain."

"Oh, I am so sorry, Sandra. The man has to be nuts."

"No, just forty-five and horny."

"Jesus, what about the kids?"

"Well, both went to Pitt and have good jobs, so that's not a problem now. Their doing great, but I don't know, I guess it is just the times. Jesus, I thought we were doing really okay. I mean, I have twenty years in at the hospital and he was still working for the furniture company where he's been for over twenty years. He said they bought a company in Florida and they asked him to go there and run it. Of course, he didn't tell me about the secretary who is also going to Florida to set up the office and I guess him, at the same time."

"What a bitch," Jamie said.

Betty came up to the table and brought Jamie a refill. "Whata you have, hon," she said in her Pittsburgh accent.

"I'm buying Sandra. Get a latte or something special, please."

"You don't have to Jamie."

"I do."

She looked back at the counter and said, "I'll take one of those vanilla latte combos I saw on the board when I came in."

"You got it, hon," Betty replied and went back to the counter.

"Okay, now, Sandra McDermott, let's talk about you."

CHAPTER THREE

When Jamie asked for Sandra to talk about her situation, he didn't realize it was going to be close to an hour before she literally stopped in her verbal tracks, looked at him and said, "Jesus Christ, Jamie, have I been blabbing away for almost an hour?"

"Fifty-five minutes in…ten seconds," he replied, looked at the clock across on the wall of the coffee shop. "Now," he said with a laugh and looked across to Sandra who he could see was crying.

"I'm so sorry, Jamie. So, fuckin sorry. It's just that…

He interrupted her and reached over to her arm, tapped a couple times and said, "For God's sake, Sandra. What you just told me is awful. Terrible. I feel so bad for you. The kids. Have you talked with them about how you feel about all this?"

"Not really. I mean they're both pissed off at him for what he did. They're furious and don't even want to talk to him…," she paused and went on, "but they have been great with me. Shit, as I said, they have good jobs and Mickey just had his first kid, a son. Millie is engaged and is getting married next summer, which I am really excited about," she paused, then added, "I guess what he did is just the way it is today, isn't it Jamie?"

He pulled his hand back, took a sip of now cool coffee, and said, "Oh, I don't know. Some men, when they get in middle age, for some reason think their pecker is all that matters in this world. It is a soft, then hard muscle that spews sperm. Period, that's what it does. Babies are created from that sperm, but the physical and mental release for some men overwhelms the reality of love, companionship, respect…all the real things in this world."

"Wow, you sound like a psychiatrist. Can you explain what you mean?"

"Sure, I mean both men and women must take responsibility for their actions. People buy because of advertising, right?"

"Yeh, I guess. So, what does that mean?"

"It means if a man or woman flaunts themselves to the other sex, then they can or should be partially responsible for the ultimate result."

"You lost me, Jamie."

"When you were explaining the situation you find yourself in, you talked about how you and your husband were in a period of your lives where you both were bored. That's the word you used, bored. So, you both were looking around for...excitement, I guess is one way to describe it."

"Well, yah, I mean Mike worked all the time and when he was off, he had his bowling, hunting, fishing with the "guys", which was his favorite way to spend time off the last couple years. Me, I worked every day and then volunteered at the Goodwill, plus I spent time making dolls, which I sold. Quite a few, actually."

"What about your kids?"

"Well, as I said, Micky's married and doing very well and Millie works at PNC with marriage coming up this summer. I mean they got their own lives. I spend time with Mickey's family, especially with the new grandson, but you know, Mike never got too involved with Micky and his family.

Then it was quiet. Both lifted their coffee cups, hers was empty. She licked the whipped cream off the edge while Jamie lifted his cup and emptied the dregs of his coffee. Both put their cups down in unison and looked up at each other. Still nothing.

Finally, Jamie said, "Okay, now what?"

"What do you mean?"

"I mean what the hell are you going to do now?"

She looked at Jamie with a surprised look and smiled weakly, saying, "Well, I guess I am going to just get on with my life, Jamie," she said quietly as if punished.

"For god sakes woman, you have got so much going for you. You have a great career in medicine. You are well respected in that field. You whole life is ahead of you. Now is your chance to sing in the chorus of the Pittsburgh Opera, for God's sake."

Sandra looked at him in disbelief. She smiled slowly and replied, "How did you remember that?"

"I may be as old as your grandfather, but my memory is still excellent. The first time I met you at the transplant service, you told me in the first five minutes of our conversation that your dream had always been to sing in a chorus of the Pittsburgh Opera. You told me you had sung for years, at school, in church and in a rock band in college. So now, Sandra, my dear, is your chance. The Opera is always looking for good looking women to dress up in costume and sing in the chorus of one of their productions. I even know the guy that runs the place. He's an old friend," Jamie paused and then said, "you want me to contact him or better yet, you want to go with me?"

Sandra looked at Jamie and tears began to slide from her eyes to her cheeks. She took her right hand and wiped them, a smile slowly capturing her round, lovely face. "You remembered that?"

"I did, so?"

"So," she paused, "Ah, yeh, I'd love that," she quietly responded with a questionable smile on her face as she didn't believe what she had just heard. Then she softly added, "You would do that, for me?"

"For sure, I'll set it up. How about you send me an email in the next day or so when you can go to a rehearsal. I'll reach out to Peter, Peter Olzewski, he's the guy, and we'll go see him. Okay?"

"Okay," she quickly responded. She reached over and took Jamie's hand, "You know something, you are a knight in shining armor?"

"Yeh, that's me. An old seventy plus knight. Just goes to show you, Sandra, one's never too old to make a difference and you, my dear, deserve that chance. I can't wait to see you belting out an aria or something. " Jamie looked at his watch, "oh boy, gotta get going, Sandra, my love." He slid his chair back, stood up and walked around to Sandra. Leaning over her, he kissed her cheek. "Send me that email and we'll go to the Strip where the Opera is located."

Sandra looked up at him as a smile spread across her face and with arms outstretched, she sang loudly up into Jamie's face, "Oh, Jamie, oh Jamie, what you do to me. Oh, Jamie, Oh, Jamie, my knight in shining armor. Oh Jamie, Oh, Jamie" and she started to laugh as the others in the coffee shop began to clap and shout, "Oh Jamie, oh Jamie, more, more."

Jamie was filled with joy as he wound his way to the front door between young folks clapping her singing. As he reached the door, he turned and waved to them. When he walked out of the door feeling so good inside that he had made Sandra happy and vowed to get her in that chorus. As he walked down the sidewalk, he realized how every time he did something to help someone it brought such a great sense of accomplishment.

It was late in the afternoon when he got to his apartment. After he got settled in, he went to his computer to look up the upcoming schedule of the Pittsburgh Opera and saw that "La Boehme" was their next production in April. He thought they would need a chorus for that one. He sent Peter an email asking for some time to talk with him this week, if possible. He went to his chair in the living room to rest his tired body. He knew tomorrow would be busy because he was switching volunteer hours. The transplant service had texted him asking him to come in tomorrow, which he agreed to, and then he would go over to the library afterwards, to begin a search for Rachel's father. 'Where in the hell should he begin,' as he reflected on how strange it was that in just a day, he had become involved in helping two young ladies literally find themselves: one a father and the other her life's dream. 'Why did this happen, he wondered?' as he pushed himself up and headed back to his bedroom.

CHAPTER FOUR

The transplant waiting room was jammed with new patients and family members, and transplanted patients. Jamie had to walk through the center to get to a corner of the research office where physicians analyzed all types of medical data on transplanted patients. Their job was to study the results and look for trends, especially if a new drug or procedure change had been implemented. The latter didn't happen often and was closely monitored, but patient reactions were vital to determine if the new medication or procedure caused any positive or negative effect on the patient. Jamie collected and entered data in the system so the physicians could analyze it. He enjoyed the work because it had meaning, and he was only there three hours, usually on Tuesday and Thursday, but many times they asked him to switch like this day due to either an increase or decrease of incoming patient data. The work he did excited him because he was volunteering for one of the finest transplant services in the world. Jamie was so grateful that the hospital volunteer service believed he could help. He knew what they did extended so many lives, and his volunteering certainly was extending his by doing this critical work.

Jamie's morning had been non-stop, and it was close to one o'clock and he had to leave. He finished up entering the remaining data, closed his computer and headed out of the office. He had to meet Rachel at the library in an hour. He grabbed a coffee and a bagel with cream cheese at the coffee shop in the library, sitting down with a paper that had been left on the table. Jamie glanced at the headlines, then quickly folded it in half and put it back on the other side of the table. 'Same old shit,' he thought.

As he sat there, he looked about the library café and was fascinated, as an admitted observer, watching people winding their way through life. He was always amazed at how everyone thought their life was unique, which it was, but he contemplated how all that mental energy expended by each human on our earth must be an overwhelming energy force in our universe. Billions of energy cells flowing constantly must be an unqualified power difficult to comprehend by the world's scientific geniuses. He often thought of things out of the box and the energy of humanity was one he pondered. 'Am I a nut case or not,' he thought, then laughed out loud.

"Hey, Jamie, you buying? Jamie came out of his mental reverie and looked towards the bright voice and saw Rachel wending her way across the open floor toward his table. "Name your poison, Rachel."

"Kidding, of course. Want something else?"

"No, I'm good."

Rachel went up to the counter while Jamie leaned back into his chair. He looked at this beautiful young woman with her whole life ahead of her. It was times like these that he was driven out of his daily physical and mental modus operandi of just living his life; of just getting up, looking around, realizing that he was still alive, breathing well, and realizing he had another day to experience what life was all about. He had lived most of his life, in essence, while she had it all in front of her. 'The way age is expanding, she'll be close to the next century when she is my age,' he thought, smiled and then wondered would this hundred and thirty-year old Library still be here? Would they still carry thousands of books? Would everything be either in everyone's' brains or in some type of miniscule disc with no need for books or covers? This last thought made him pause with his thinking. 'Glad I won't be around.' Rachel walked over with her large coffee and what looked like a bagel.

She looked at him, "Jamie where you been? What have you been thinking about?"

Jamie smiled, "Oh, I was just looking a bit ahead in time. I was wondering if this old library will still be here when the 22nd Century comes around?"

"That's quite a long time away," she calmly replied.

"Well, you will be close to a hundred in age, which at that time will probably be normal, assuming there is still an earth." He looked at her and smiled, "Just kidding, Rachel. But you are a healthy woman and by that time, I'm sure people will be living well over a hundred years."

She looked him, smiled slowly and said, "You know Jamie, I asked to see you today to talk about, guess what, today. I appreciate where your mind may wander to. I can understand that, but I gotta pull you in and back."

"I'm back, Rachel. My mind often wanders around." He sipped again and said, "Okay, let's go find your Father."

They were at the library for hours until she had to leave to begin her shift at the bar. Normally she started at 3PM, but she switched with another bartender so she could meet Jamie and was going to work a night shift. During their work, a plan was created that would include Rachel having a DNA test. Jamie had read that in many cases it helped to locate parents. They had also pulled out City Directories for the area in Pittsburgh Rachel believed she was born in, looking for clues from a few names that she had picked up over the years.

Jamie stretched and said, "When I go home, I'll get on my computer and do some digging around. I have five spellings of what his name might be. Michael, the first name and Collins, Cullens, Cullen, Killen, or Kellens. All you know is that you Mother called him Mike and you think she said Collins or something like that. A truck driver, right?"

"She said he drove long distances and one time he just never came back. I was about two years old at the time and Mom died when I was twelve without telling me hardly anything about him. There was no marriage license or bills…nothing except a neighbor who told me when I was in high school that he was Irish or Scotch or something like that, who drank a lot of beer when he was around which wasn't very often. My grandma met him one time and she died before I was even interested in finding him which by the way was only when I started college. I kept my mom's name, Cochran. Still do."

"Okay, get going and I'll start working on it. Do I have your email address?"

"Yeh, it's on here," she replied as she took a card out of her wallet and handed it to him. "I can't thank you enough, Jamie," as she paused then said to him, "can you do me a big favor?"

"Of course, whatever you need."

"Would you keep this to yourself. Don't tell anyone, especially at the Pub. I don't want anyone to know, if that is okay."

"That's a good point and mum's the word as we used to say."

"Thank you and I guess you could change that to dad's the word," she said with a twinkle in her soft, lovely face.

"Even better, dad's the word," as Jamie slid his chair back and stood up slowly, stretching. He closed his leather notebook, zipped up his jacket as Rachel gathered up her purse and put on her backpack.

"I'll email you when I have something, and we can meet again. Is that okay with you?" he said as he tapped the table.

"Perfect, Jamie, perfect", as she stepped back and took off through the room to the front door of the Library as Jamie watched her disappear.

'What a great kid,' he thought as he headed for the main hall. The bus was on time and he sat by the window. It was one of his favorite past times, to look out of the windows of either the buses or subway cars he rode and observe life on the streets. He loved the solitude of his rides because his mind could wander all about, whether at the people on the street or across from him sitting alone deep in their own thoughts. What really got to him was what looked like the disparity of so many people. 'Disparity', he thought, 'what a strange word'. He knew it meant inequality and so much of that had been created when the City of his life had gone through difficult times when it's driving force, the mills, had disappeared.

Jamie noticed a black couple across the aisle, probably in their fifties, dressed almost in rags. He turned slightly and the two, a large breasted, narrow faced black lady in a yellow jacket that barely covered her body sat next to a wide faced, dark skinned African American man. Jamie kept looking at the man because he reminded him someone, he knew from a long time ago, but couldn't think who it was. The two didn't talk; they just sat there looking straight ahead 'Why is there so much unfairness, so much fucking disparity in this fucking world", he said to himself.

Another night of frozen dinners and five minutes of the news featuring gun shots and political mumbo jumbo sent Jamie to an early trek to his bedroom. He lay thinking of all that he had to do with his new ventures and his mind drifted between finding a man somewhere in the country for Rachel, to hoping he could get Sandra an audition which was his last train of thought as he drifted away. Some time in his sleep he dreamed of walking into an old red brick building in a run-down part of town and coming up to an old friend of years ago, Sam, the Marine veteran, who was sitting on what looked like an old barber chair. He threw that wide smile at Jamie and yelled, "Where you been man, where in hell have you been?" which made Jamie awake in the darkness of his room. "Whew, that man's face on the bus was Sam's", he muttered out loud, "that was too real".

CHAPTER FIVE

It was just another day, but when he got back to his apartment, he was whipped. Everything had gone well with no surprises, but it was nonstop from an extra-long session at the library as he tried to complete a new project given to him of an important section on the Hill District of Pittsburgh, which was an important and historical section of the City. The "Hill", which was what it was called, was a mixture of immigrants from all over Europe and a special place for African Americans from the South, who were able to find work in the booming industries of Pittsburgh in the early days of the 20th Century. As he ate his dinner and tried to read a National Geographic magazine, he realized what his body was saying to him, 'Old man take it easy on me'. He went to bed early but as he lay waiting for sleep, he began to think again of Sam; Sam Westfall, the African American whom he had dreamed about the night before. He was a man that had such an impact on Jamie in his young life decades ago. If Sam was alive, he would be eighty or more. Sam's life story as Jamie remembered, drifted through his mind. He was a man who had nothing at birth, yet, as far as Jamie knew, when he met him, he had created a purposeful life after serving in the military. He was raised by his young mother and her mother, never meeting his father. Where is Sam now, he wondered? Is he even alive? For some reason, he vowed to find him. He had to see how this fine man was faring all these years later. He helped Jamie once, maybe saved him from harm and he vowed to find Mr. Samuel Wescott. He had ended up working with Sam as he was building his architectural career. He had never forgotten what this Marine veteran was trying to do for African American children in the poorest neighborhood of Pittsburgh. He could still visualize Sam's broad, dark face with a smile he couldn't forget and wondered if he somehow continued doing what he seemed to really love doing as his life's work for young people. He would try to track him down after all the intervening years since Sam had literally come into his life out of the blue and saved him from potential great harm.

He lay there remembering the day when it happened forty years ago. At that time Jamie was working for a small firm doing grunt work for the top two architects in the firm. His main job was gathering data on the sites they were working on like water levels; mining that had been done underneath the properties; and all the other details that must be known before a building can be designed. It was a very hot summer day in August as he would never forget, and he was walking through some vacant land and buildings along the riverbank in the South Side of Pittsburgh. There were railroad tracks back about fifty feet from the shoreline which apparently were to be moved. He remembered he found it hard to believe because there were two sets of tracks. When he asked Mr. Duncan, the big dog in the firm whom he worked for, about the double tracks, Duncan told him that the C & O Railroad had agreed to merge the tracks with ones that already ran alongside Mount Washington. Apparently, the other lines were now part of the same conglomerate so the lines along the river could be taken out. It was a coup, no doubt because it opened up a vast, empty space for construction and Duncan & McKenzie had the contract to create new apartments and retail outlets along the river. This was big stuff for that time, the seventies.

The heat was unbearable, and Jamie was plodding over cement blocks and railway lines in disrepair when he suddenly heard a noise beside an abandoned cement building to his right. He stopped and as he did two black guys came around the corner of the building, stopped, laughed and came up to him. They said something to the effect, "What's you doing here, white trash?" or something like that. Jamie didn't say a word but looked around. "You goin' run white boy? You know no white guy can outrun a black man, so do us a favor and give us all you got in that fat wallet of yours," said the biggest of the two with a smirk across his broad face Jamie would never forget.

The second one, who didn't say anything, came up to Jamie. He was thin, much shorter than him, but wiry with no smile on his face, just dark black eyes that penetrated him. "Give me all that shit you got, fairy face," he growled at him. Jamie replied that it was just architect's stuff and they laughed, obviously having no clue what that meant.

The big guy came right up to him and grabbed Jamie, throwing him to the ground. He turned him over and began to frisk through his back pocket and finding his wallet, he yanked it out and opened it. He pulled out two five-dollar bills which was all Jamie had, causing him to kick him in the groin so hard that it caused him to stop breathing. The next thing he knew they both were on top of him, kicking and punching him and slowly he faded.

As if in a dream sequence, he suddenly heard grunts and oofs and someone yelling. "Get your nigger asses out of here before I kill's you both, you dirty motherfuckers."

Slowly Jamie opened his eyes and looked up into a big black face with wide open eyes looking straight down at him.

"You okay buddy?"

Jamie couldn't say anything but nodded his head and tried to pull himself up. The man said, "Take it easy. Just stay calm. Those fuckers are gone and they ain't coming back."

That's how Jamie met Samuel Wescott. After slowly walking to a diner with him, they ended up talking quite a while over lunch. Jamie remembered so well what he learned about this man that day and the days after he spent with him those many years ago.

As Jamie continued to think about Sam and his life which he learned about the year he worked with him. Samuel Wescott, born Samuel Abraham Lincoln Wescott, was raised in the Homewood section of Pittsburgh. As a little boy, Samuel lived with his mother and grandmother, no daddy about. He was a strong boy and stronger young man, so much so, that after high school, he got a scholarship to Pitt and played two years of varsity football, even went to New Orleans to the Sugar Bowl. Sam had always wanted to go into the Marines, which he did after he graduated from Pitt and had quite a military career. His first years were in post-war Korea and then Viet Nam and then to various assignments all over the world. His last assignment was at the White House, where he served as a Marine liaison. When Sammy was discharged, he was only forty-one. He had twenty years in with the military, a college degree from Pitt, and was married to a French woman he had met while stationed in France. What did he want to do with his life was what he asked himself the summer he was without a job for the first time in twenty years? He went back to his roots in Homewood and was appalled. The area had disintegrated. Empty houses; weed filled lots; hoodies walking around acting tough and mean; and people scared to be outside. He was taken aback and depressed about the conditions he saw. After a few weeks of snooping around, he realized that many of the young girls had kids just like his mother and that most of the fathers of those kids never came around, just like the father he never knew. The girls were getting welfare for the children and the boys who had penetrated them and deposited their sperm inside them, just walked around with guns and sold dope, mostly to white people who drove through looking for a fix. It was a nightmare for this strong and responsible man. He decided that he knew his next mission in life. He would set up some kind of assistance program for young black kids and their mothers, especially the single ones. He worked at a bar and went to classes on the GI Bill at the University of Pittsburgh on starting a new business. Over the first year he looked all over Homewood for a place to work from and finally found a vacant building centrally located that he thought he could fix up. He visited the schools to explain what he wanted to try and start. Sam, who looked like a pro football tackle was received with a lot of skepticism which only made him work harder to get his concept up and running. In the meantime, he hunted down families that just needed handouts of food and some medical needs which he bought from his own money. It gave him an insight into how bad it was for so many young people, both children and especially young mothers with no support from errant fathers.

Samuel slowly began to go to meetings around Homewood, from church groups to City meetings trying to assist families. He got a few mothers and students to help him create a volunteer organization to set up a list of families in Homewood who were in dire need of help, for food, medicine and clothing. He also tried to help some young black boys who were on the fringe of gangsterism to try and find a way to keep them interested in something else, like playing basketball and touch football. Sam's goal was to try and lead them out of the wilderness of their neighborhoods. At first, the young black boys were skeptical of this old Marine snooping into their lives, but he was successful in first helping a few young boys. The gang element in

Homewood didn't threaten him like they first were doing. He tried not to police them, just offer help to some of the young boys he found either in the street or through some helpful teachers in the schools. He got some grants to help him, plus developed a strong volunteer force of single mothers and church members, to scour the alleys and back yards of the old, rundown houses for people living in despair and they found plenty. Even the single mothers, who were reluctant and distrustful of Sam at first, finally came around.

How Jamie had met him was pure luck and so fortunate for him. For some reason which Jamie never did ask, Sam was in the South Side of Pittsburgh that day. He was out of his bailiwick of Homewood, but the ex-Marine was still on duty as he quickly dispensed Jamie's assailants. Sam helped Jamie up off the ground and after shaking off his clothes, asked him if he could buy him a burger which he agreed to. They spent hours at a small burger joint, looking at the Monongahela River flow by and just talking. He gave Jamie a brief resume of his military career, but mostly he talked about how he was trying to save young lives, both male and female, in his neighborhood of Homewood. Sam gave him a quick history of Homewood which had gone from one of the most elitist places to live in the late 1800's when the likes of Andrew Carnegie built a home there and many of his business cohorts followed suit as Homewood was a place for the very well to do. It took about a hundred years for Homewood to deteriorate into a ghetto type neighborhood with over 90 percent African Americans as all of the while folks had long moved. It suffered like the rest of Pittsburgh when the mills closed, but as Sam explained his mother and grandmother stayed put, raising him as best they could. He then asked Jamie what he did, and he told him he was an architect which seem to give Sam pause, as he then asked him if he could give him a tour of Homewood and look at some of the derelict buildings he was uncovering. Jamie said he would like to do that, and they phone numbers. Jamie asked Sam if he wanted a ride home and Sam said that a bus would be fine, and they parted ways as he walked down to the corner to a bus stop. Over the next year, he worked with him and he was amazed about what he discovered in the old rundown Homewood. He couldn't believe some of the hidden treasures of homes built at the beginning of the Twentieth Century that were falling apart, but repairable.

Jamie looked back on that year as an exciting time, as over the year, he helped Sam create a foundation to buy three old classic homes for just a few thousand dollars which he designed to be rehabilitated. Within a year they were completed, and both sold which provided some badly needed money for Sam's work. Unfortunately, Jamie's architectural job became too much to continue helping Sam, as his company began to ask him to travel all over the country and overseas on new projects. He called Sam many times, but eventually he completely lost track of him and his work. Now, almost forty years later, as he now had time, he began to think of that man in Homewood and decided he had to find out if Samuel Wescott of Homewood was still alive. If he was, he would be in his eighties and if so, Jamie vowed to go find him.

He lay there and thoughts kept coming to him and for some reason he remembered another event of years ago. Clearly, he remembered a beautiful spring day at McConnell's Creek, a fast-flowing stream north of Pittsburgh. He could see the event as if it was happening and he couldn't figure out why except that it involved Warren Decker, who Jamie knew in high school and was now a national political figure. On that day a young girl drowned in the fast-flowing stream and Jamie saw Warren, a football star in high school, just watch her go. It had always bothered him because Warren was literally the big man on their high school campus, and he did nothing to try and save the young girl. Jamie was a friend of Warren in high school, but after graduation they went their separate ways. Warren became extremely successful and wealthy. Currently as a Pennsylvania Senator, he was a prime candidate to be running for President next year. Jamie helped Warren and his wife Margaret put an addition on their home near Fallingwater a few years ago. He could never get the nerve to ask him about that day. When he read about him and saw him on TV, he could not get that spring day out of his mind and why he didn't try and save the girl in the creek. He thought it strange how events of long ago were finding their way into current thoughts as if they were unresolved situations of a long time ago. It was odd because in one situation, it was about Sam, who worked to help young children survive and the other about Warren Decker, who Jamie saw not trying to help a young girl who eventually died as she floundered in a creek right in front him. Jamie believed there had to be reasons for these thoughts recurring about Sam and Warren. Something was telling him to find resolution about them both.

As light from a streetlight filtered in through his window, he groggily laid with his head buried in his pillow and his mind that could not stop, began thinking again about Sam. He would be seventy-five in a month and he guessed, if Sam is still alive, he would be eighty-five in December. His birthday, he could never forget, because it was on Christmas Day. He was ten years older than Jamie and about a hundred years brighter and God knows how much more now, if he is still alive. What in the hell could have happened in forty-years? Let's see he thought Nixon, Reagan, Bush 1, Clinton, Bush 2, Obama and now, incredibly, Trump and maybe Biden. As a Pittsburgher; six Super Bowls, a couple of World Series and a bunch of Stanley Cups, plus the incredible rebound of one of the world's great cities. Jamie knew much about the latter, because he had designed five classic buildings in that time frame around the rivers here. Oh, and twenty or thirty around the world. Oh, what a braggart, he thought, but where in the hell is this man from his past, one Samuel Wescott.

He looked over at his clock. It was close to 1 o'clock. He turned over in his pillow to try and sleep. His last thoughts were about Sam and Warren, as his thoughts slowly faded and he slowly fell into a deep sleep.

CHAPTER SIX

The next morning Jamie woke up in a calm mood after his late-night thinking about Sam and Warren. It seemed to generate a sense of how important it was for him to find out where Sam was, if he was still alive and maybe contact Warren, which would be difficult as the man was a powerful man in Washington, D.C. As he lay there, planning his day ahead, he decided the best and only thing he could do would be to concentrate on searching for Sam. He got up, did his morning rituals, and dressed for work at the transplant service. There was some time left before he had to leave, so he went into his living area with a yellow legal pad, along with a couple sharp pencils, which were his tools when he did any kind of research or planning work.

With his computer in front of him, he searched Google to find information about Samuel Wescott. Ten names came up and one man was in his eighties. He typed the name in Google where he found a reference and picture of a man who had written stories. Jamie looked closely at the picture, but the face of the man didn't look anything like what he thought Sam would look like. This Sam wrote stories about places he'd been and places he still wanted to go to before he died. Jamie kept looking at the picture of this very dark man; his eyes were the key and then, he thought maybe it was him. He got up and went to a wooden cupboard in his living room and pulled out three leather picture albums. It took him quite a bit of time to go through the pictures because he had just stuffed many of them in the folders and had never taken the time to put them properly in the album. As he opened one stack, he saw it, the picture he could never forget of the lady who had two grandchildren and was taking pictures of them in Schenley Park one summer afternoon. It was about a month after the incident when Sam asked Jamie to join him for lunch and take a hike through Oakland. Jamie remembered he had dressed in jeans and a sweatshirt and they had lunch at a burger place in Oakland. After an hour or so of just jabbering away, Sam asked him if he was ready to start their walk through Schenley Park, that he was tired of sitting there. As they walked, Sam leading the way, they continued to talk about many things. After a while, they sat down at a wooden bench in the park and that's when they saw a lady taking pictures. Jamie remembered Sam yelling over to her to see if she would come over and take their picture. She came over to them, asked them to slide closer together and carefully snapped a couple pictures. She asked Jamie for an address which he gave her. Two weeks later he got three pictures that she had taken. In a week or so after that, Jamie stopped by Sam's building where he organized his work details and gave him copies of the pictures. Sam smiled as he looked at the pictures of them with their arms over their shoulders. Over the ensuing years, somehow, Jamie had misplaced two of them, but right now he looked at the one he liked the best. It was a great picture and he had to see that smile again. The more he looked at the picture and the guy in that Google picture, he was sure it was Sam. There was no personal information in the article, only that he had been in the military and had taken lots of pictures while in the service.

Jamie checked the time and realized he better get moving if he was to get to the hospital on time because he wanted to do a quick stop at Café Latte, his morning work ritual. He was quickly out the door and, on his way, zipping up his rain jacket as it was grey, and rain was falling lightly. In a short time, Jamie was sitting at his favorite table looking out at his favorite street in his favorite kind of late winter weather; gray and windy. As usual, pensive, Jamie began to think about himself, his own life. His first train of thought came up with the fact that at this stage in his life he had done just about all that he could possibly do. He stirred the coffee, even though there was no cream or sugar in it and gazed out into the slanting rain now pummeling the street outside. As he sat staring through fogged up window of the cafe, his mind began drifting until he was startled by two young people across the store, probably in their early twenties, who were laughing uproariously over some video on a blonde girl's iPhone. Of course, Jamie knew it wasn't a phone anymore, it was a media monster that brought the world between inches in the palm of one's hand. The boy had doubled up in hilarity and his blonde partner kept clicking on new visions and sounds of absolute goofiness that kept them rollicking in humor.

Jamie who had turned from the rainy window, now looked calmly with a smile on his face at young exuberance. Suddenly the boy looked at his watch, jumped up, followed by the young girl and they began to pack up their respective belongings. They snapped shut their phones; zipped up their jackets; adjusted their head wear and headed for the door. Their comic relief was over, and it was on to their current life's work, probably classes at the Academy across the way. Not a care in the world; their whole life ahead of them and Jamie suddenly felt hollow inside and a tightness gripped him as he had deep, negative thoughts about the world they were blindly heading into. A pessimist or just an old man. This was the question he wrestled with daily as he, the older soul, who still read the newspaper, but now only three days a week and watched some of the news of this media driven world on TV. He saw them go out the door and followed them as they ran across the wet street. They disappeared into the door of the building of their school, continuing their life travel. He mused about their age and his own, smiled slowly, took a sip of coffee and put his cup down.

Jamie kept looking at the rain swept street, then sat up, looked at the wall clock and realized he had work to do for the two young ladies after his shift at the hospital. He stirred his coffee and thought how lucky he was they had come to him for help. This would get his mental wheels turning for two ladies smack damn at the early stage of their lives. 'Jesus,' he thought, 'I got to get going to help them with what I promised'. He finished his coffee, stood up quickly and said out loud, "Super, got to get moving," causing several customers to look over at him as he headed out of the coffee shop. He looked up the street as a 74 bus was wending its way down the puddled street.

The visitors lounge was crowded at the transplant office. His mind was still racing with all that he suddenly had on his plate and his volunteer work which had really been a blessing. 'Wow', he thought as he walked into the volunteer lounge to get his jacket on. He was really excited about all the avenues of life he had to walk down in the coming weeks. When he signed a deal in Tokyo over twenty years ago on a bank building, he was exuberant then about what he was doing with his life. It had been exhilarating to see his design exciting people and this moment was similar; he felt reinvigorated about helping the girls with their lives. He was in a great mood as he worked his way to where his desk was located where he would sit doing his work.

Jamie got to his area and went over to the nurse's message center where he pulled out a stack of medical records that he needed to enter into the patient's file. It was a noisy, busy location with nurses, doctors and administrative people going this way and that in this hubbub of saving lives. He remembered talking with one of the nurses about a patient that he'd seen arrive, who was jaundiced from liver disease and apparently only with months to live. She told him that was a normal body reaction to their disease. Weeks later he happened to see the same patient who had been transplanted and he was amazed by their natural skin color. This atmosphere of assisting these patients made him feel positive about doing something to help them. He never felt his time was wasted, just the opposite, that not only were the patients getting a new lease on life, but he was also.

"Jamie", he heard. He turned and Victoria McPherson pounced on him holding out a piece of apple pie. "Take this, Jamie, it's my fiftieth birthday today and the docs pulled a surprise party for me in the nurse's room."

"Well, Vickie, my God, fifty. You don't look a day over seventy, if I say so myself".

This rotund, vivacious lady roared back at him, "Jamie you, old bastard. You always have a comeback. Here, have some of this pie, it is delicious."

"Thank you so much. Funny thing I was just inputting medical reports on some of your patients. You have been busy, Vickie."

"Nonstop, old boy, nonstop. Thanks for all you do, Jamie. You are most appreciated, believe me."

"I appreciate being here because it does so much to help me feel like I'm helping you all, in some way."

Victoria patted him on his shoulders and moved on down the hallway. "See you later, Jamie and thanks again." Jamie went back to his computer.

He finished his work at the transplant center and lunch at the hospital cafeteria before walking down the hill to the library. He had found an isolated area off of the main collections section where he could plan and work quietly. For the first few minutes he sat and wrote on his legal pad. In front of him was a Webster's Dictionary and he remembered the word codger which he wondered its derivation. As he read the history of the word, he laughed quietly because it described himself, "a character, an odd ball". He looked at the yellow pad and began to write down things he had to do; wanted to do; and should do. Then he just sat there, staring straight ahead. Two different problems to solve; one might be easy but his calls to Peter at the Pittsburgh Opera had not been answered or returned. He may have to go to the Opera Center to catch him so he could find out when he could talk to him about how Sandra could try out for the chorus. She had mentioned to him that she was practicing tonight with her church choir, so he thought that maybe he could stop by to hear her sing before talking with Peter. So that was a plan for Sandra, but how even to begin to search for Rachel's father? That was going to be really tough. Where in the world should he start?

Over the next couple hours, he scoured through Pittsburgh records of Collins, Cullens, Killen, and Kellens with a first name of Michael or Mike. He found about fifty names and narrowed it down to about twenty within a potential age range with what he guessed would be close to Rachel's mother's age when she was born. Rachel was now twenty-five and her mother was thirty when she was born as guessed by her daughter because her mother never talked at all about her birth. By five o'clock he was tired. He put his legal pads and pencils into his leather portfolio and left the library. He walked in his vigorous manner so he could get the most out of the exercise for both his body and his heart. Jamie was feeling better about his life now than he had since Louise died and was as excited in a way like he was years ago when he was scurrying around designing projects whether here or elsewhere. He seemed to now be thinking every day about all he wanted to accomplish in his lifetime. Would it be twenty more, ten more, or next week? 'Christ', he thought, 'enough, just keep moving, thinking and filling time with fulfilling projects, concepts, and get back to writing that book that had been evolving around in my brain for years.' "Wow", he said out loud, as he rounded turned the corner of Fifth Avenue just about hitting three young women coming down the street. "Oh, God, I'm sorry, ladies, the old boy is daydreaming."

They laughed and went on their way to the intersection. Jamie watched them never stop talking and looking at their iPhones as they crossed the street without looking for traffic. He shook his head at their lack of precaution and headed towards his apartment when he had an idea that one of the regulars McDonough's Pub know something of Sam.

CHAPTER SEVEN

Jamie pushed in the heavy oak door and saw immediately that the bar was jammed with an assortment of old timers he recognized and new timers dressed in all the garb of now. As the door swung shut, he heard a couple outbursts of "Jamie" coming from, of course, the old timers and only a few turns of heads from the young ones. He waved at Tommy McNeill and Jerome O'Brien, two guys who lived most of their current lives on the padded bar stools of the Pub and who Jamie thought might know something about Sam. He walked up to these two and noticed two middle aged women next to Jerome's side of the bar stools.

"A couple of hot shots, if I ever saw any," Jamie said as he came up to them.

"Takes one to know one, old boy" piped up Tommy, as he hoisted a pint glass with foam halfway up the glass. "What are you doing here today, it's not Friday, or is it?", as he laughed looking at Jerome beside him as he added, "Some rough days for you?"

"Not rough, just a bit crowded," as he looked over at Tommy. "Looks like you got into a new keg, there, Tommy, old boy."

"New it 'tis, Jamie and you should taste it," he replied and then turned back to the bar and yelled, "Millie, old girl, give my man Jamie a new one."

At that point a young new one sitting at the bar on the other side of Tommy, a girl with flaming red hair in a bun on top of the back of her head, turned and got off her stool. "Here you go, sir. Have my seat, won't you."

"Oh, no, darling, I can't take a chair from a lass looking like you," Jamie said with a smile on his face.

The redhaired girl smiled broadly herself and replied, "If I didn't know better, Jamie is it, I'd think you were putting the hit on me."

The two guys, Tommy and Jerome, plus two girls sitting beside where the red head had been sitting, all roared in laughter. The red head then sat back down beside her two friends. It was a glorious scene of joviality. Jamie slowed down his laughter, patted the redhaired lass on her shoulder as he passed her and sat down beside Tommy, as a beer with a huge white foamy head was put on the bar in front of him.

"So, what's up, old timer," Tommy said, leaning down toward Jamie.

"Oh, keeping busy, with my two volunteer jobs, that's all. What's up with you?"

"Not much. Same old, same old," Jerome replied as he also took a sip then turned back to Jamie, "When you get our age, you never know. We're getting up there, old buddy."

"You're right about that," Jamie paused and said, "so guys it's good to be sitting here. Actually, I've really gotten back into a groove. My volunteer work at the Carnegie Library and at the transplant center is keeping me busy and I got a couple jobs helping some girls get some information." As soon as he said it, he realized he had better explain that one. Before Tommy or Jerome could respond, "Just some work at the library."

"Whooh, two young girls. Aren't you the ageless wonder," Tommy replied!

"Not me, I'm just helping them with a couple projects. One is actually trying to find her father and the other wants to sing in the Pittsburgh Opera. I know a guy for that one but finding the father for the other one is going to be tough. So, boys, I am keeping busy."

"Sounds like you are, my boy," Jerome said with a smile and trying to also stuff some pretzels into his wide-open mouth. He was a big man, with a barrel chest sprouting some gray hair peeking through the triangle of his t-shirt covered by a blue sweatshirt.

It was quiet for a few seconds as they all took sips. Tommy turned as a group of new customers came through the front door. "Here comes the army of young ones, guys."

Jamie looked at the young office types heading for tables, not for the bar. Then he thought of why he stopped in and looked at Tommy. "Hey, Tommy, back when you worked around town, did you ever come across a black guy from Homewood named Sam Westfall?"

Tommy looked first at Jamie and then turned to look at Jerome as the only noise came from the newbies giving their order to Millie. After another few seconds, Tommy leaned toward Jamie and said, "Had to think for a couple seconds on that one because when you said that name something hit me right away, but I couldn't remember why. But the more I thought about it, it hit me. Yeh, I know or knew the dude."

"Knew," Jamie replied immediately.

"I guess he's gone, but sorry, don't know for sure. Last time I heard about him, must have been five or six year ago," Tommy said.

"Where did you know him from?" Jamie asked.

Tommy replied, "I used to see him a while back at the veteran's club in East Liberty. I think he was in Korea."

"He was and 'Nam, for that matter. He graduated from Pitt and then spent twenty years in the Marines, even two years at the White House. But I knew him when he was just starting up a program to help kids in Homewood where he grew up. I helped him renovate some old houses he could use for some poor black folks who lived there. I lost touch with him when my job took me all over the world. When's the last time you saw him?"

"Oh, Christ, probably…at least ten years ago. I think he tended bar there at the vet's club, so maybe someone there might know something about him."

"Jesus, Tommy, terrific. Thanks so much. When do they open?"

"The better question would be when do they close. Open at seven in the AM and close at two in the next AM, at least that used to be their hours. I haven't been there in a long time."

"If I wasn't so goddamn tired, I'd go tonight. Think I'll stop by there in the morning before I go to the library. Jesus, thanks, Tommy." He turned back and looked ahead at the mirror facing him and smiled to himself as he realized that things are meant to happen and stopping in here meant he was to find out where he might find Sam. Jamie then looked down the bar and yelled at Millie. "Need a round here, my dear." He laid a twenty on the bar and slapped Tommy and Jerome on the back, waved at Millie and headed out, realizing that his schedule the last couple of days was a bit tough on his body, more than he realized.

As Jamie got to his apartment building, he realized he was too tired to go to Sandra's choir practice and he texted her from his kitchen. His evening was quiet as he had a microwave dinner and a show on Netflix he wanted to finish about a great detective in Sweden. He watched the program until ten and tapped to the local news. As he sat back, he saw a headline flashing across the bottom of the screen that he couldn't believe. It was a bulletin stating that Senator Warren Decker, born in Pittsburgh and a leader in the polls to be a candidate on the Republican Party for President next year, had died of a heart attack in Washington. Jamie was shocked. The man he had been thinking about over the past weeks, his classmate who had not tried to save a young girl in a creek, was dead. Jamie sat there stunned as the TV kept on going. He switched to CNN and listened to them highlight the career of Warren Decker, as they plied together highlights of his life. There were events he spoke at or interviews he had given over the years, and then several of him and his wife at the last Republican Convention. Jamie was absolutely in shock. As he sat there, he recalled his last time with Warren when he was doing the work for him near Fallingwater and how lovely was his wife, Margaret. She was a formidable woman and Jamie was saddened to think about what she must be going through. He would send a sympathy card with a note of condolences tomorrow.

The next morning, Jamie rolled over and checked the clock. He could barely make out the hands, so he pulled it off the stand, and saw it was almost seven. As he lay back down, his first thoughts were about Warren and realized that he hadn't been close to him since those days in school, except for the work he did at Fallingwater. The afternoon by the creek would never be solved or answered, so he should just let that memory slid away in peace, because it made no difference now. He realized he had to get up. As Jamie dressed and mentally planned his day, he decided to skip the Cafe Latte' and instead get a coffee at the Starbucks at the corner, then head over to the vets club where Sam used to work in East Liberty before heading to the library.

Coffee in hand, he felt really good and strong this morning, as he walked with a sun booming towards East Liberty. He could have taken a bus or Yuber, Uber, or whatever they call that new cab service. 'Give me a Yellow Cab any day' or better yet, my dear beloved legs', he thought as he crossed with a green light. He could see the beautiful East Liberty Presbyterian Church steeple rising up ahead. Based on what Tommy had said, the club was on a back street in the block opposite the massive church in the historic section of East Liberty.

It was a very old and dark brick building of two stories that had a narrow front door with a square glass opening about eye level. Jamie pushed the door and it opened easily. He looked in and it was like he was back in the seventies. The bar was big, old fashioned and it was dark, even though the day outside was brilliant. Band music played from speakers on the light green wall behind the wide wooden bar out of the twenties, he guessed. There were four old black guys at the bar, two slumped over and the other two yapping away with a wide screen TV blaring away from the same wall farther down the bar. A wall mirror covered the space above the bar, side to side, with a slanted crack going from bottom to top. There was no bartender. Jamie walked up to the guys talking and sort of waved a hello to them, but they paid no attention to him, they just kept talking and he thought he heard the magic word of the day, Trump.

Jamie walked to a bar stool near the overhead TV and flipped his leg over and sat down. The only sounds were coming from the TV game show and who he thought was a Pittsburgh singer of days gone by, Billy Eckstine's voice coming out of the speakers. He sat there for a minute and just looked around. There was a bulletin board at the side of the mirror nearest the door with pieces of paper tacked to it. Underneath the mirror were shelves of bottled booze of all different kinds and mostly the cheapest brands as far as Jamie could tell. Still no bartender.

Jamie sat there thinking of the times many years ago, when he would frequent a place like this when he was young. He always loved to just nose around places like this just to see how the "other "half" lived, as he would tell himself. The truth was he liked "slumming it", as the terminology went in those days.

Finally, one of the old guys at the bar turned toward and he looked at him and said, "Lookin for someone, boss?"

He realized one of the guys had asked him a question, so he responded, "Well, yeh, actually I am. I'm trying to find an old friend I used to work with, oh, forty years ago who I was told used to bar tend here years ago."

The guy turned all the way to face Jamie. "Who would that be?"

"Sam Wescott," he answered.

The man turned back and looked at the old, cracked mirror that he faced. Jamie didn't say anything. He waited as the man turned to his buddy next to him and leaned over, whispering. After a few seconds he turned back to Jamie and said, "Sam the Man. He's still with us and my friend here says he is still working in Homewood at the old fire station that he turned into some kind of place that helps the kids in that area. Joe, here, says he's had that going for as long as he can remember."

"You mean he's still alive?" Jamie surprised, responded quickly.

"Guess so. Only way you're going to know is to go over there, I'd say." At that his friend jerked his sleeve and he turned back, listening to his friend. After a few seconds he turned back to Jamie. "Seems the Mayor was over there a couple weeks ago helping them celebrate some new project. My man here also said he' thinks he's eighty-four."

"I can't thank you enough," Jamie said, paused and added, "I'm Jamie Sloan, can I buy you a drink for helping me?"

"Of course, you can, 'cept the bartender is down in the basement."

"I'll get it," said his buddy, as he slid off the stool and walked around the wooden bar. "Want something, Sloan?"

Jamie waved him off, "No, I have to get over to the library where I work, but thanks anyway," he said as he laid a ten-dollar bill on the bar. "That enough, guys?"

The guy closer to him said, "Yeh, that's good and thanks," as he paused then added, "Whata you do at the library, Sloan?" asked the guy closer to him.

"Oh, I just volunteer. Right now, I'm going through some old records," Jamie paused then said, "Keeps this old guy out of trouble."

"Trouble at your age, wow," said the other guy, who put two bottles of beer on the bar between them.

"Hard to believe, but thanks, you've been a big help to me. I'm going to look up old Sam later today." He slid off the stool and waved to the two who just looked at him as he walked to the front door. He took a couple steps and stopped, turned and went back to them.

"Forget something, boss?"

"No, I was just wondering if I gave you my phone number, you could pass it on to Sam if you or any of your friends talk to him."

No one said anything for a few seconds and then the bigger guy nearest to Jamie said, "Sure, man give it here. Maybe I'll find someone who knows where the old dude is."

Jamie took out his notebook and pencil, wrote his number on the paper, then handed it to him.

"I'll see what I can do and thanks for the beer," he said as he took a sip.

Jamie said, "Thanks so much," waved to them and walked out onto the street.

CHAPTER EIGHT

Later in the morning, Jamie was completely enmeshed in a new project at his desk behind the main desk of the library staff. Several times his mind flashed back to the news headline of the night before about Warren's death and he still could not believe what happened. He deliberately shut out those thoughts and went back to focus on the work in front of him which concerned a rich benefactor of over a hundred years ago who left three boxes of pictures to the Library that were taken in the early 1900's by an amateur photographer. The pictures were of the rivers of Pittsburgh, loaded with coal barges and of the buildings that made up the downtown of the early 20th Century. Jamie went through the boxes and was amazed at the clarity and specifics that the photographer, who he found out was only in his early twenties when he began his photography career. He spent the next hours putting the pictures into categories by Pittsburgh locale.

He was so involved with the picture project that he realized he needed to spend time finding Rachel's father and he remembered an idea that hit him earlier this morning. Several years ago, when the Post-Gazette newspaper was publishing seven days a week, he had met a lady who worked in the back room for reporters finding information on people and events of the past. He could not think of her name until it hit him when he was flipping over a picture of a boat on the Monongahela. It was called the Lady Jane, and, in a flash, Jane Nesbitt's name popped into his brain. She was a hardworking, resourceful woman who had five kids and was married to a guy since high school. At the time Jamie was doing a building project on the North Side and working with a real estate reporter to get background information on the site of the Olympic Building built in 1905. It was an extremely historic location and Jamie had promised the City and the local professional organizations that specialized in preservation, that his project would protect the building, in fact he promised and did just that. It was and is a beautiful brick edifice now being used as site for high tech internet equipment for a firm based in the Netherlands. It was one of his proudest accomplishments as an architect, but Jane

Nesbitt had been a life saver by coming up with terrific information, pictures going back into the 1800's on that location. She became a good friend, but he hadn't heard anything about her in years. She could find anything and so he decided to get a quick lunch in the cafeteria and contact Billy Andrews who still worked at the Post-Gazette to see if he could tell him where Jane was living since, she retired a few years ago.

As his luck had it, Billy was still working at the paper and gave him her phone number and email address. As he sat in the corner of the cafeteria area of the library, he called the number.

"Hello," came the familiar voice of his old friend.

"Janey, girl, it's your old architect buddy, Jamie Sloan."

There was nothing coming back at him, so he added, "Jamie Sloan, you do remember the Olympic Building?"

"Jesus Christ, think I need a beer, because this tea I've been drinking is doing things to me, 'cause I thought I heard this name, you say Jamie Sloan?"

"I did say Jamie Sloan, because it's him, me."

"I'll be a son of a bitch. Jamie, my God, it's been years. How the hell are you?"

"I'm good, really good."

It was quiet for a few seconds and then he heard her say, "You Jamie, I remember when you would call me at the Post -Gazette, you always wanted something. Never me, which pissed me off", as she paused then added, "so don't tell me you're calling me now after all these years cause you want something and I know for sure at our age it ain't me."

"Well can't say for the latter Jane, but I have to admit I thought of you because I am looking for someone, actually it's for a young lady who I am helping. She's trying to locate her father."

It was quiet again and then Jane said, "Well, I'll tell you what. I live on the North Side, and what you should do is stop by and tell me who you're looking for and I'll see if I still have it in me find him. My contacts at the PG are still there but I've become a wizard with my computer in my old age, so maybe I can just find this guy."

"When can I do it?"

"Best time for me is in the morning 'cause my brain is rested."

"How about tomorrow?"

"Ten bells would work for me."

She gave him her address and they talked for another few minutes and Jamie hung up, ecstatic because Jane would scour the internet or wherever she needed to find Rachel's father. 'Wow', he thought, that was a coupe' and then he realized he still hadn't been to the Pittsburgh Opera to see Pete about Sandra, so he decided to head out to the Opera center in the Strip.

It was late in the afternoon when he got to the Pittsburgh Opera's building and after he entered what look like a rehearsal facility, he saw Peter in the back row of the darkened space watching a screen with obviously a production number which Jamie did not recognize. He knew literally nothing about opera, but Peter had been a friend for years since they met on another project Jamie was involved in on an old theater that a small group had bought to make it into a theater for light opera productions in Squirrel Hill. Jamie and Peter quickly became friends, because even though Peter was an operettic music nut and Jamie had no clue about or interest in opera, but they both loved Baseball.

Peter was a tall man who played shortstop at Pitt and was even drafted by the Padres, playing two years in the minors until he broke his collarbone skiing at Seven Springs. He was never the same, baseball wise, but quickly switched his interest to his first love music, opera music. His mother taught music, plus he grew up listening to opera, which his father also loved. Peter had a great tenor voice and sang in high school and college even while playing baseball, which was a strange combination for a young man. Peter was hired by the Pittsburgh Opera about thirty years ago and worked his way up into a managing role which he still held. Peter worked on getting young singers into the Pittsburgh Opera career program which apparently, he was very good at, but his primary role was building the opera into a profitable enterprise which, according to what Jamie knew, he had. It had developed quite a reputation nationally and with his guidance, they built a separate facility not far from downtown Pittsburgh where Jamie was standing right now.

"My God, the real Jamie Sloan," came a brusque voice from the tall, now heavyset man with a silver and black goatee, mustache and horseshoe shaped curve in his silver hair sitting in the back of the darkened center. As Peter came down the steps and up to Jamie, he grabbed him and gave him a bear hug. "So good to see you, old buddy. Got your messages, but man I've so goddamn busy, sorry."

"Wow, still have the bear hug, Peter," Jamie replied as he stepped back and said, "no problem. I know you are a busy man, and it was good to finally get to your neck of the woods and get your infamous bear hug."

"You know me, full steam ahead. Say, you want a cup of tea or some wine? Got something over in my office."

"A little wine might be good. I don't want to take too much of your time if you're in rehearsal," Jamie replied.

Peter took his arm and they walked past some stage props into a dark hallway. "In here, Jamie. Grab a chair. I'll grab some vino."

Jamie sat on a heavy, dark leather chair across from Peter's desk, piled with files and pictures. He was back in a few seconds, holding a bottle of red wine and two glasses. "Some Pinot Noir, ok?"

"Perfect," Jamie replied. Peter put the glasses on the edge of his desk, pushing some files to the center. He poured wine in the glasses and went to his leather chair behind the desk, and sat like he probably always did. He leaned over and handed a glass across to Jamie who reached over and took it from him. "Ah, tastes good. What a treat. A good one and my old buddy, Jamie." He paused looked at Jamie and said, "Okay, what's up?"

For the next few minutes, Jamie explained his volunteer work and how he had met Sandra Cochran at the transplant center. She is a mom with two grown kids, a transplant nurse who works extremely hard, and with a husband who just ditched her. She is now wanting to do something she has always wanted to do. One major desire in her life."

Peter smiled when Jamie used the word desire and he smirked, "And it wasn't you, old pal, eh?"

Jamie smiled back and said, "No, it wasn't me." He then went on to explain how Sandra told him the other day about a dream she has had since she was a kid to sing in an opera. Even now, with her busy work schedule, she has sung every Sunday in her church choir. She mentioned that she read that the Pittsburgh Opera needed vocalists for the chorus to back up a production of the "La Boehme". Her lifetime dream was to sing for the Pittsburgh Opera, and she remembered me talking one day about going to the Pittsburgh Opera with my wife. She asked in passing if I knew anyone there that might help her get an audition for the chorus. Jamie then said to Peter how surprised he was by her question because of their old friendship and added, "So that's why I'm here, Peter old friend", as he emphasized old friend"

Peter looked at him for a few seconds and didn't respond and then quietly said "You know when I was a kid, about ten, I heard "The Four Freshmen" sing on TV and I was mesmerized by their voices. It was that moment that as a kid I knew what I wanted to do in life. I wanted to sing. So, when you tell me you got a woman, who has raised two kids, who sings in a choir and has always wanted to sing in the Pittsburgh Opera, I say to you, your timing is perfect, as we are having some potential chorus singers in here tomorrow morning to see if they can sing in our chorus. Tell her to be here at nine am sharp, okay?"

Jamie's leaned across the desk and put his hands on his shoulders and said, "Peter, my man, thanks so much. I don't know if she can because she works at the transplant service. but I will call her. She will be ecstatic. I can't wait to tell her." Jamie spent another half hour talking to Peter about their lives, mostly about his kids, who didn't live in Pittsburgh anymore; a daughter in Seattle and his son who was a singer working in London.

When Jamie left the Opera center, he stopped on Penn Avenue and called Sandra. He asked her if she could be there tomorrow morning at nine o'clock and she literally cried out that she had plenty of sick days and would be there. She couldn't stop laughing and crying at the same time. She was so excited and wanted to know what she would be singing and how many would be there, plus other questions he couldn't answer. He told her he had no idea and that he couldn't be there, but for her to just stay calm and follow Peter's instructions. He added that she should be there a half hour early and be ready to belt out some music. He couldn't help laughing at her complete happiness which made his day.

As Jamie sat in the bus, his thoughts went back to his meeting with Peter, which was so congenial and the outcome just perfect which made him feel good that it had worked for Sandra. He came out of his thoughts as he realized his stop was at the next block. He got up, grabbed the safety line and headed to the door. In a few minutes he was walking down the tree lined street with barren limbs still awaiting spring warmth. He felt good getting home because he was exhausted. So much had been accomplished in the week and there was so much more to do in the coming days. He sat watching the evening news, but soon his thoughts were about Warren again and he was truly sad that this man had died before he was able to achieve probably what he wanted to in his life. Earlier at the library he had picked up a Wall Street Journal that had a front-page article about his life and also quite a bit about his wife Margaret who apparently had a very independently successful life. He remembered the time he worked with her on the house near Fallingwater and how impressed he had been with her knowledge of architecture. She knew exactly how she wanted the addition to fit in to the very old structure.

That night Jamie slept so well that he again had trouble getting out of bed in the morning. Once he did, he spent the next minutes doing his ritual of stretches to keep his aging body as limber as possible especially with all that he had to do this day. Somehow, all he could think of, was getting a bus over to Homewood and seeing if he could find Sam. He thought back to how long ago it had been since he had been in Homewood. He'd read about attempts to rebuild the now predominantly African American community which had become one of Pittsburgh's poorest communities during a time when the City itself had been revitalized by new industries. Why old Sam might have hung around he knew would be a great story if he was a reporter for the Post-Gazette? Hopefully he was still there and alive and well.

Jamie walked out of his apartment building to make his ten o'clock meeting with Jane Nesbitt. After he was done, he planned on going to the library to pick up where he left off on the project which really interested him plus look up articles about Homewood where he might find some information about Sam. They were his two goals today. Walking was for him, like yoga must be to others; a time of peaceful rejuvenation from the noise of the world, of people, of just about everything in this day and age. He wondered why people have to make noise. Jamie could hear the different cadences of the birds. They seem to repeat their messages without any increased volume or noise; just communicating without the hysteria humans seem to create, just to make sure others around them, hear them as if to make them special. Jamie loved silence. He smiled, thinking of that moment when he will pass to a different modality, either something or nothing, yet it will be quiet, he was sure, no matter where death leads him. His smile continued as he heard a man shouting from a car that passed him. Jamie looked at the Caddie racing away down the two-lane quiet side street with the driver waving his right hand at a bump of a head belonging to an obviously smaller passenger. 'Power", Jamie thought. As he continued his trek that word stayed with him. Power over what? Your destiny? Your role? Your own viewpoint in the world you live in? People need or seem to need to know exactly what their role is in their environment. 'Why do they', he wondered. Why can't people just live their life, following the paths they choose, dodging here and there roadblocks and taking new paths when necessary without forcing others off the pathway. He loved his walks when he could just think and process this journey called life.

Jamie came to an intersection with the park to his left and across the way was a ballfield where he used to play fast pitch softball. He crossed over the street to the fence that surrounded the field. He stood looking at the field where he started playing during the summers in his early twenties as he began his work as an architect. The team was made up of young guys from a Presbyterian church that he attended at times. It was a time, when he was beginning his career, that he continued the Presbyterian faith in deference to his mom and not to his once a year, church going father. As he thought of the church, he remembered the repetition at the Presbyterian services when he was growing up. The same songs, every Sunday, it seemed, and the same sermons. The one highlight he remembered was the Presbyterian minister, Reverend James Donaldson who was the minister when Jamie was in high school. Reverend Donaldson was a man you could not forget. As Jamie kept looking at the ballfield, he could visualize this stocky man in his black outfit standing high above his parishioners; about six four and two fifty pounds, who continually pushed up his glasses as he looked down at his middle of the night written sermon. He was a common man, never overindulgent about living a life of purity, maybe because, he himself did not. The Reverend was a good man for a young man to talk to about one's future prospects in life because Jamie had no clue about what to do with his life, as if anyone at that age really does have control over their future existence. The Reverend had simply and repeatedly told him to try and follow his passion, whether it be work or finding a mate, which, as it turned out, Jamie had. When Jamie learned of his death in Palm Springs, California, years ago, he was saddened but always smiled when he thought of him because he was a good man; one of the good guys, as Jamie always thought of people who he felt were positive and helpful to others.

Jamie took a last look at the ballfield, turned and headed down the sidewalk. As Jamie turned a corner, up ahead he saw the apartment building where Jane lived. He felt good about being with this old friend and beginning his task of finding Rachel's dad. He knew Jane would lead him in the right direction because he had looked her up on Google and she was still working by writing articles for local magazines and national publications.

After having croissants and sipping coffee in her living area, they moved to her dining room table. Jane began in earnest to go through the information that Jamie had brought with him about the man who had many possible names. Jane began to work on obituaries, then trucking companies in the Pittsburgh area and then got into VA data, which listed people who had served in all the services. Based on Rachel's age, her father was probably twenty to thirty years old when she was born. She came up with three men who might fit the bill. The most likely suspect became Michael Cullens that she traced from the Army, to Continental Trucking, and to now living in Phoenix, Arizona, where he currently worked for a contractor doing logistical management for Amazon in the Southwest. She found out he had also gone to college at Arizona State, after being stationed there his last years in the Army. He had apparently never returned to Pittsburgh.

Jane learned he had a sister who lived in Penn Hills, a suburb of Pittsburgh and two brothers in California. But the really critical information was that Rachel had two stepsisters and one stepbrother. Jamie was amazed how much she had found out in such a short time and as he was leaving, he hugged Jane with a promise for lunch with Rachel after he told her of what she had found out. As he was about to leave he asked if she could check a man he was looking for in Homewood, Sam Wescott. She looked at him for a second and typed his name into her computer while Jamie watched.

"Well, there are a couple articles about Sam, a Marine veteran, who has been providing food for young black kids in Homewood for years. A couple months ago he was given some citation by the Mayor for the work he had done. Here's a picture of that meeting. Jamie looked at the picture and it was Sam, for sure. That same smile and his body was still large and wide as he remembered. She found several other references to Sam's work and one mentioned his grandkids who were now helping him. Another article was about some of the kids he had helped who were now working; having their own families; and helping Sam.

"He's quite a guy, I'd say," said Jane.

Jamie said, "Thanks so much. I can't believe he's still at it and still in Homewood. He is alive and well which is incredible, and I can't wait to get over there to see him again. Thanks so much, Jane for getting all this for me."

"It was fun and seriously, it was great seeing you. So glad I could still help you Jamie."

Jamie left her apartment, heading to the hospital. Thinking back to his meeting with Jane he was astounded about how much she found out and how quickly she did it. It is an amazing informational world we now live in. As a lover of novels, he knew that this story of Rachel and that of her father would have been a great plot to write about. He knew it was a great story and now he wondered, how will Rachel react and what could she really do. As he walked up to Fifth Avenue, he was filled with wondering, how will this man, a husband and father react if he finds out he has a daughter he never knew existed. Jamie thought that maybe he shouldn't tell her, but quickly dismissed this idea because all parties should know. He smiled thinking he's got so many stories developing especially after he gets over to Homewood to hopefully meet up with Sam. 'Now that is a story,' he thought.

He got to the hospital and was quickly immersed transferring data into the data system at the transplant center when his phone rang in his pants pocket.

"Hello," Jamie said, expecting a spam call which is usually what he gets when he heard a voice say, "Mr. Sloan?"

Jamie immediately knew it was Sam. He stammered, "Is this Sam?"

No response and then he heard the all too familiar voice of forty years ago, "I am as I have always been, Sam the Man," came the absolutely, exact voice.

Jamie stammered, "I cannot believe I am actually talking to you, Sam. I think I have already gone to heaven and heard from my first Archangel."

"Well, you ain't in heaven, 'cause if you were, you wouldn't being hearing this voice."

Jamie laughed and said, "Well, all I can say to you is I have to come and sit down and just talk with a man I have never, in all the days in between, ever forgot about. I am so fucking…pardon the language because you never did like swearing…but sorry, I apologize…but I am so excited to hear that voice I have never forgotten and a face I can't wait to see again."

No response for a few seconds and then, "Well, Mr. Sloan, I'd say it was time we had a visit. See what else we can do to this world."

Jamie was stunned as he listened and remembered the slow, deep voice of this man of so many years ago. Finally, he said, "I just saw a couple articles about you and you're still doing what you started all those years ago."

"Yeh, still at it my man, still at it."

Jamie stuttered a bit as he said quickly, "I have to see you, Sam. Where and when?"

Sam laughed and said, "Well, I got a class at 1:00 o'clock at my school over here in Homewood," he paused. "3:00 o'clock will work fine. If you remember how to get here?"

"Well, not quite but give me an address and I'll be there. Three o'clock will work for me."

"Sounds good to me, Mister Sloan."

"Hey, Sam, you started out all those years ago calling me Mister Sloan, but gradually you called me Jamie, which I insist you call me now. I know Jamie sounds like a twenty-year old, but James has never worked, so its Jamie, okay?"

No response for a few seconds and then the low, deep voice said, "See you at 3:00 PM", pause, then "Jamie". Another pause, "Can't wait to see you."

"Oh, the address?"

"How are you coming?" Sam asked.

"I'll be catching a bus from Oakland."

"Take the 86 and tell the driver you want to get off near the old fire station near Brushton. Got that?"

"Got it, and I should be there by three. I'll be the old white guy coming through the door."

Sam laughed that great laugh Jamie had always remembered, "Whoa, well I'll be the old black guy in the easy chair. See you then," he said, and the line went dead.

Jamie closed his phone and gave out a huge sigh as a smile came to his face. "Wow, haven't been this excited to see someone in ages."

CHAPTER NINE

Jamie caught a bus in Oakland which took him through an area of Pittsburgh he was only familiar with from when he visited Sam over forty years ago. It really wasn't that far from where he lived now, but throughout the ensuing years, he had never been back to the Homewood section of Pittsburgh. When he first met Sam, the area was still doing fairly well as the mills were still open, but even then, there was much rumor and speculation about the mills possibly closing, which they did. As he rode out Frankstown Avenue he pondered who he would find after all these years? Would he still be the hero, Samuel Wescott, he remembered, or would he have become someone else? Recently he had been thinking about Sam and Warren Decker for whom he carried different impressions over the years. Jamie was about to meet up again with Sam, so maybe this was literally a "meant to be" situation, which had become a favorite expression of his when life literally took one's life in its hands. Thinking about Warren, ironically, just yesterday, USA Today had a frontpage story on his recent death which included an interview with his widow, Margaret Decker. At the end of the article, Margaret Decker stated that she had no intention of being involved in politics as many reports had rumored. She clearly stated, she was going to devote her life to projects she had been involved with over the years that provided private funding to help the lower classes in the country. Jamie was very impressed with her philanthropic commitment to helping those in need. As he thought about what she had said in the article, Jamie thought how ironic it was that he was just about to meet a man whose life is devoted to providing assistance to lower class folks in the downtrodden section of Pittsburgh's Homewood.

Sam's address was an old, two story brick structure that was once the Homewood fire station built in the twenties. As an architect, he loved looking at old buildings of that era, mainly because they were built to last as they had. Jamie stopped outside on the crumbling sidewalk and just scanned the building which he could tell had recently been cleaned and windows replaced. The woodwork surrounding the windows and in the roofline was a deep red. It was an attractive building which spruced up the street filled with boarded up buildings. Jamie went to a heavy wooden front door and pushed it open. He walked into an office area with three empty desks with computers and hall that went to the back. He walked down the hallway and came to a door which he opened. A large, tall, dark man walked up to him. Sam's face hit him right between his eyes; he was magnificent. Older for sure, his gray hair telling the tale, but he was still trim, and his square shoulders were as if he was marching in a parade when he was in the service. The same wide smile that stretched across his face with deep, penetrating dark eyes that bore down on Jamie.

"Mr. Sloan, I presume," he said with that sly smile on his face.

"Sloan it is, but Jamie to you, old man."

Sam laughed, that laugh of his which Jamie remembered which was loud and rowdy. "My God, it is so good to see you, old friend." He grasped Jamie by the arms, then hugged him. His arms wrapped around Jamie and they stayed embraced until Sam picked Jamie up and held him off the ground. "Still got the arms, young man," he said as he laughed. Then he set Jamie down and stood back, "Well let's go back to my office and have some of my special Jamaican coffee. We got a lot of talking to, old buddy."

They walked into an office where a young woman of dark skin and deep black hair, was standing next to a brown skinned young man who Jamie noticed resembled Sam in body structure. Sam walked up to the two who stood almost at attention and said, "You two, I want you to meet an old and I mean old friend of mine from the early days when I had nothing except my military money and a lot of bills to pay for starting to help our young folks. He literally came to my rescue. Jamie, this is my granddaughter Germaine," he said holding her elbow.

"Mr. Sloan, a pleasure to meet you," the young girl with a beautiful smile replied. "Sam has talked much about you since you talked yesterday."

Sam then reached over and pulled the young man over to Jamie and said, "And this young man is, guess what, my grandson, Marty, named for guess who, Martin Luther King. Marty, Jamie Sloan."

"So great to meet you, Mr. Sloan," the well-built young man said as he grasped Jamie's hand tightly and with an almost identical smile span as his sister and grandfather.

For the next hour plus, they talked. His grandchildren had left and it was just Sam and Jamie sitting across from each other at a dark and ancient wide oak table as they talked back and forth. At first, a lot of laughs about when they first met. Jokes galore as Sam told one about Jamie talking to a preacher from a Baptist Church, the Reverend Leroy Collins, Jr. The Reverend constantly chewed out the white man, Jamie, because he was a big-time architect who represented all that his people didn't have. It took almost a year, Sam recalled, before the Reverend called Jamie, Mr. Jamie, which is an African American's way of calling a person with respect. From that day on, everyone except Sam, called him Mr. Jamie.

Eventually they talked about what each was doing now, in their older ages. Sam was adamant about his current school and self-help programs which he said had finally began getting grants. Just this morning they received a grant of twenty-five thousand dollars from a private foundation. Sam went on about how his program had grown over the years and how his current goal was helping kids find work after high school or college scholarships, if they wanted to go to college. He emphasized that this program was also being designed to assist young men and women, who had been incarcerated, learn needed jobs skills in the changing new world. Sam was adamant about how the country was changing with technology and there was a need for people who could work with their hands and minds, to create or fix equipment that is part of this country in this new world. Sam talked as he always did, in a slow, methodical, but always right on the subject matter. He talked slowly and meaningfully about the plight of his hometown when he got home from the service. It was literally coming apart at the seams. He smiled several times when he talked profusely about the kids of young men and women, he had pulled out of the maelstrom of extreme poverty who had succeeded in their lives. He was their surrogate father and now, as he expressed it to Jamie, he was the surrogate grandfather to so many kids. That was the highlight of their talk, as he expressed how thrilled he was by the lives of many of the children he had helped in the years gone by. He then expressed that for a long time he had concern about how the program would go one after he was gone. He quietly said to Jamie, that the two he had just met can do it and will do it. Then he said quietly when "I go I will really go in peace".

Jamie was most impressed about what Sam said as they were close to wrapping up. He got volatile when he said, "So many kids have no fathers," he had said several times. "These guys and girls think sex is just a plaything for them. Never changes, meanwhile babies are born, and fathers disappear," as he paused, obviously on a subject that really bothered him, but he straightened up and continued looking at Jamie, "I know as a black man who studies and reveres history that our people still have a society that accepts black men just taking black women as they please and moving on. Don't get me wrong, Jamie, it goes for white men or men of any color, who literally just hit and run. It goes back to how my father, who I never saw in my entire life, just ignored what he had created and that my mother and grandmother were totally responsible for my care. I've told that story a hundred times without regret when I tried to get organizations to try and help find fathers of my kids and all it got me, was that some charitable organizations stopped supporting me. I am adamant about that, but for some reason, many charitable groups think I cannot criticize anything black men do or have done. They hate reality. These black boys or any boys, have to be held responsible for their actions as do the little girls who haven't got a clue what they're doing when they spread their legs for those hit and run dudes. I have made a lot of progress over the years Jamie, which I feel good about, but there is so much more to do on this front. This mentality I see every day in this little cross section of what goes on all across this country in black communities," he paused, then added, "this problem continues to be one of my major priorities. I have tried to change that, and I have so much more work to do." When he finished with that message, his head dropped on his wide chest until slowly it rose and he smiled, "Well, Jamie, old boy, you have come back and you now have the whole update on Sam the Man."

Jamie was quiet and then said, "If I'm an old boy, then you are, for sure, an old man, but what an old man. You got me again, Sam, for sure. I, right now, after my career as an architect ended and losing

Louise, I sort of went into a funk. But I have finally regained an incentive to concentrate on fulfilling my life until I can't. I decided to volunteer at the transplant service at the University of Pittsburgh Transplant Center and at the Carnegie Library in Oakland. That has been my new routine and it's been invigorating. Oh, and I'm helping two young ladies I met at the Library, one to find her father, who she's never met, and another to fulfill a lifetime dream of singing in the chorus of the Pittsburgh Opera. So, old Sam, I'm in a good groove, but the icing on the literal cake is sitting here with you," he paused and added, "Sam, I left you forty years ago, but not now. I want to help you right here where we worked together forty years ago."

They looked at each other without speaking and then Sam said with his great smile spreading across his face, "I think we were supposed to be again, and ironically, I've been looking for someone to design and monitor the rehabilitation of this old fire station and the other properties that we've picked up," then he paused and added, "this my man is what is called divine intervention."

"Divine it may be, which would not surprise me and you can count on me. I'll get my schedule worked out and let you know when I can come over. Tomorrow I'll be at the library, but I'll call you. I can usually come in the afternoons, so let me have your phone number and email address."

Sam laughed, "I have a phone but no email address, but we got one. But just call this number here", and he gave Jamie his cell phone. Jamie wrote down the number and gave it back to him.

"Okay, Sam, how much are you paying these days," Jamie said with a serious look on his face.

"You'll get a minimum wage, you realize that?" Sam said with a smile on his broad face.

"That's fine with me," Jamie replied," paused and added, "how much is it now?"

"Zilch," Sam added quickly.

"Didn't know you spoke Polish, Sam", he quickly responded.

CHAPTER TEN

Jamie had a calm, settled evening after his incredible meeting with Sam. In the morning, he was up and about, full of energy, no doubt because of being with a man who was such a fine, rare person. Jamie got to the library on time and got right into the work on the new project he really liked on the floods in Pittsburgh history. Over the next hours he worked on this project on floods in Pittsburgh in 1935 that would have been covered in the newspapers. She had a request from a writer who was doing a book on that historic event and the data was now available on the computer data bank that the Library had developed. As Jamie downloaded the information, he found it interesting.

He was deeply into reading an article when his phone rang. It was Rachel. "Where are you, Mister...," then said, "Jamie?"

"At the library. What's up?"

"You got some time to see me today?"

"Of course," as he looked at the clock on the wall he added, "I'll see you at two o'clock this afternoon in our usual spot, okay and I got some info I think you will find very interesting."

"Oh, wow, super. See you at two," and she tapped out.

Jamie paused for a few seconds and then went back to his project. He printed out copies of the newspapers including the Pittsburgh Courier which was the newspaper that covered African Americans and was the leading paper in the country on their news items. He found out the flooding affected them a bit differently because the consistent rains flooded hillsides and caused great damage to their old and crumbling structures. It was interesting to read the articles especially after spending time with Sam yesterday. It added to his perspective of how blacks were treated and how amazing it was that a man like Sam became what he had become; a truly dynamic human being. He turned off the newspaper system and just sat there as he thought of life; the only time for human existence. In our terms, years, nothing in the timeline for the Universe, but all that we had. He was mesmerized by where his thoughts were taking him and wondered why he had recently become so interested in the meaning of human life. Was it just his age? He remained sitting, pondering as his thoughts returned to humanities existence in our Universe. A topic, literally for the rest of the day or his life, for that matter. What is our life all about was the thought he was having when he was jolted to the moment, realizing that he was to meet Rachel in ten minutes downstairs in the main library reading area. She seemed excited when he told her earlier, he had some information for her. As he returned to the projector in front of him, all he could think of was the continual flow of lives that were covered in these pages of a newspaper over the years. Pages of stories of peoples' lives; born; murdered; achievements; failures; marriages; divorces; death; accidents: everything that can happen to Man, is feed into a system so others can read and know about all that has happened to other humans. A strange element in our way of life, however, it had its values as demonstrated by the information he had found about the floods of years ago and also, he had found Rachel's father; at least he thought he had. So, it had value, of course and now he was going to share it with her.

When he got downstairs, he came over to Rachel who was already there. He was glad to see that she seemed calm, but he could tell she was excited. He had typed up a memo with all the data Jane had uncovered. Jamie read her the information and she sat there entranced as if in a dream. He looked at her and slid the memo across the table to her. She picked it up and tears began to run down her cheeks as she read. Slowly she looked up and smiled slowly.

"Wow, now what do I do. Looks like I have a father in Phoenix, Arizona, and aunt in Penn Hills here and possibly, a half-brother and two half-sisters.

Jamie replied, "Looks that way. I guess the next thing to do is for you or you and I to explore more sites online that will highlight all that and maybe pick up more information on them, like in Facebook. I didn't want to do anything until I talked with you."

She looked at him and said, "Could we?"

"Yeh, for sure. We can get all that and even check out the company he works for. Get all that and I'll be glad to help."

"Any pictures?" Rachel asked hesitantly.

"I didn't go any further until I talked with you, but there two things we can do. Check the company site and then find out the high school and suburb he either lived in or lives in now. Once we have some of that we can explore different sites. I'm sure we'll find out a lot. These days there is so much available."

Jamie could tell she was interested, not knowing how to react or what to do next. He found out quickly as she leaned across the broad wooden desk and gave him a kiss on his cheek. "Thank you so much, Jamie."

Jamie smiled and replied, "Well, your quite welcome, my dear. This is an extremely important life thing for you, for anyone, for that matter."

She smiled as she mulled over the paper on the table that had her whole unknown life before her. For a minute she reread the information and Jamie sat quietly across from her. Then she looked up and said, "What do you think I should do next?"

Jamie said, "Well, once we have all the information, I would read it all over again and again. Take it all in, then take a hot shower, lie down and just think about what you really want to do. Then think about your fathers and your half-sisters, and brother. I'm sure after that process you will come to a decision as to whether to proceed or not," he paused, "maybe a letter to your father might be the best way to start."

"A letter," Rachel said, looking up. "No one writes letters today," she said somewhat sounding exasperated.

"Old school, that's me. You asked me and I told you," Jamie replied a bit exasperated. "Do what you think best," and he pushed back his chair, got up and looked across at Rachel saying, "If you think I can help you further you know where I'll be, right upstairs," and he started to walk away.

"Are you mad at me, Mister Sloan?"

"Mister Sloan. Where did that come from?" as he paused looked at her with a slight smile and said, "Okay, Miss Collins, no, I just want you to think of the affect, the shock of a man now in his fifties with children a bit younger than you, who finds out from a text, an email, or through Facebook or some other impersonal message that he has a daughter. How the hell," he said as his usual calm voice rose for emphasis, "do you think this man will react to get a fu....," he looked at her and said, "text from a daughter he never knew he had?"

Rachel was stoned face as if she hadn't realized or thought about that question. Neither spoke for a few seconds as Jamie started to turn to go again Rachel said, "Oh, Jesus Christ, you're right, I never thought about him. I've always in some way hated him because of what my Mom had said when I began to ask questions. I thought of him as a guy who just left my Mom and of course, me."

Jamie had turned back to face her as she sat at the table. He said, "You are a fortunate, intelligent young woman with a great future. Your Mom deserves so much credit and maybe her husband, your stepfather too, for giving you a base, a foundation that got you here today. Listen to me, child, inherently, maybe there is some inborn virtue in you from that father you have never known. He may not be an evil man. He may not even know you exist. Do you know if your Mother ever told him?"

Rachel looked at him with a faraway look as if seeking a vision of her Mother and her Father when they were briefly together. She didn't respond right away as Jamie just stood looking at her until she replied, "You know I don't think she ever did. In fact, I remember her telling me about ten years ago when I was in high school when I was quizzing her about him after she admitted how I was conceived, that she had never told him of his child, me."

Jamie walked around the table and came up to Rachel. He leaned over and gave her a hug. "Take some time and then call me and we'll figure out a way to contact him. You have to do something to let him know softly, quietly, not harshly. Know what I mean?"

She turned up to him and patted his arm, "That's a plan and thank you so much for all that you have done and want to do. It means so much to me."

Jamie smiled as he straightened up and said, "How about we meet in the next day or so after you've had some time to process this. This is really tough stuff. You…we gotta do it right."

She smiled, "You're on. I'll call you and we can meet right here. This is where it started and this is where we'll figure out what to do," she paused, "you don't know how much this means to me, what you've done."

"Rachel, you've made my day. I'm so glad we or you are going to work out a way to meet your Dad. Oh, by the way, my dear, get ready for a couple of reactions. We don't know how he will react. Hopefully, positively, but you never know. You must relax and realize he may be hostile or upset or something that you don't want, so calm down and we'll go into phase two, okay?"

"Okay, Mister…," pausing she went on, "Jamie, okay," she said moving her chair back and stood up. She went to him and hugged him tightly. "I'll call you, probably tomorrow or no later than the day after."

Rachel picked up her phone and leather backpack then walked out into the hallway with a parting look back at Jamie.

When he got to his apartment that night, he realized how tired he was as he seemed to be these days. He lay down into his leather sofa and slumped into its heavy, soft comfort, unable even to turn on the TV to see local news. His eyes closed and the day, which was incredible for all that had happened came back to him in his thoughts, from meeting Sam and then imaging what it would be like to be home when you receive a phone call from a daughter you never knew you had. Then he smiled, as he remembered something that had happened at the library today that was now, hysterical. A large lady, probably his age, sitting at another table across from him, who apparently had lost her purse, came over to him, looked right down at him and intimated that he knew who took it. He had looked up at her and said, "Took what?" She was dressed up in a suit out of the 'Fifties and just stared down at him, then she suddenly turned and hurried out into the hallway, headed towards the lady's room, he assumed. He watched the hallway then went back to what he was reading, but a minute later he looked up as the woman hustled back in with a large, jammed black purse over her arm and sat back down without looking over at him. It had made him chuckle to himself as he thought back then to the work he was doing about the horrific flooding in the Hill District of

Pittsburgh in 1937. All these interconnected thoughts as his mind had worked in overtime and he realized he was just tired.

Finally, he roused himself, got up and went into the kitchen where he took out a quart of his favorite green pea and mushroom soup. After it heated and with a cold Yuengling Dark Beer, he settled down in front of the TV and watched in the usual numbing sense, the absolute absurdity of his beloved America. He kept punching the clicker and finally went to YouTube for a talk by one of his favorite poets, T.S. Eliot. Jamie had read Eliot's poetry over and over, especially the last years since Louise had died. She wrote and loved poetry, especially Eliot and would read in front of the fireplace of the home in Squirrel Hill. He would come into the room and she would be staring off through the large window that opened up to their back yard where the giant pin oaks stood. Sometimes he would just sit down on the floor as she would calmly and quietly recite his great lines that now, Jamie, really loved to read. Now he would read Eliot and his mind would wander off of Earth into spaces beyond. He also would turn on YouTube and watch Eliot reading his poetry. For some reason his lines spoke of a life beyond this earthly one. Eliot spoke quietly and looked right at the camera in an obviously old, black and white reading of his poetic lines.

It didn't take too long until Jamie was nodding off. He never remembered dreams but as it turned out, it didn't seem like a dream at all. He was drifting through a foggy night somewhere in a woody area that reminded him of a place in West Virginia where he went as a kid for summer camp and got lost. It was dark and he couldn't find the right trail to get back to their cabins. His underwear was wet because he'd peed his pants a few minutes earlier when he heard what he thought was a wolf howling and it scared literally the piss out of him. It was so dark and all he could hear were strange noises of the woods, but none were from his fellow Scouts who were with him at this summer camp. Suddenly the moon escaped the flowing clouds above him, and the trail was illuminated so he could see lights way up ahead which caused him to run as fast as he could. When he got to the top of rise in the trail, he looked out over a valley which was bathed in moonlight with no lights at all that would be the camp. He stopped and was scared.

Slowly he began to walk down the hillside. He was now at the beach looking for seashells in tiny puddles of sea water. He loved seashells and, in a few minutes, had his small pocket filled with them as he heard a call. "Jamie, Jamie, where are you?" It was his mother and he felt so good and he slowly came out of his thoughts and realized he was on his sofa with his head across a pillow. He sat up and couldn't remember anything about where he had been except an echo of his mother's call to him that he could never forget. His mother's soft voice, when she was calling him, he always remembered. As a kid; as a teenager; as an adult, when she used that firm, yet soft voice it penetrated him even as it still does whether in a dream or just thinking of her. Jamie slowly got up, turned off the TV and lights, then headed into his bedroom where he hoped a real sleep awaited him because so much was opening up for him to do in the days ahead.

CHAPTER ELEVEN

Morning came and Jamie slid off the bedraggled bed and sat on the crumpled sheets, listening to rain pounding off his bedroom window. He got up and went over to the window and pulled back the drapes. It was dark outside as a slanting rain hit off the window. A smile came to him because he and rain were simpatico. He loved it's refreshing cleansing of the earth. It was a great start to this day which he was loaded with so much to do. He bustled around his apartment from brushing teeth to getting dressed to eating his usual bowl of cereal to gulping his deep, dark coffee. He was ready and headed outside into his favorite type of day; gray and rainy. He decided to head on over to the library and skip his usual latte so he could continue the work on the floods especially in a day like this one because the transplant service had texted him not to come in that day due to some office rearrangement that was going on which worked out well for him.

His raincoat was at least twenty years old, but it flowed gently over his body providing him dryness and comfort in its aged look much out of fashion as he was in this day and age. His old Steeler hat was pulled down, so he stayed dry and warm in the cold morning. The walk to the bus stop was two blocks away and he made it safely and only his shoes were damp as he huddled under the bus stop shelter, squashed up against three others trying to stay dry. No one talked, but not because of the tightness of their haven but because they were all yapping and tapping on their cell phones. Jamie was laughing quietly to himself as he thought of this world in the beginning of the second decade of the 21St Century; constant communication. What in the world did people have to talk about, constantly?

He peeked around the corner of the shelter and saw a bus rounding the curve with its large windshield wipers sweeping across the water laden windows. There was some pressure from behind him as the bus pulled up to the stop. Everyone moved slow as an older woman wrapped tightly in her gray raincoat led the way up the wettened steps of the bus after they were lowered. It was civil, no one pushed or shoved as all found seats in the half full bus. Jamie fortunately had a window seat and was by himself. Looking through the misty window, he thoughts went over his day ahead until he realized his stop was coming up.

Jamie worked his way to the middle door as the bus came to a jolting stop. As he stepped down on the sidewalk, the rain hit him square in his face. He pulled up his collar and headed along the sidewalk to the library entrance. He climbed the stairs and entered the ancient structure built by the entrepreneur, Andrew Carnegie who read books as a kid in Scotland. The Library was a gem within the university atmosphere In the Oakland area of Pittsburgh. Jamie went to the elevator, past the new book displays, he noted that he didn't recognize a single author. He wound his way to the elevator door and glanced up to the clock.

As the elevator slowly moved up to the third floor, Jamie went over how he was going to prioritize all that he had to do. Prioritize was the key word and the first thoughts that came to mind was to talk again to Rachel and find out what she was going to do; possibly go to Sandra's rehearsal, but the most important thing was to have another session with Sam about how he could help him. As the elevator door opened, he thought of Margaret Decker and her loss, plus reading about her interest in helping underprivileged children. Her interests were so similar to that of Sam and his efforts to provide support to children and families living in poverty. Could there be a way for him to bring these two individuals with similar goals together?

For the next several hours, Jamie didn't leave his desk except to make two cups of coffee. He completed his library project for the day and as he sat in front of the computer, an idea came to him about setting up a schedule of things he had to do. He typed in SCHEDULE and began to outline the various personal projects he was working on. After a short time, he saved the file and then printed a copy. As he looked at the copy, Jamie realized that he had phone calls to make to Peter about how Sandra had done; follow-up with Rachel; go see Sam; and the possibility of contacting Margaret Decker when he thought it was appropriate. Tomorrow night, he may be going to the Strip to listen to Sandra's first rehearsal as she was asked to be at tomorrow night's rehearsal. His new schedule that he had come up with worked out perfectly because Rachel had left a message that she wanted to meet him for coffee at the Starbucks across from the Library because she had come up with a plan, she wanted to run by him.

Jamie decided to call Sam and set up a time to go see him.

"What's up, old man?" came the deep throated response.

"At my age, not much," as Jamie paused, waiting for a snort from Sam which he got, "but, I need to talk about something that I've been thinking about since we talked. Does this weekend work?"

After a few seconds Sam responded, "Well, this weekend we have a whole bunch of kids' events, which you're welcome to come see, but don't think we'd have much quiet time. How about Monday before you do your volunteer work?"

"That is perfect and what's going on Sunday afternoon? Do you need any help?"

"Can always use help, especially from an old white dude."

"Well, this old white dude will be there around, what, two o'clock?"

"Three's better because I could use you to judge something for me. How's that sound?"

"Perfecto. I'll be there. If something comes up, I'll let you know."

Rachel was in a far corner in Starbucks leaning over a propped-up laptop as if she was writing her great American novel. She never noticed Jamie sidling up to her table and even when he sat down in a chair beside her. He didn't say a word and then she looked, turned her head to him and smiled quickly as she shut her computer. "Hey, Jamie, I'd say pull up a chair, but you already have."

He noticed she didn't have a drink on the table, and he asked, "I'm going to grab a coffee and a muffin or something. You want anything, I'm buying!"

She leaned back and said, "Well, I had something earlier, but you know, I could use another jolt. How about a latte with whole milk and a shot of whipped cream, oh, almost forgot, a shot of sugar free vanilla?"

"Whooh, let's see. A sugar free vanilla latte with whipped cream and whole milk, right?"

"You nailed it.

"Anything to eat?"

"Oh, yeh, a wheat bagel with cream cheese."

"Got it, be right back. We got some talking to do."

Jamie was back with a tray and put her latte and bagel beside her as he sat down. He took a sip of his coffee and said, "Okay, Rachel, you wanted to talk to me."

She smiled, straightened up and said, "First, I have to apologize for how I reacted when you gave me the info about my Fath…Dad."

Jamie quickly responded, "Don't have to. It was a shock."

She added, "Two, how I am going to handle this, is all I have been thinking about since we talked."

Jamie smiled and said, "The important thing is what you have done is a critical event in your life. Finding out your real name and your Father is a life moment, so don't feel bad about how you reacted," he paused, "so, what have you decided?"

"That's why I texted you. I want you to give me your opinion, as an older man, as to best way to approach him…my Father?"

Jamie sat back took a sip of his coffee, looked away and out the window of the busy coffee shop. He didn't say anything as he just looked out the window as Rachel fidgeted looking at him, as if concerned he wouldn't give her any help. Then he turned back and said, "I think I would send him a letter, a picture and a summary of your upbringing. The key word is summary. The letter is one introducing yourself as believing that you are his daughter, very calmly and nicely with no expectations of anything. You just want him to know that you understand from your Mom vaguely how it happened and that you have no ill will towards him, you just want him to know of your existence. I would tell him how well you are doing with your life, college, personal situation and that…", as Jamie pauses, "that if he would want to, you would like to meet him."

Rachel was crying as her head bowed on to her chest. Slowly she rose and said, "Oh, Jesus Christ, can I do that and even if I do, what if he doesn't answer?"

Jamie took hold of her right hand and held it gently, "I have a feeling he will want to meet you. Why I don't know, it's just a gut feeling."

Rachel looked at him and said, "Do you think?"

"I do, I really do. I mean the guy seems to have a solid working career and from what I can tell hasn't bounced all around the country. Seems like he's been in Arizona most of his life except when he was in the service, so he sounds like a rather normal, down to earth kind of guy."

Rachel moved slightly away from Jamie and picked up her large, leather purse and put it on her lap. She pulled out an envelope and gave it to Jamie. "Here, can you read this? Tell me if it sounds okay, at least for the first shot."

Jamie took the envelope, pulled out white, folded stationery, separated them and took the first page. He began to read.

CHAPTER TWELVE

Jamie put down the letter as a smile spread across his face. He looked at her for a few seconds and said, "You nailed it, Rachel. This is perfect, at least from my viewpoint. I think any rational man would be overwhelmed with this clear, honest declaration and would want to meet you. Better yet, he would want to know you. Who you are? What your life is all about? So, I say, send it asap."

She leaned over against him and put her arms around his shoulders and gave him a hug and said, "Thank you so much for leading me when I didn't know which road to take. I thought for a whole day not knowing what I should do, but then it hit me. I remembered your last words about how he would feel finding out he had a daughter, not my thoughts about how he should be so excited to find out the same thing. What if I find out something like this in twenty years? Anyway, as you also said, it took a while, but I didn't think of it for a day and then decided to make my decision and what you read is what I did."

"There's a mailbox at the corner. I'd take it there now and you'll feel a weight off of your shoulders. I know you will."

She smiled and replied, "Okay, I'm on my way," as she stood up. "You gonna hang around? I have to get over to McDonoughs. Maybe I'll see you there," she said as she smiled at Jamie and headed towards the door.

He moved his chair back and said as he stood up, "Hold on, I'll walk out with you. I have something here at the Library to take care of, but I'm ready for a cold one at McDonoughs, so I'll see you there. But more importantly, let's meet right here a week from today or sooner, if you get a response. Is that a deal?"

She reached out and took his hands in hers and said, "You'll be the first to know. As I told you, my Mom's been dead for years and I only have two aunts, so I don't have anyone else to tell. But at least I have you and who knows what may happen after my...," she pauses, "Dad knows."

Jamie responded, "Okay, love finish that high-priced bagel and let's get to the mailbox," with a chuckle as he stood up.

"Okay," she replied, "I can't believe I'm doing this. It was so hard to do?"

Jamie reached out to Rachel, putting his hands on her shoulders and said, "Rachel, it had to be. My God, after all these years, to be writing to a father you have never seen. It had to be, but you did it and I think and hope it will be one of the most important decisions you will ever make and maybe one of the most beneficial to you. It will certainly be one you will always be proud of, whatever the outcome because you have reached out."

Jamie and Rachel left Starbucks, walking up to the mailbox on the corner. She opened the door of the curved blue mailbox, looked back at Jamie, smiled and then turned back to the opened door, dropping the letter into the slot.

They both stood back and looked at the mailbox, then he patted her shoulder and they separated. Jamie waved at her as she headed to the bus stop and he crossed over Forbes to see if his boss Lee might be at the library today. He hadn't seen them this week. He wanted to make sure he was doing the project correctly. He took the elevator up to their research location and Jamie found Lee at a computer in his office. He turned to Jamie and said, "Well retiree who never stops working, what's up? Jamie explained to him that he just wanted to make sure that he was getting the data correctly for what Lee wanted.

"It's right on, Jamie. I checked it out yesterday and you have a good handle on what we are trying to save."

"Well, that's good, I was worried I might be putting too much information down next to the picture."

"Oh, no, it's good, really good."

"Okay, well I'll see you next week, Lee," Jamie said and headed for the stairs out of the library. He felt a bit tired, yet he knew he needed to walk a longer route to get some exercise after sitting so long, especially because he wanted to stop by McDonoughs for a beer and just relax. It took him almost an hour by going the long way, but he felt so much better after the walk and he was glad to see the

McDonoughs sign over the front door. When he opened up the dual doors and entered, he was surprised by all the people at the bar. Bart was serving drafts to a group of people at the corner of the bar. At the far end and he saw Rachel pouring a shot for a guy in front of the large screen TV. As she looked up, she saw him and raised her hand, waving for him to come to that part of the bar.

Jamie wended his way to a stool and sat down, seeing Tommy and Jerome down the bar in a deep conversation. He gave out a sigh of relief because it felt good to be sitting here awaiting a beer after such a phenomenal week. He turned and looked all around the bar; it was really jammed. There must be some office parties because there were groups clustered around tables at different spots, going out into the dining area. It was a weekend in Pittsburgh.

"Here you go, Jamie," he heard Rachel's voice and he turned, looked into her lovely face. "This one is definitely on the bartender."

"Oh, wow, if I had known, I would have come sooner," Jamie responded as he lifted up the mug and took a sip. "Ah, makes my day, darling."

"Well, you made mine, so we're even."

Suddenly he heard, "Hey, Jamie, old sod, how the hell are you?"

Only one voice like that in the world as he looked down the bar to see Tommy waving at him. Jamie lifted his mug a bit and waved toward him, "Doing fine, Tommy, doing just fine." He waved his mug at Jerome beside him and added, "Tell your driver there, it's nice seeing him to."

Rachel was still standing behind the bar and Jamie looked at her and said, "You got a lot of parties going on? Bart must be a happy camper."

"Oh, he is. Fact he's back double checking the kegs because the beer is really flowing today."

"You hungry, old man? yelled Tommy.

Jamie raised his right hand that had pretzels, shook them at Tommy and then took a bite out of one. "Their good, Tommy, you should try some."

At that moment Rachel came back in front of him and said, "How do you eat, Jamie? What do you do, cook yourself?"

Jamie looked across the bar at her and replied, "Sure, every night, it's nothing but French or Italian or even some Scottish fare like lamb, which I love."

"Wow, I'm impressed," she replied.

"Actually, I do have them, but it's all from my freezer. I can't cook worth a damn."

"You want some pierogis; made today by my friend's Polish mom from the Slopes. You should try them. How 'bout it?"

Jamie looked at Rachel and said, "Oh, God, I'd love some. Bring them   on.
He was in heaven a half hour later as he devoured the tiny pierogis like he hadn't eaten in days, washed down with a second draft. Rachel stood back with her arms crossed looking at him and said, "Must have liked them, Jamie," she said laughingly.

"My God they were incredible. Thank her for me and please let me pay for them, please."

"Not tonight, not tonight," she responded then suddenly darted down the bar as Bart was waving at her.

Jamie went back to his draft which he had just about finished when Tommy yelled down to him, "Well Jamie boy, did you find that missing nig…black man?", he said sarcastically with a smirk on his face as he looked at Jamie before turning back to Jerome and laughing.

Jamie slowly put down his mug and looked at this man he had known for a while from just being here and said bluntly, "I guess you are referring to my friend of forty years…," pausing and saying loud, slowly and clearly, "you Mick…white man?" His eyes bore into Tommy.

Tommy seemed stunned. He just stared at Jamie as if he had never seen him before. Then he turned to his bosom buddy Jerome, who was glue eyed. Tommy turned back to Jamie and said, "What do you mean by that, you Protestant bastard?"

Jamie did not budge, but straightened up, slid his beer back on the bar, turned to Tommy who straightened up on his stool, never taking his eye off him. Jamie looked right at him with a tight face and said, "You Protestant bastard, you said?"

Tommy was stunned and he turned back to Jerome beside him and then back to Jamie. Then he said defensively as he looked Jamie standing there looking at him with a scowl on his face and tightened fists, "I was talking only about the man you were looking for that I told you where you might find him."

"I thanked you for that, didn't I, Mick."

Tommy was stone faced and replied, "Mick, is it?"

"It is, from this Protestant bastard," and Jamie walked down toward Tommy, who began to slide off his chair. Before he stood up, Jamie had him by the arms and put his fist into his broad red face. "That black man has more guts than you and your white buddy next to you could ever dream of having. Don't you ever talk about that man in that way when I'm around. Do your bullshit between yourselves, but not around me," as he pushed back his shoulders. "I might be an old Protestant bastard, but I'll take you on anytime. What say white man, are you ready?"

Tommy was shocked. His face was drained, and he backed away to his stool. Jerome who had got up, came around and looked at Jamie and realizing that he was steaming, grabbed Tommy's shoulder and said to Jamie, "Hold up there Jamie, he didn't mean no harm. He knows a lot of black men."

Jamie took his hands off of Tommy, looked at the much larger Jerome and said, "What the fuck does that mean? I know a lot of Micks too. Most of them are decent folks like I thought your buddy here was. You'd think he would remember what his grandparents went through a hundred years ago and what black people have been going through for hundreds of years right here in the goddamn United States of America," as he paused, stepped back from Tommy, wiping his sweating face, and still looking menacingly at Jerome. Then he turned and walked back to his stool. He picked up his mug, finished it and turned, waving down the bar at Rachel who was standing there with frozen look on her face and walked out.

CHAPTER THIRTEEN

Jamie for a change, slept well. During the morning he went back over what had happened at the bar and felt really at peace with his reaction one he had never done before in his life. Normally he would have either turned away from the perpetrator or looked at them without comment, which always bothered him. He wasn't a fighter, physically, but if the person or persons were intelligent and it was more or less a discussion of different beliefs, he could be engaged. But the attitude expressed by Tommy had hit him right in his heart and he was actually furious in a flash. As he thought about it, he slowly began to smile. It made him feel good, actually.

Jamie spent the morning and the afternoon, straightening up his apartment with the news on and coffee brewing after a bowl of cereal with bananas which got him fixed for the day ahead. Sweeping the carpet was an outstanding achievement as he hustled as fast as he could because he had to get to the Strip later that day for Sandra's rehearsal. He even took a nap, which he hadn't done in a while. As he was getting dressed, CNN had stories about a virus from China that apparently was now in the in Seattle and New York. It was causing great worries in the White House. He turned off the TV, finished his last coffee and headed out the door to catch the bus. He didn't want to be late for the rehearsal at five.

It was an astounding setting in the large cavern with a stage which Jamie could see had a group of at least thirty men, women, boys and girls gathered in a variety of dress awaiting their individual call. Apparently, Peter wanted to hear them individually first, before they sang together. Jamie waved at Sandra standing bravely in the middle of them. She was dressed in a pale blue ball gown as if she was going to a dance of some sort. He sat back, waving once to Peter who had nodded at him as he went back to his seat about half-way back in the rows of the rehearsal hall. Jamie's thoughts wandered as singers came up to the front of the stage and sang their hearts out to various pieces of music from, he assumed, all kinds of operas; an artistic field he knew absolutely nothing about. Then, Sandra's name was called, and she moved slowly, but confidently up to the stage with a single microphone hanging down from above. Orchestral music played which, strangely enough, Jamie recognized, not the name of the opera, but the music. After a few seconds, Sandra began singing in a slow, quiet voice. As the music gradually became more intense, her voice rose beautifully to a new level that surprised Jamie. He realized, no matter what Peter decided, this lady had a great resounding voice, and he was so proud of her. She finished and went off stage. Next they were all together in a choral setup and sang for another hour, the songs of the show. Jamie was astounded how well they sounded for a group that hadn't sung together. When the rehearsal was over, he walked up to Sandra and put his arm on her shoulder and said, "Sandra, you were incredible. What a lovely voice. I am so proud of you and the whole choir was incredible."

She smiled and turned, then hugged him. "You don't know how I feel. It was a dream come true. What happens, happens, but I did sing one of my favorite arias at the Pittsburgh Opera."

"My dear, you were sensational."

He got back to his apartment and spent the rest of the evening looking at his notebooks and draft copies of the book he had started years before. By ten o'clock, he was bushed, and as sat in his sofa watching a PBS story of the Russian Revolution in 1919. As he watched this fascinating program, Jamie wondered what had happened to all the fire and energy that had engulfed people to literally give up their lives for what they thought was the idealism of Communism. Jamie understood their frustrations with the world of that day, dominated by Kings and Queens, who had no good reason to be in charge of the destinies of people. What a system that caused millions of humans to die, mostly the young and poor, while a few rich people stayed safe and got richer from the war itself. No wonder Communism inspired the intellectuals and the poor to want a new, fairer system. As the 21St Century unfolds, Jamie wondered, is there such thing as a fair system as he thought about all that Sam has been doing over the years. Maybe our attempt at democracy was the fairest, maybe the best system, but then he thought of all the politicians in America who just sucked off the system. Maybe some kind of new revolution was in order.

Jamie settled back against the sofa and thought of how well he was feeling even with all the activity over the last days. He thought about the rehearsal and that you can't beat people doing what they love to do, especially in our world of so much negativity. He also felt good physically, even this late in the day. He had eaten well, got some walking in, and certainly was working his brain with all the various projects that he was involved in and excited about. As he relaxed, he thought of Scotland and remembered the maps on his desk he had picked up on the British Isles over a year ago which got him thinking about a trip to Scotland. Something he had always wanted to do. Maybe a trip to where the Sloan's lived centuries ago would be good for him. Then he thought about Sandra's rehearsal at the opera and realized what a productive day it had been. He smiled and laughed saying, "What the fuck", he was on a roll and at his age he should be so glad he could do just about anything he wanted. "What the fuck", he said again with a smile as he was using this self-expression to put reality into his age bracket of a life that he in essence could and should do anything he wishes. At this point in his life he was the only person affected or concerned about his situation, so anything was literally on his table for him to pursue. This thought made him smile again as he headed to bed.

The next morning Jamie decided to call Sam and cancel coming by later that day but would come by tomorrow if that was okay. He spent the day loafing around, which he hadn't done for a while. He got up from the dining room table where he had a special breakfast of scrambled eggs and bacon, his favorite with four pieces of toast smothered in strawberry jam and three cups of coffee. As he sat there, he realized he hadn't felt this contented for some time. A thought came to him that he should get back into some of the various projects he had put aside over the years. He went into the small wood paneled room that was a second bedroom which he'd made into an office and sat down at his computer. He had a good computer arrangement; with a big screen, combined with his reading glasses, gave him excellent vision when he spent time on Google and other information sites. Jamie pushed up his glasses that always sunk onto his cheeks, and typed in Michael Cullins, Phoenix, Arizona on Google. He found several articles about the company he worked for where his name and a picture appeared. Jamie could actually see a resemblance to Rachel. He printed this data to give to her.

Jamie then checked his architectural company's website to see what they were up to and was excited by all the projects they were working on, many overseas, one actually in Edinburgh. This brought him back to thinking about making a Scottish trip. He did the next best thing and went back to the internet sites about Ayrshire where the Sloans came from. He then typed messages to Cousin Hugh and several other Sloan cousins who lived all over the world. He would invite them to a Sloan get together next summer in Pittsburgh that Hugh had emailed him about weeks ago. It had been ten years since the last one which Jamie vividly remembered. He thought back to the job in Edinburgh and then to his Company in which he still had a large financial stake. A thought came him. What was going to happen to all the wealth he had accumulated during his career? He immediately realized he needed to contact Jeff McDonald, a guy he had known since college, who still worked on estate planning. Jeff had said to him many times, that he'd better set things up or they would be a mess and very expensive if he didn't do an estate plan.

It had been a productive and peaceful day. As Jamie sat there, he did feel a bit tired, yet he had enough left in him to get a legal pad to write down things he had to do. He wrote a note for Monday to contact Jeff about his estate. As he sat back, he felt a new energy in his life by meeting Sam again. He now understood how important it was to contribute to society by helping those who may never have a chance at a good life.

While Jamie ate a late dinner, he turned on the TV to check the news and weather for the upcoming week. The headlines were all about the virus from China now being called the Corona Virus, that apparently was spreading like wildfire in the U.S. Tomorrow the White House and some special medical group was announcing how this country will deal with it. The reporter was stating that the country may be put on some type of mandatory shutdown if the virus, which apparently is dangerous, builds up. 'This could be dangerous', Jamie thought as the reporter stated that the virus was especially dangerous to older people. How would it affect his work at the transplant service he wondered and even the library? As he sat there and watched the reporting, from adding up the new cases and deaths in areas of our country, which at first were limited to Seattle to now appearing all across the country, especially in New York City. There was talk from State governors and from the White House that the potential of this virus could cause a major disruption in the way we live. There was talk about closing down cities and people staying away from each other. Apparently from what was known so far, the virus spreads from human to human by touch or vapor spray from people coughing. He squiggled in his sofa and had an awful feeling. CNN was reporting the history of plagues of the past and the one ten years ago which caused thousands of deaths. As they continued their reporting, it had hit New York City and Governor Cuomo of New York State was going to announce restrictions on people in the City tomorrow. On the other hand, CNN was reporting from Beijing that China, apparently, had taken care of the virus that may or may not have started in the city of Wuhan in December. CNN said the Chinese government denied any knowledge of any major viral attack and said there were few incidents of the virus in Beijing. 'Where is this going?' Jamie thought as he turned off the TV, put his dinner utensils in the kitchen sink and headed for his bedroom.

CHAPTER FOURTEEN

Monday morning Jamie awoke early and lay in bed watching the sunlight pour through the window. He had such a peaceful and calming day yesterday, but he had to get up because he couldn't forget the headline news that kept coming back to him when he had CNN on last night. When he got downstairs, he turned on CNN and the virus was their only topic. They were reporting with greater intensity, the growing number of deaths due to the virus called Corona. The Department of Health and Human Services had announced guidelines for people wearing masks in public and standing six feet from one another. A special task force had been formed by President Trump was going to be on the air later today, to give an update on the viral attack. Jamie sat there stunned, as he wondered what the hell was going on? How would this affect his life and all that he had been planning? He decided he had to set things up with Sam as soon as possible before things come to a halt based on the news reports. How could he handle this pending crisis and still fulfill the work he wanted to be involved in? Then he realized everyone in this country was probably thinking the same thing.

When he left for the bus, it was another typical Pittsburgh morning this time of the year, cool and wet, but the news on the TV continued to trouble him. As he waited on the sidewalk, all he could think about was all he had to do. Sam was first and then Jeff McDonald about his estate, which based on what he was hearing about the virus, he had to get set up. As for his two young lady friends, he'd done what he could, but he still wanted to find out if Rachel had received any response from her father and when Sandra would perform for the first time. Other than that, his volunteer work was still on for the week, as far as he knew. The library today and the transplant service had switched to tomorrow. Local news said there was talk in Harrisburg, that the State was contemplating closing all facilities from work to schools because of the spreading and deadly virus. But, Sam, he had to see today, no matter what. His work was too critical, virus or no virus. The more he thought about it, they would be the least protected if in fact the virus hit Pittsburgh. The library was jammed when he walked through the entrance with people carrying out books in their arms. The guard told him that the rumor was that libraries would be closing this week because of the virus. He was overwhelmed mentally when he walked towards his desk to do his volunteer work as he saw people carrying out books like they would never get another one.

His boss, Lee, waved at him as he walked toward his office.

"Jamie, I think this will be the last week we'll be open. It's not official, but I'll let you know, then added, "From what I'm hearing it may be by Wednesday. No one knows yet."

"My God, is it that bad, I asked."

"Apparently so. Just got a headline on KDKA's app, that we've had our first cases in Pittsburgh," Lee said with an unusual serious look.

"Wow," Jamie exclaimed. "Well, I guess we have to just see what happens. I can get that one project done today, I think."

"Okay, do what you can. I'll keep you posted."

Jamie worked past two o'clock, longer than normal and finished the photo project. As he cleaned off his desk, he took out his phone and dialed Sam's number.

"Hey, my man, what's up?" Sam answered in his deep voice.

"Need to see you, today. Does that still work for you?"

"Three bells are perfect. Okay for you?"

"I'll be there," Jamie answered. "See you,".

He got off the bus a few blocks from Sam's building. He wanted to get in some walking. He'd felt so tight in his legs from sitting at the desk in the library.

Sam was by himself sipping on a cup, probably green tea which he was drinking when Jamie was with him before.

"How's it going, old timer?"

"Well, I'm still perking along," as he paused and put down his cup and motioned for Jamie to sit in the overstuffed, leather chair across from him. "Grab a seat, Jamie, I got some talking to do to you."

Jamie sat down, sinking deep into the ancient chair. He straightened up and said, "Wow, this is some comfort zone, Sam. Feel like I'm in an old mattress.

Sam laughed and said, "Yeh, that came from the Steelers old office. The old man, old Art himself, Mister Rooney, sat in this very chair. His son gave it to me a long time ago."

Jamie looked surprised and sat up, turned slightly to look at the leather on the arm rests on both sides of the chair. Then he said, "You mean, Art Rooney sat in this chair?"

"Well, Dan said he did, and it came from their office."

Jamie smiled and replied, "Never know what I'm gonna find out from you, Sam. You always were and still are, a man of surprises."

Sam straightened up and said, "Surprises, don't have too many of those anymore, I sorta think it was some greater power sneaking up this old man and trying to tell me something."

Jamie's face tightened and he replied, "Why do you say that Sam?"

Sam quickly said, "Because I realized, that when I was explaining my plan to you about this work I do, it helped me concentrate on developing a future plan. Explaining to you, made me understand exactly what I want to do from now on. So, you coming back and wanting an outline of what I'm doing here, gave me a chance to put it all together. Now, man, that is a good omen," as he paused then continued, "We talked, or at least I did, explaining the other day what I want to do with this program that I've had here for all these years. The irony is that you come waltzing in my door when I have been trying to figure out exactly what we can do to help the increasing numbers of poor black folk's kids who could go down the economic drain and will never have a chance for a fulfilling life. This country is a great one, no question, and this even applies to a lot of my brethren who have made it into the upper echelons of this country. The life problem, however, for most young black children and their mothers is still here. For me, Jamie, the last ten years, especially, have been awful for me, not personally, but for what I can't do for the kids from single mothers who live off welfare checks and don't or can't work or get any support from the fuck and run crowd, as I call them. These are the boys and men who just get their rocks off and walk out the door. It's what my father did, and I still see this happening all the time among my folks."

Jamie said, "Hasn't the City, County or State, controlled by those who are responsible to help poorer folks, come through?"

"Yeh, a bit, here and there. The Churches, black and white have also helped, but it's all piecemeal," he paused, "but what gets me is they don't address the problem of really going after the men who create these kids. You know what I mean?" he said.

Jamie quickly added, "I do, I do, but it seems that it's never really been addressed for all people."

"Oh, you're right, but I know mostly about my black children and their runaway fathers. Their moms, or others help them, file claims and stuff if they can, but even if they do so and are supposed to get payments, most never get a dime. The mothers or someone helping them can spend the time going through the process, but even when they do, these guys never pay squat. You see Jamie, it's not just after school stuff. It's not just helping kids be exposed to the internet with computers. It's not just finding clothes at Goodwill for them or buying stuff at CVS when they can't get it themselves or their mothers are unable. Jamie it's about an overall program of support that flows from day one, meaning they are getting decent food, going to school, not getting beat up at home, and then maybe working, going to college or serving in the military. Or, the alternative and worst case, set adrift back into the same dismal neighborhood of welfare, drugs and more babies. But I have finally got some great folks helping me, including my own grandkids and finally, at my age, I can at least see the endzone, Jamie. But I never stop worrying about them kids out there", as he paused, then added, "So my goal, now, is to structure the whole program better, tighter and expand it as much as possible to help all young kids, both black like me and white in this town, and who knows, maybe elsewhere", as he again paused, "because I have seen it work for so many. And with you on board, man, I think it can be done."

Jamie was stunned. Not by what Sam proposed, but by the blanket coverage he wanted to put in place. He didn't know how to respond. It was quiet for a few seconds and then he said, "Well you're right, Sam, I was meant to come back to see you. What you have been doing and are doing, is all I've been thinking about since we talked, which reminds me, of something I want to discuss with you."

"Okay, let me hear what you got to say," Sam said.

Jamie looked at Sam and replied, "During the past years I've thought about, practically every day, about what I can do positively in my last years. I now have my volunteering which has been great and rewarding for me. But then all of a sudden you and your face pop into my mind and I started to look for you and thank God, I found you. So, here I am now, sitting across from you and we're both still with it at our age. Maybe, as you intimated the other day, this renewal of ours and the timing of it, was driven by some ultimate power we both know exists, in some fashion. So, whatever is going through that eight-decade brain of yours, I'm ready to be involved with you in this phenomenal work you've been doing and that you want to expand. Count me in, Sam, count me in."

Sam roared his lion laugh. He leaned over in a convulsive state and then slowly his head came up as he calmed down, looking deep into Jamie's eyes. "Wow, my man, you want to come on board this ship of mine big time, hallelujah, brother," he pauses, "how much time you got today?"

Jamie quickly responded in a laughing way, "To my life or for you?"

"Both," Sam replied with his own twinkling of laughter in his deep dark eyes.

"The rest of this day if need be," he responded. "Lay it on me, Sam."

Sam looked at Jamie and said, "Okay, we gonna be a team again, which relates to what I've been thinking so much about over the past months. You coming here, at this time in both our lives, I believe, was meant to happen by a force beyond our understanding. So, let me ask you something, okay?"

"Fire away, boss," Jamie said.

Sam answered, "Do you know what a moment is?"

Jamie slid up a bit in the cavernous chair, looked at Sam and said, "Of course. A fraction of a second…a space in time…a quick event," he paused then added, "or if you're a historian or a writer, I guess you use moment as a short time period; a second, I'd say. Don't know, that's the best I can do. So why did you ask?"

Sam leaned back and said, "Because over the past months, years actually, I've been doing a lot of meditating. You know that Hindu stuff? Well, for some reason I got books on it and grew to really like it because it literally gives you pause to just think about this unique time, we call life. Life, what the hell is it really? Oh, I could really go on. You got me started, Jamie."

Jamie replied," No, Sam, you got yourself started, so keep going. You're on a roll and I want you to lay it on me. I'm intrigued."

CHAPTER FIFTEEN

Sam took a sip of his tea, briefly looked away from Jamie and then turned, looking at him, eyes on eyes. Jamie had not felt that affected by another person. His look was, as if he was speaking from a mountain, as in Moses depicted speaking to his people. Jamie wiggled a bit in his chair, adjusting to Sam's intensity. It was quiet in his file filled office which seemed out of place for whom he was looking at. Jamie thought for a flash that they should have been in a monastery, somewhere, probably in Nepal because, as he tried to return the look that Sam was giving him, he knew he was going somewhere he had never been before.

Sam sighed and said, "My friend and truly I mean that because I know that you are coming back to me literally out of the blue, was meant to be. A power: a power of this universe sent you back to me," as he smiled, paused and went on, "and I know you are too wise a man to laugh at what I say because I knew you back then and now as a wise man. What do I mean? I mean that you can laugh; you can enjoy a cold beer; you probably enjoyed making love to your wife, who you mentioned the other day died ten years ago, and most important to me, you are a completer. What is a completer? A person who likes to start and complete whatever he starts. You started with me, oh, what was it 1979 or 1980, in helping me organize food and helping me fix up those derelict buildings. In doing so, you were helping me in my beginning, to help some of the kids in my neighborhood while you were struggling to get your start as an architect. What you did for me, affected me; that you would give up your time to help me when you yourself were struggling. I've never forgotten what you did. For me, I have seen thousands of good things happen to my kids and thank the Lord, so to speak, I also had a woman who gave me love, respect and a couple of super kids and grandkids who now work with me. Man, what else could a man hope for. I have seen some of those kids I fed and monitored and admonished for foolishness that comes with youth, go into some successful life stories, which makes all that has been done so worthwhile. And, I have lived to this age of mine, still with a mind that works and you, who helped me at the beginning, have come back to me," he paused again as Jamie was in kind of a stupor, just listening to this sage, who now went on, "yet Jamie, there is more to come because I want you to listen to what I have learned and now believe in about this thing of ours, we call life. Do you want to hear it?"

Jamie was mesmerized and didn't know how to reply except to quietly respond, "Please go on, Sam."

Sam straightened his large body into almost a military position befitting his early career and lifestyle as he continued, "Jamie, it all comes down to one word," as he paused and then said, "Moment." He said that one word with a slow clarity, it was almost as if he was talking in a biblical way, then he repeated it slowly, "Moment...human life is only a moment in the trajectory of this Universe. Our Earth is a grain of sand in the ocean of the universe and we are likewise a grain of sand in the ocean of our world. Think about that, if you would, because that is the analogy of life that's come to me lately."

Jamie was startled by the change in Sam's demeanor and face; he was serenely intense. He had that look that he was secure with anything going on within himself or in anyone he was looking at. Many times, when he spent time with Sam forty years ago, Jamie would leave the century old brick building where he first started his work with black youngsters, wondering who Sam really was? The man had been in the service; in war in Vietnam; at the White House; and then came back to his decrepit hometown and neighborhood and devoted his life to helping black kids literally survive. But even then, to Jamie he seemed almost godly; always pure, honest and never changing his philosophy, that the little kids he served just needed a chance to survive and help to succeed in their lives. Jamie told Sam after working with him back then, he should have been a priest; a guru; a minister or someone of religion, who served humanity for good. He would laugh and say, as he did every time, that he knew what his purpose in life was and in essence he was a priest, guru and minister, but in his way. Jamie could never argue with that and looking at this man now, forty years later, as lean and tough looking as he always had been, Jamie knew he was looking at someone who was a special human being and he, Jamie, was meant to be sitting here this day looking at him. He smiled and said, "I have a feeling more of this philosophy is on its way."

Sam smiled and said, "Much more but remember that key word; moment. It is the focal point of humanity; yours, mine, everyone who ever has or will exist on this earth or probably anywhere in this Universe where some creations like us or not like us, exist for their moment."

Jamie didn't move, he couldn't. He was frozen. As he looked at this man older than himself by ten years, his thoughts focused on one thing; either Sam had begun to drift mentally, or he was on a new, visionary tract. Then without thinking further he knew it was the latter. Sam was too brilliant a thinker not to have delved deeply into whatever he was focused on. But why now and was this revelation the first time he had spoken to anyone about his new beliefs? As Jamie looked at the seriousness in Sam's face he knew immediately, for some reason, that this was his first expression to anyone about his beliefs that had developed. Jamie then reacted by saying, "Sam, why now and why me?"

Without hesitation Sam replied, "Because, my dear friend, you coming back to me was supposed to occur because it has never ended from when we last met; there was a synchronization when we first met and worked together that has been reattached by you coming to see me. No question about it."

Jamie smiled and said, "I don't doubt that, but I need to hear more about this "moment" philosophy."

Sam replied, "I firmly believe that Man has made up God to fill a need, but actually God may be just a name that simulates what I and others call, the Universal Energy. I mean, Jamie, do you believe that the Universe just happened?"

Jamie did not know how to answer, but did say, "Never thought of it much, that way," he paused, squirmed in the sofa and added "but I have always been puzzled by those shows I've seen, especially the last couple years, by scientists who spend their lives looking out into space. Since we launched satellites and space craft that can see where we could never before, I've been fascinated by what they have discovered. But to answer your question, Sam, that has nothing to do with believing in the Universe. I mean I believe in it. It does exist. It's out there and we, Man on earth, are just a small part of it. That I do know and believe, but did it just happen, wow, how the hell would I know?"

Sam immediately responded, "That, my dear friend, is what I expected you to say. How would you or anyone know, except, that we know it exists. We are in it, although a tiny essence which gets back to my first and most important point, that is, we, humans, on this earth of ours, are just a tiny and I mean a tiny element in the Universe. Our lives, which is our total element of existence, are likewise a microscopic element in and of Earth."

"So, Sam what are you trying to tell me?"

"Not trying to tell you anything, except that my belief is that our lives are simply moments in the unknown magnitude of time. Every human beings' moment of existence is a creation of the Universe and all resides in a three-pound receptacle right here in each human species," he said tapping the side of his head. "That three pounds is the finest computer system ever created which then makes me believe that in this Universe, humanity, even though developing from tiny cells in water, has developed and adapted over billions of years in a never-ending function of the Universe," he paused again and added, "have I lost you?"

Jamie was speechless and mindless. He didn't know how to reply, so he didn't, he just looked at Sam who was now smiling with lines crisscrossing across his cheeks. He recovered a bit and said, "No, you haven't lost me, it's just a bit much. I could tell that you had created a comforting belief system and I think I know what you're getting at and frankly I also think we may be closer in our aged beliefs than ever, Sam. "

Sam smiled, saying," I felt that. But I need to go on because…," he looked past Jamie and waved past him and said, "Come over, darling," he said.

Germaine walked up to Sam's desk with two cups of steaming water. "Some tea Pops and for you Mr. Jamie, if you would like some."

"Sure would, thanks," Jamie replied.

She put the cup on the table next to Sam and handed a cup to Jamie. "You two are awfully quiet in here. Marty and I were getting worried," she said with the a smile Jamie automatically knew where it came from.

"Your grandfather was just explaining some things to me Germaine," Jamie said and paused, adding, "that smile of yours certainly runs in the family."

"You know, you should see Marty when he lights up?", Germaine responded. "He looks like some TV star I used to watch, can't think of his name, but he saves it, you know what I mean, for when he wants to use it. When something hits him to make him laugh, his whole face opens up like a great big brown bear."

Sam injected, "I try to make him laugh sometimes, Jamie, just to see that smile."

Jamie laughed and added, "Well if I was in the room with the both of you when you let go with some laughs, don't think there would be much room left."

"We are one happy family, Jamie, 'cause their Grand Momma, my beloved Isabella, was one funny lady."

Germaine quickly said, "Granddaddy does not think he is funny, Mr. Sloan. But you know, we know that humor is what makes his seriousness work so well. You know what I mean?"

"I do. Ironically, as you were talking, I was thinking about what your grandpa, Sam, as I call him, was just talking to me about. It was serious, deep stuff and all of a sudden, I thought of his smile, that over the years I've never forgotten, which made me realize that he is the epitome of a complete man. He knows the seriousness and the humor about being a human being. So, thank you for bringing me some tea and for explaining how humor is ingrained in your family. So, refreshing, just like the tea, I might add and thanks for it."

"You're welcome and I'll leave you two alone. If you want more tea or anything, ring that bell, Gramps," she said as she looked at a small brass bell on the table next to Sam. She turned and left the room.

Sam took a sip of tea, put down the cup and said, "Okay, Jamie, let me throw one more bit of cosmic philosophy, as I call it, on you. Okay?"

Jamie put down his cup and said, "Fire away."

"My Moment Philosophy as I call it, is also tied in with this mindfulness stuff popular on that social media. To me that crap is temporary pop stuff for people to make money. What I believe is that our moment is our opportunity to excel. It's all the time we got, Jamie. We are the minimal; our brain is the unique and minimalist unit paired up with the unique and maximalist exposure we call the universe. It's almost like, a minus and a plus equaling a neutrality; or the ultimate power, if you will." He looked at Jamie and said quietly, "Got it?"

"Whooh," Jamie exclaimed. "You adding your formula of equal minus and plus gets a neutral power?. Is this a new Einstein code?" Jamie responded seriously.

A roar from Sam, as his grin crisscrossed his face and he slapped his thighs, "Whooh, Jamie, Einstein I am not, but Sam, I am, I am," he rollickingly roared.

Jamie returned with his usual held back smiling technique, "Sam the Man, you don't know how great it is to be here with you and I can't wait for more of your "moment" dissertation."

"I've only just begun, Jamie," Sam responded as he took a sip of tea, emptying the cup.

CHAPTER SIXTEEN

Over the next hours, Sam and Jamie talked back and forth, mostly with Jamie trying to interpret Sam's newfound beliefs. It was near six and Germaine, then Marty came in trying to get Sam to take a break for spaghetti and meat balls, which apparently was a specialty Marty had mastered. Sam said to Marty that he needed a half hour and then they would eat, but he needed him to make sure they had some dark, red wine. Marty left and Sam turned to Jamie, saying, "Wine, Jamie, what's it made from?"

"Well, it comes from grapes, Sam, even I know that."

"That's my point in this whole discussion. Elements from outer space; the universe; out there, billions of miles away, the elements are what creates anything. But where do they come from? Oh, and speaking of elements, have you been following the news about this virus, Jamie?"

"I have and it is about to paralyze this country."

"All countries, Jamie, all countries. The Universe is speaking to us humans, I believe. It is saying that we are not invincible. We are all just part of this whole mysterious, totally unknown space we call the Universe."

They conversed back and forth about their belief systems until Marty waved them for dinner. Jamie had not had spaghetti in a long time, and it was scrumptious. He hadn't wiped a plate with a piece of bread in years. The dark red sauce was delicious. As the two young folks cleaned up the table, Sam and Jamie sat back sipping on red wine without talking until the two young ones had gone back to the kitchen.

Finally, Sam looked at Jamie with that look of his, bore into him and said, "My belief system is mine, Jamie. I have not talked to anyone about my convictions which I have recently, and finality understood. Oh, I was a devout Christian since I was a baby. My mama was a typical black lady who sang in the choir of her church almost until the day she died. I was in the service and for those years, wherever I was stationed, I attended church. When I got out of the Marines and came here, I went back to attending the same church where my mama was buried. You will laugh at this, but several years ago when I finally took time to sit back and relax here in that very chair in the living room where we first talked, I began to watch, now you're going to laugh, Jamie, National Geo. I was fascinated by the shows about the Universe. I learned about billions of miles between everything in this space of ours. I learned about how we know literally nothing about these billions of miles and that we, humans, on this tiny, round ball of rock with some billion-year-old oceans and mountains ... are absolutely nothing in this Universe. When I say nothing, I mean in comparison. We are miniscule in the universe, yet what we are and what we experience in these moments, of what we call life, is everything. Then poof, it's gone. Yet, Jamie, as I just said, it...life, for us, for all humans, is everything. Afterwards, nothing...unless that force that we know and call energy, is in some way part of some Universal power system that we know nothing about." Sam stopped, wiped his face with a handkerchief because he was sweating so much from the intensity of what he had just said.

Jamie again could not respond. As Sam looked at him slowly, quietly for the first time, his mind began to wander why this man, who he had not seen in forty some years, was exploding his newfound philosophy to him? Ironically, Jamie understood, indirectly, that at his age of eighty-four, one begins to seriously think about death and the life one has led. Along with that, as per his own mindset of recent times, one may think about where humanity has been and where it was going. At least that is how he was now, at this moment, as he looked at Sam who was stoic, just staring calmly at him. 'Where is that man's mind, right now', Jamie wondered. He sat up and replied, "Wow, Sam, that's quite a bottom line you just laid out. I've noted since we hooked up again that you hadn't lost your incredible sense of reality. You don't live in maybe's or could be's, you just live in what is, if you know what I mean?"

Sam smiled and replied, "I know just what you mean and that is the best description I can accept of me, because I only believe in what is, however, Jamie, what I have just described to you is my belief in a controlling universal force we know nothing about."

Jamie responded, "Okay, Sam, I understand what you are saying, and we are living in this Universe that is in control of everything, but Sam, you and I are two old men who have known each other for half of our lives who are facing just a few more years of our existence. Pardon my language, but what the fuck does this new philosophy of yours have to do with me, Jamie Sloan, reigniting our friendship and wanting to help you support poor young people find a better life for themselves. What does that have to do with what I wanted to talk to you about today, tonight, now, which I haven't even had time to do so," he said, exasperated.

Sam's face looked away, then back at Jamie as he finished. "I guess I didn't tie them together very well, but it has everything to do with what I'm doing and you being here with me, everything. It has everything to do with what I will accomplish here for my young people now and the ones I have helped become productive people in this world. I'm still helping them and this new sense I have of this world we live in makes more logical sense to me than I have ever felt," he said abruptly, pausing then added, "if I misunderstood you, so be it, you are still a man I trust and value."

"Sam, you did not misunderstand me" Jamie responded then went on, "but, actually, I do believe in what you have been saying to me. You said it better than I could have because I too have come to believe that we humans are temporary inhabitants of this earth. Earth will go away some time far away in the future within this Universe itself," ...he paused, "who knows, maybe the Universe is temporary, we don't know that there isn't something that even the Universe is within. But Sam, that's way beyond the years that you and I have left. We have to deal with the reality of our existence, now, Sam. Ours, Sam, nothing else, no one else's just our conscious time. So, Sam, I want to come back in a day or so, whenever it's convenient for you to tell you. What I want to do to help you with now; key word is now. How I can help you in this present time, now, because what you have said to me today is literally the big picture and I want to tell you about how I want to help you in, let's say, the little picture...our picture."

Nothing for seconds. It was quiet. Jamie was done, silent, he just sat there. Sam did not respond, then he slowly turned away and looked out the darkened window. The two grandchildren could be heard saying good night to each other out in hallway. It was also dark in the room except for the small light on Sam's desk. Finally, Sam cleared his throat and said, "You truly are a wise and good man, Jamie." He rolled his chair back and stood up for the first time in hours and came around to Jamie with his right hand out. Jamie stood and they shook hands, then hugged tightly. After a few seconds, Sam leaned back and said, "Let's get a nightcap…a small one and you can be on your way and maybe you can tell me what you wanted to talk about."

Jamie did not reply but followed Sam into the kitchen where he went to a cupboard and pulled out two, small glasses. He poked around in a shelf and brought down a half empty bottle of Glenlivet scotch. "Neat, Jamie?"

"Neat," Jamie replied.

As they stood there with their glasses in hand, Sam said, "Okay, lay it on me, old friend?" as he walked back into his office area with Jamie at his side.

Jamie took a sip, looked across at Sam and said, "Last week you showed me computer reports of those you have helped over the years; those being helped now; and prospective kids who really need help. The categories are well defined, and funds needed are obvious to help these kids. Sam, I want to help by donating $100,000."

Sam put his drink down on the counter. He looked at Jamie. He turned and Jamie could see a tear coming down his cheek as he said, "Will I say something like, oh, no, Jamie old friend, you don't have to do this? Pardon my language of the Marines, but fuck no, I won't say that."

Jamie replied, "I knew you wouldn't. No bullshit, that's you. But that my friend is only the beginning. I am shooting for more with only one request."

"Whooh, whooh, okay", Sam paused then said, "what would that be?"

Jamie responded, "I've been thinking about what you have done and are doing and what you have told me about. It seems to me what you are doing is probably what many people around the country do in different ways and what the governments try to do, that is assist poor children and their parent or parents support them. It must be a massive and totally uncoordinated function of society and I would like to find a way to coordinate all the potential children who need help into, first a local and gradually expand nationally. All these organizations and government systems, would be coordinated into some type of system designed to help all disadvantaged kids and families in this country," he paused and added, "but with one proviso."

Sam replied slowly, "And what would that be?"

Jamie said firmly, "That administrative expenses will be closely managed. Over the years I've been involved with many non-profit organizations and I know for a fact that with some there is waste in the allocation of funds. The administrative expenses are extremely high, which means the funds donated are not used to benefit those in need."

Sam said, "Oh, man, I understand your concern and you are right on. I personally will watch all of our administrative expenses."

Jamie added quickly, "Sam, it won't be just me because I vow that we will work to find other people to be primary benefactors, in fact I've been thinking about contacting a person who might be able to help you. He pauses, then goes on, "Margaret Decker's husband, who was a Senator from Pennsylvania recently passed away. In a newspaper article, she indicated her interest going forward would be to focus on helping underprivileged children and their families. I have known she and her husband since high school and feel comfortable contacting her to see if she would have interest in talking to you about your program. If you agree, I have her email address and would like to contact her tonight."

Sam seemed stunned. He looked at Jamie as he slowly finished his drink and poured himself another one. He said, "Where in the hell have you been all my life, Jamie Sloan?"

Jamie smiled, "Good question. I don't think I've been anywhere as you can tell from what you have told me today. Whether you knew it or not, I was right here beside you and I sure am now. Haven't been anywhere, really."

"One thing," Sam said, "ironically, my belief system is currently giving us humans the ultimate test, if you've been listening to the news.

I think the Universe is testing humanity once again with the virus which, based on the news, is spreading rapidly in this country and around the world. How we deal with this virus will be another test of our ability to preserve humanity?"

Jamie replied, "I caught the news this morning and it is getting really serious. It will be a challenge if it stops our country cold as it looks like the Feds are talking about. But you know, as I was thinking when I was listening to you and how I could respond to you, something hit me, Sam. If it does bring our country and the world, for that matter, to a standstill, the people it will affect the most will be the kids you have been helping all these years. Maybe we can organize asap because your folks will be needing help more than ever when and if this country comes to a halt."

Sam rubbed his face and replied, "Your folks now, Jamie boy. So, let me ask you, can you be here tomorrow morning, early?"

Jamie replied, "I can and will be," as he paused and then went on, "but what I want to do is get more monetary support for your kids. I know what I said sounded like a campaign slogan for some politician, but that is the mantra I have to believe in since being with you. I feel unfairness of it all and want to find ways to level the playing field, so to speak. What's go me scare is this goddamn epidemic is going to do to these kids and their parents."

Sam responded, "You are right, Jamie. This will be a test, that is for sure, if this thing really takes off, but I must also think about the long haul. So, we must intensify our services," then he paused as his train of thought changed and he added, "You and I, well you may be, but I may not be around too much longer to keep this program going, so what you said earlier about funding is a blessing for me and all the kids here now and who will be here, especially if this virus epidemic takes hold." Sam then stepped forward and put his hands on Jamie's shoulders, his still solid body wider and taller than Jamie and softly said, "You're being here at this time is a message from what I was talking about earlier. Why now? Because the Universe is challenging this specimen, we call humanity and at the same time brought you to me to help me during this time."

Jamie tapped Sam's shoulder and said with a smile, "Something got me to Homewood and you, and I guess the Universe is as good as any to blame. I'll be here as much as I can after my volunteer work is done, so get used to me, old man."

Sam looked at Jamie and replied, "Well, you may be here more than you think because Germaine told me earlier that that public places may be shut down soon. But whatever happens, my focus will be on keeping us afloat. We can start setting up backup alternatives if things get really rough and maybe even expanding during this difficult time as you were just talking about. Take advantage of a bad situation."

Jamie responded, "It's been a good session Sam and thanks for your dissertation. It's got me thinking. You mentioned you were having a staff meeting early tomorrow morning , so I thought I would stop by before I go to the transplant office.. You be up?", Jamie said with a smile as he started to walk to the door.

Sam looked at him with a querulous look on his face, "Every morning I'm up way 7AM, so if you can make it at that time, I'll make you some great coffee", he replied as he led the way out to the door.

Later that night Jamie sat at his computer and found Margaret's email address. He sent her an email sending condolences; asked how she was doing; and if there is anything he can do to help her. He then explained that he read the newspaper article about her interest in working with underprivileged children and families, which ironically, he was now doing with an old friend of his here in Pittsburgh, Sam Westcott. He wondered if on her next trip to Pittsburgh if she would be interested in getting together with him for coffee.

CHAPTER SEVENTEEN

Jamie woke up early after a restless night and checked his emails. He couldn't believe what he saw. It was a reply from Margaret thanking him for his condolences and saying that it was so ironic he had contacted her because she was flying into Pittsburgh tomorrow to settle estate issues with her attorneys. She stated that she would love to see Jamie and would it be possible to meet Sam Westcott tomorrow and learn more about his organization. Her plane arrives at 10AM and her appointment with her attorneys is not until the next morning. Jamie immediately responded and wrote he would contact Sam and coordinate a time with him. He closed with it will be great to see you tomorrow. He called Sam immediately to tell him that his friend Margaret Decker that he had mentioned to him yesterday, would be in Pittsburgh tomorrow and would like to meet him. Sam was elated and told him that anytime tomorrow would be fine. Jamie emailed Margaret back and said Sam is available whenever its convenient for you. Here is Sam's address and my cell phone number. Look forward to seeing you tomorrow.

Because of Margaret coming tomorrow, Jamie left a message with the transplant office and changed his volunteer schedule for later today. He then called Sam to tell him he wanted to come over and prepare for the meeting tomorrow with her. Sam was up for that.

Jamie was amazed because Sam was up and full of energy at this early hour for his staff meeting. His two grandchildren, Germaine and Marty were there, along with three other people he hadn't met before, but who were introduced to him by Sam before the meeting began. Sylvan Brown, a lovely, dark skinned woman who had three young kids and policemen husband; Jeffrey Epstein, a graduate of CMU, who grew up in Squirrel Hill and was their computer online expert; and lastly, Barbra Brewer, a heavy set, tan skinned woman in her forties, who raised two kids now at Pitt because of Sam. She had worked for the State of Pennsylvania for twenty years and decided to join him. Sam began the session by going over the role of these three staffers. They were primarily working on a logistical trace of all the children ever in his program from day one; ones currently in the program; and lastly, the potential children who were in the process of being accepted. Sam then went on to talk about their biggest concern of this morning was the potential and pending closures of schools due to the State and Federal governments trying to stop the spread of the covid virus. They all sat stoically as Sam quietly talked about the challenges they would face if everything shut down because of the virus. Fortunately, he said, most everything they did was online; every child; every support mechanism, from private donations inventory to all government programs that they had uncovered was available on their site, which they would be able to refer to if they had to make emergency plans if things happened the way they were being portrayed in the media.

Sam then introduced Jamie to them all as an old friend who was with him at the beginning and was now coming on the team to add some age into the group which caused a chuckle from the group. He then raised his hand and they quieted down as he said they had a new benefactor who was beginning with a donation of a hundred thousand "big ones", he said with a smile and a pat on Jamie's back. The staff cheered in unison with Jamie receiving a couple more slaps on his back from a smiling Sam. Jamie said that he was already involved at the Carnegie Library and the University of Pittsburgh Transplant Service as a volunteer but would begin to come by at least two or three days a week to do whatever Sam or they needed to be done.

It was getting close to nine, as Sam put up his hand and said that Jamie had to leave, but asked each of the others to give a summary of their current duties and what they needed to do that week. Each summarized their workloads and Sam added, that he would concentrate on working out an emergency program if and when the schools closed which would affect all of their children. The last thing Sam did was to set up a schedule for the rest of the week and that by Friday, the complete interior of the building from the basement to the space under the roof would be completely cleaned and organized by next Monday morning. He had a contractor friend who was going to go over the building and make necessary repairs of any structural problems he found and would give Sam a blueprint of additional structural repairs that needed to be done. Jamie volunteered to help with this work which Sam acknowledged with a wave of his hand.

With that, Sam closed the staff meeting, and they all went to their workplaces.

Jamie and Sam spent the next several hours planning for tomorrow's meeting with Margaret. Jamie explained to Sam about his history with the Decker's. He gave him Warren's rise in politics to where he was a Senator from Pennsylvania and in line to run for President as per the media. His sudden death had received major coverage as it did with Margaret because she had been very active in international work for the United States. Sam acknowledged he remembered Warren as somewhat a neutral politician, not really left or right. Jamie said that Margaret had stated several times in interviews that she wanted to spend time now working to on coordinating Federal and State government programs that were supposed to help underprivileged children. Sam perked up when he said that and how he had always been critical of how ineffective the various programs were that helped young children and their parents. Sam went on to say how glad he was that "lady Margaret", as he called her, wanted to work on coordinating all the millions of government dollars set aside in so many different programs, that he had lost count. That was something that had always bothered him and if she could help with that, it would be great. Jamie agreed he would like to help in working on streamlining all the sources available. As they concluded their meeting, they did their usual hug, and Sam went into the main office area as Jamie headed outside to catch a bus.

He still had time to get some work done at the transplant office. He got situated at his desk and began his data work, but after a few minutes, Jamie thought back to the morning with Sam and his remarkable band of five, who were the core of his operation. They were obviously dedicated to helping Sam's cause. Then he realized he had to concentrate on this critical work he was doing because it had to be perfect. This data had to transferred exactly as presented with no mistakes as it was patients medical results. For the next hours, he concentrated on the work and finished what was needed to be done that day.

With his work done, Jamie headed down to the Carnegie Library to see if he could find a couple books because he realized he had nothing to read. He'd been so busy working and now with his new commitment to Sam, more than ever, he knew he needed some downtime and reading good fiction always helped him to relax. For close to an hour, he slowly worked his way through new books and pulled out some he might want to read and took them back to a table off to the side of the main library. As he read the book covers about the novels, he thought about Sam's comment about how he had always been concerned about the mismanagement of current programs that were supposed to provide assistance for low-income families. Jamie realized how ironic it was to be bringing Margaret and Sam together who seemed to have such mutual concerns.

Jamie sat beside the books he had pulled and relaxed as he hadn't done for quite a while. This was the atmosphere that had always put him at ease, a library and books. He drifted in thought to what he was now involved in and where it all came from and where it might go. He couldn't stop thinking about his morning session with Sam and what he had committed too. It was almost a dream come true because his life, conservative in his views of life and generally politics, was very liberal in how the "have nots", people of lower classes were treated by governments and unfortunately the "haves" in this world. His best friends as a kid were black and Italian who played two streets away from his Victorian house. His mother had not a racist bone in her body and encouraged him to accept all people. Throughout school, the service and college, he was close with many who were underprivileged folks. He worked closely to rebuild and build facilities around Pittsburgh and in other cities with no salary for low-income families. underprivileged folks. He spent time in Puerto Rico building living sites for poor Puerto Ricans who were, even in that diverse country, set aside from the white, Castilian Spanish folks who dominated that island. Slowly the country had gradually accepted all those with black skin especially after the favorite and most popular Puerto Rican of all time and Jamie's personal hero, Roberto Clemente was killed in a plane crash in 1971. It seemed that helping to mend centuries of division between blacks and whites, as it was gradually doing in America itself, had become a mantra for him. He wasn't sure why, but he believed, down deep, that it went back to his mother, with her quiet, persuasive attitude of hating bigotry. She had grown up with a father, as wonderful as he was, who was bigoted against black folks. His mother had deeply rejected her father's belief system and passed her beliefs quietly onto Jamie, who was now carrying on her belies which made him feel so good inside. He thought how amazing it is that genetic threads can positively bind and affect children long after the provider of same, his Mother in this case, had passed on. Of course, the opposite also occurs, which is why so many others continue bigotry into the next generations.

As he sat quietly in the silence of the library, he thought of Sam's philosophy about how we, humans on this earth, are just a moment in what we call time. He took a deep breath and smiled again, chuckling even at how life is a pinball machine as the ball bounces all over the place. He now had to concentrate, like in the old days of designing a new building out of nothing, on helping Sam build on the foundation of what he had had created. A library was a thing of beauty for mankind. A quiet place in our society of noise upon noise. An institution that had been in the same location for over a hundred and twenty years that still provided the same altruistic mood for thousands over its life span. He had to get going so he moved his chair back; he had much to do.

Jamie walked toward the bus stop on Fifth Avenue as his mind continued to work overtime in thinking about tomorrow. So much going on and he hadn't eaten much all day. He had tried to keep an eating routine that was based on quality and healthy foods over the past years. When Louise died, he ate terribly; and he gained twenty pounds. Finally, he began to watch his diet and eat less and healthier, plus walk, instead of ride, all the time. He lost that weight, plus another ten pounds and began to eat more at breakfast and always had a lunch.

Sitting at the kitchen table, Jamie began to eat a frozen meal of macaroni and cheese with slices of tomato. He stopped, put his fork down and thought how fortunate he was and said out loud, "Here you are at an age when most men are struggling with health issues and have nothing to do in their lives, and you, Jamie Sloan, have a nice warm apartment with food in front of you, clothes on your back and people who you are working with each day who seem to appreciate your efforts and an old black friend who has opened up his life and beliefs to you. Jesus Christ, you are so fortunate," Jamie proclaimed out loud in his empty kitchen of his empty apartment.

He immediately took his fork and devoured the rest of his dinner and sipped the remaining amount of deep red wine. He sat back in his chair and said out loud, ""Okay, Jamie old boy, tomorrow is another big day."

CHAPTER EIGHTEEN

Margaret arrived late morning. She arrived with her associate, Gizelle, a French lady who apparently did a lot of her research, plus was her personal pilot and driver. After a walk around the site when Jamie had explained the expansion locations, they went back to Sam's office where Sam started by giving Margaret his background, how he started, where he was now, and where he would like to go. They all listened as Sam talked non-stop, as if he had another twenty years ahead of him and Margaret, as they both ended up calling her, seemed to buy into his every word. They spent three hours together, the last one with Sam's two grandkids and three person crew. They were laughing and drinking Sam's special coffee, with a sprinkle of a small bottle of twenty-five-year-old Glenlivet which he said he hadn't tasted for five years because it was only used for special, special occasions. Sam was absolutely in his own heaven as Margaret pledged three things to him, but looked at Jamie as she said it, because they seemed to have developed a connection. Jamie was impressed with this seventy-plus year-old woman who looked twenty years younger. He noted when she talked, she had a twinkle in her eyes like the old TV star, Phyliss Diller. She hadn't changed much since he had last been with her, but as she was then, she was a charmer, but a really honest one.

After listening to Sam, she said she felt as if she had walked into a place where she was supposed to be. She had always wanted to be associated with an organization that truly helped young people and who really, truly needed help. She felt that this was the place. Sam's face lit up as she went on to say that she wanted to start, for openers, a one-year plan, by establishing, a local and then a national structured program for underprivileged children which Jamie was astounded at because that was what he had envisioned to Sam. Then she talked of working to integrate a high-tech system to coordinate national, private organizations of a similar goal and tie it into current government programs because Warren had told her so many times of the dysfunctional and overlapping systems within the Federal government. She said she felt it could be done and more importantly, they must establish a national organization or federation of similar groups to include children of native Americans; children of immigrants; and any unrepresented elements under United States control. When she paused, Jamie looked at Sam and he hadn't moved. He just sat with his arms crossed with a slight smile across his face.

Margaret went on to say, that all children in need, could and should be supported and their parent or parents also. Her mantra sounded close to what Sam had talked about and Jamie was astounded by how these two adults, one in his eighties and the other her seventies, had almost similar beliefs along with his own. But what amazed him more was that he, Jamie Sloan, had somehow, brought them together and he was right in the middle of one of the most exciting things he had ever been involved in. He had built some beautiful buildings during his career, but nothing as powerful as what this group of eight, led by Sam and now with Margaret Decker who had come out of nowhere except from Jamie's past.

On a break, Jamie told Margaret he needed to clear up something about Warren that he had witnessed. They moved to a small room off to the side of Sam's office and sat in two old leather chairs facing each other. After he went over what he had seen at the creek that spring day years ago, she looked at him and said that she was so glad he brought up this terrible event because it had haunted Warren his whole life. She told him the tale of more than fifty years ago at McConnell's Creek located north of Pittsburgh that Warren had repeated many times to her that haunted him. He was devastated by what happened and what he didn't do that day. She described how excited she had been in high school, a junior, and that Warren, a senior, and probably the most handsome boy in school, had asked her out. They had gone with a group of his senior friends for a picnic. Most of them swam in a small indentation in the swift moving creek upstream. Warren spent time building a campfire downstream from them for a sing a long that night with parents as chaperones in cabins that night. It had been an exciting day until Marsha Snowden, a real daring girl, dove into the main creek downstream which was roaring along. None of their group saw her go in, but suddenly they heard screaming and looked down the creek at Marsha flailing her arms. The nearest person to her on shore was Warren. He ran to the creek bank, looked down at Marsha flailing her arms and was yelling at her. He looked around as if looking around for someone to jump in to save her. Then he got down on the bank and kept screaming, looking around, but didn't move toward jumping in the violent stream. Marsha kept sinking and coming up as she was carried downstream. Several boys ran down to the creek bank and Skippy Young, took off his shirt and pants then leaped into the water. He came up and kept looking around, as his body was swept along, but still a long way from where Marsha was last seen. Finally, Skippy grabbed a tree branch, that was hanging over the river and pulled himself into the riverbank. Warren leaned over the roaring creek and helped him up. Marsha was never seen until three days later and several miles downstream. where her body washed up against a bridge pillar. Margaret added that their group watched this awful event

Even then, many people asked Warren why he didn't jump in, and he would always say the same thing that he thought she could get into the shore, but then it was too late. It was at that point that Jamie interjected and told Margaret that he had been on the other side downstream with a church group for an outing. He saw the girl jump in and begin to scream as she was swept downstream. What surprised him was that Warren was right where she dove in and saw her come up, watched her struggle, but did nothing until her screaming stopped, as she went downstream in the violent current. Jamie said he ran up his side of the creek, but there was no sign of her, and he couldn't believe that Warren, the hero of the football team, with a big, muscular body could not have tried to save the girl. He did nothing and for all the years since, Jamie wondered why he hadn't tried to help her.

Margaret took his hand and said, "I wondered too because I was saw it happen. He was a different person after that happened. We stopped dating and it wasn't until I was working in New York and Warren traveled there on business that we began to date again. One night I asked him what had happened that day and could he have done anything to help her. He looked at me a look I'll never forget, and he slowly said that he thought she was strong enough to pull herself out and quickly changed the subject to his work travel. Other than that mystery, I fell in love with him because I felt a closeness to him, I had never felt with another person, let alone a man. It wasn't until our honeymoon in Canada, that Warren, the great athlete, explained to me that he never learned how to swim. In fact, he was afraid of any kind of water; a lake, a river or the ocean, which we never visited throughout our marriage, until we discovered Cape Cod. For some reason, he had a violent fear of water. It wasn't until we went to Wellfleet on the Cape, that I got him in the water, cold as it was. Gradually, he got over his fear. Apparently, when he was twelve years old, he was thrown into a deep lake at a boy's camp and almost drowned. From that moment until Wellfleet, he feared water. He was crying when he told me about that day and that he was ashamed for not trying to help her. She paused, then smiled at Jamie and said slowly "Well, now you know."

She went to say that Warren never forgot what he didn't do. In fact, he set up an anonymous fund for Marsha Snowden's family's grandchildren in her name, which they were told was because of what happened to their daughter. He could never tell them or anyone about why he hadn't or couldn't help her. It troubled him his whole life, she said, and Jamie knew she was serious. Jamie felt ashamed that he had held such a negative opinion of such a successful man for all the years but was so glad that he now understood. He thanked her and she was so pleased that her husband's dilemma had been clarified for him. For Jamie, her coming to Pittsburgh had literally taken a monkey off of his back because what he had thought of Warren over the years. So, as it turned out, meeting her had been a blessing understanding about that terrible event of years ago, but now, in this time, ironically it became a bonanza for Sam and all that he had wanted to do all his life.

But that revelation was not the topping on the cake, that came when Margaret said that when she went to the lady's room earlier, she had a called her banker in Boston to find out if they could set up a transfer process for funds to be set aside for Sam's program, the amount to be decided upon in the next day or so. She asked Sam to have his finance person set up a special account tomorrow so the funds could be transferred to Sam's bank as soon as possible because what she heard from her contacts in D.C., the President and Congress were going to react with some type of plan to handle financially the looming virus attack. She told Sam that the funds would be put into a special account that he should have his accountant and bank set up. Sam was ecstatic and called his accountant who said he would come by that afternoon to talk with Margaret and Sam about how to set up an account. She wanted to make sure it was titled properly with the name of his current organization until they came up with a new name to make it sound more national in name. The two of them were head-to-head across from Sam's desk as Jamie finally had to excuse himself because he had to get to the library. Margaret got up and gave Jamie a hug and said that she was so grateful to him for introducing her to Sam and what he had done, and she wants to be a part of it. Sam saluted Jamie as he turned and walked out, they were still jabbering away

He walked an extra six blocks to get a bus to loosen up his cramped knees which tightened when confined and gradually he could feel his legs opening up as his mind was on fire thinking about the meeting. As he rode on the bus, he first thought over the meeting at Sam's and then as usual, his eyes wandered around the collection of humans one encountered when on public transportation. He always wished that the political leaders of this country could ride public transportation just once to get the sense of who their constituents really were. The man across from him, maybe his age, who was stooped over, barely able to stay up in his seat; the lady in a wheelchair at the front with legs the size of loaves of bread; and the young black girl with three really young girls surrounding her on two seats in front of him. Where were these people's lives going to be in the days and years ahead? How unfair that he had everything, and these folks literally had nothing, at least based on what he was looking at. Looking around, the passengers represented mankind, including the disabled. Why in this world are so many out of the accepted mainstream? Then, he changed mental direction, thinking back to Sam's "moment" philosophy, that their meeting was a special moment; a moment that brought two people together who had never met before, yet they are now committed to help other people who just needed a chance in this life of ours. "Whooh," he cried out, as he saw seeing his stop up ahead wondering where in the hell he had just been.

The lady in the wheelchair unhooked her clamp that was attached to a siderail as the bus stopped and the driver opened the door while the floor panel dropped to the level of the sidewalk and she rolled her chair up to and down onto the sidewalk. In a flash she was off as Jamie got off behind her and followed her to the light at the corner. The bus roared off and he was right behind the square shaped lady with a bright red sweater as she rolled her wheelchair across Fifth Avenue headed for the library. He could see books stacked in a side pocket. 'What a lady', she is, he thought.

As Jamie waved at the police lady at the door, he watched the wheelchair lady head into the main library with no hesitation where she was going because she rolled right up to what Jamie knew was the European fiction racks. 'How wrong can you be?', he thought. He had put sorrow and negativity upon the people in the bus who looked overall, despondent, when in fact, how the hell did he know anything about them? He'd seen the older, chubby lady in the wheelchair and immediately made assumptions of all society, when in fact she knew exactly who she was and what was important to her. A lesson learned as he reached for the elevator button.

As Jamie sat down at his desk, he couldn't stop thinking about what Sam had been talking about in regards his vision of humanity within our Universe, especially after the phenomenal meeting of the morning. He hadn't reacted immediately to his monologue, but the more he thought about what he had said, the more he realized that it coincided ironically with how he was viewing life now, so different from when Louise passed on. As Jamie thought back to Sam talking to him, he realized it related to him, because it described how the mind does control Man. Nothing new there, but Sam was carrying it further, as he described humanity or each man's life as a nano-second; lives are a flick of a moment of time. Life literally it just a flicker of light, a moment in the cycle of universal time. Since leaving Sam that night his mind was churning overtime thinking of what he said that each of our lives are our just a moment; life is just a moment. For us, maybe eighty years is old in today's world, but to the Universe, it is just that; a flash. He could not forget that analogy. Something else he had said was that even though our lives are literally nothing timewise within the universe, within our own life span, it is our own universe and is everything time wise. "Two times; ours and the universe", he had said and ended by stating, "both are limitless". He came back to this moment he was in; his job at the library and back from all that he had experienced in a day he would never forget.

His felt a tap on his right shoulder. "Jamie, have a second?"

Jamie was startled, looked up at Lee, his boss at the Library. He sat up and said, "Sure, Lee, was daydreaming for a moment, what's up?"

Lee said slowly with a sad look on his face, "The library may be shutting down at the end of the week. This virus thing is starting to affect everything public and we may be shutting down until it passes. I'll get an email off to you by tomorrow afternoon."

"Man, this thing is getting serious, I guess. Okay, I'll look for the email," he said. "I can finish this up and start the South Side work when I come back. Just let me know."

CHAPTER NINETEEN

Jamie was down because if the library was closing, he knew the transplant service would probably also close. It was depressing, but then he thought back to the meeting yesterday afternoon with Sam, Margaret and the infamous genius Xavier Zaquill Lee, better known as the X Man, Sam's financial guru. Even now, as tired as he was from the jam-packed day, he couldn't stop smiling when thinking of this man. He had left their meeting when the whole crew was together in harmony, planning how they were going to expand Sam's business even with the pending pandemic scenario playing out. As he sat there looking out the window, the bus picked its way toward his stop, thing back to the extraordinary time he had just spent with his new partners.

There was so much that happened and Jamie's sense of humor was usually only for him, however, humor, at times, can make a serious meeting unforgettable, which apparently is what happened when Sam's financial guy, Xavier Zaquill Lee, met Sam's new partner, Margaret Decker. Apparently, as Jamie later found out from Margaret, their first encounter earlier that day was hilarious and yet extremely successful as it involved a most critical next step in the relationship between Sam and Margaret. From the get-go, they all had hit it off, personally and productively in their newly found mission. Margaret said that the experience with Xavier Zaquill Lee, who was the financial backbone of Sam's ventures, was hilarious. The X Man, was how he was introduced to her by Sam. She went on to tell Jamie about their meeting and that for the first half hour, Sam and the X Man talked about their lives together and Margaret just listened. They went on about how they first met in the Hill District of Pittsburgh listening to jazz when they were in high school. Sam went on about his joining the Marines while the X Man took courses in bookkeeping at a small Pittsburgh college named Robert Morris. After Sam got back from the service and was bouncing around Pittsburgh trying to figure out what he was going to do with his life, he bumped into the X Man, literally at a funeral of one of the guys they knew during their jazz days, Bubba Watson, who was a numbers man in the Hill. The X Man told him he was doing accounting work and if he ever needed any help, to call him. Sam explained that he wasn't sure what he was going to do with his life at that time. Then Margaret said that the funniest thing was when Sam talked about one night, he was eating dinner at his mom's house when a commercial came on the TV. Sam said he wasn't watching the TV, but he heard a quartet singing a song Sam knew as "Exactly Like You" which he remembered Earl Garner, the great jazz pianist from Pittsburgh, playing one night at the Crawford Grill in the Hill District. Sam always loved the song and when he heard it as a commercial that night at his mom's, he listened. It was a commercial but as he watched and listened, he began to laugh when he realized it was about an accounting firm and their slogan was "XZackLee, likes you". It was a commercial by Zacq Lee's company and he was stunned as a picture of the X Man , whom he had seen at the funeral, was superimposed on the screen with the music playing in the background. Margaret said she just sat there and watched these two like she was watching a comedy show on TV. She went on to say that Sam said he was stunned with the commercial and began to laugh, but quickly wrote down the phone number for the company, "XZacqLee Accounting" with a slogan at the end, "Your numbers always up." With Margaret as a one-person audience, they had gone back and forth, about how important their friendship was, and Sam went on about how important the X Man had been to his work over the years. Sam explained that when he began and Jamie was there to help him at first, he thought how he wanted to be able to do more for them. Jamie had gone to his career and he didn't know who to turn to for advice. He knew he had to have some kind of accounting system, so he called the I Man, who was an old friend and an accountant, and he pointed over to. The I Man waved and Sam said he would explain more about his role later on,

As Sam then explained to Margaret when he walked around the old neighborhood he was dismayed and almost demoralized as to how desolate it had become. It was poverty stricken, which it certainly was. Work just wasn't available for anyone, but mostly for black men and he realized how terrible was the atmosphere for so many young black kids who lived in dilapidated homes with many other brothers and sisters and in so many cases, their single moms.

Margaret then went on to express to Jamie that it was apparent how much Sam was affected by what he found when he returned to the place, he grew up in. She said she could sense how hurt Sam was about how bad it had become and then how sad it was to hear him quietly talk about growing up in that now desolate community without a father he had never known. She said that his voice got more forceful, when he said he finally realized his mission in life. Somehow, he was going to find some way to provide support for these children of his black race. He had learned so much in the military and had met many white men and women who were appalled and disgusted how black America had been treated, so he believed there was underlying support amongst all people within this country for attempting to give children a chance to find some fulfillment in life, but in his case, he was going to concentrate on young black kids. to say what he did at first. Sam said the first thing he did was to approach grade schools within his old neighborhood, talking with principals and teachers, plus the support folks who were trying to help the young students.

She said he talked about this white guy, one Jamie Sloan, came out of the blue to help him some forty years ago, then he just came back out of the blue to help him again and then he brought her to him. He went on to explain to her how he gradually developed a basic support system over the next years that was just food oriented at first before it gradually grew into a multi-effort of support for single mothers and for those who worked, having places for their children to go after school. He went on to explain that eventually he came up with summer programs and finally, as he watched some of the young children become high school graduates, he began to set up a support system of seeking scholarships and working with coaches for some boys and girls to get sports scholarships. It had become a full-time project for him and over the years he ended up with volunteers, black and white folks, plus over the last years his grandkids began to help him who were technically advanced using computer technology. He talked about how help even came from some students at CMU, who volunteered to help set up some programs to monitor the activities of all the students. By the time he was done talking, Margaret said she was mesmerized by his total honesty and complete dedication to what he could do to help to these children.

She said that as Sam finished talking, he looked at her and pointed over to the X Man, who had remained silent while Sam talked and said, "if I had not had this man sitting over there, I would not have been successful in my dream. That man there, Margaret, that man, Xavier Zacquill Lee, or the X Man, made it possible with his financial wherewithal and extreme dedication over these years."

Margaret went on to tell Jamie, that she was impressed by what she had just witnessed from these two men and their honest commitment to what they were doing. She could not believe she was here listening to them. She said it was quiet for a few seconds after his introduction and then the X man started slowly to talk, as Sam sat back. He went on to explain about working tirelessly to find funding for scholarships and projects for the kids to be involved in during their school years where they could work and get paid for their efforts. He explained that he was married with three kids who all went to Pitt and two of them worked for his company which now had twenty branches around Pittsburgh and Western Pennsylvania. In fact, he had satellite offices in three other cities: Chicago, Cleveland and his latest Washington, D.C. Sam interjected at that point and said that with the X Man providing financial structure and with several new grants, he realized that finally, his mission had a chance to really have an effect on underprivileged children in not only his old neighborhood but maybe in areas all over the poorer sections of Pittsburgh. He went on to say that the X Man, had become a less than silent partner to Sam's life work and had organized all of his financial data, plus donated thousands over the years. As Margaret reflected on their meeting, she said to Jamie, that listening to these two cemented her initial reaction to what Sam had done, Jamie was doing and wanted to do. Jamie sat back and smiled, 'she really is sold on helping Sam'.

Jamie's straightened up in his seat in the bus and looked out at the streets, as he rode toward his apartment, but he couldn't help returning to what he had just witnessed. He thought back to when he got to Sam's office, Margaret was on her iPhone and Sam and a tall black man, who he thought was the X Man based on Sam's description of him, were deep in conversation in the staff room. Jamie was seated across from Margaret as she snapped shut her phone and looked across at him. She immediately started to tell him about her earlier talk with Sam and the X Man. She told him he talked about his business and helping Sam and his kids, except for his own family, was the highlight of his life. She added that his laugh was incredible. Margaret went on to say that she could not believe where she had been her whole life because she never felt closer to these two men in two days than she had been with hundreds of people, men and women she had known during her whole life. They were so honest, and it wasn't any man, woman stuff; they were genuine and thoroughly bent on helping young kids have a chance to succeed or be "fulfilled", as Sam would say over and over. She was overwhelmed by what she had come into and was so glad that Jamie had rejoined them, so she could thank him for bringing her into this cauldron of good will.

As they sat across from each other, Margaret had looked over into the office area where Sam and the X Man were with the staff. She said Sam began waving at her to join them. She she got up and went into the staff room, passing the X Man, who was on his way to Sam's office. Jamie was checking his phone when he looked up and the tall black man with a wide smile on his face stood looking at him.

"Jamie, the white guy I've heard so much about over the years. I'm Xavier, or the Man, as our good man Sam calls me," he said to Jamie. Guess we just missed each other way back," he said

Jamie smiled and said "Yeh, somehow we did. I have heard so much about you from Sam." With that he stood up and went up to him. They hugged each other before backing away and sizing each other up. Jamie looked up at him and said, "Well how do you think our Sam is doing, X Man ?"

The X Man didn't respond immediately, he just looked away and then came back at Jamie, "Well, I look at it this way, the man knows people. He knows them better than they know themselves, usually, except maybe you and me," he said, as he broke out into his high pitch laugh, "but I do think the old babe he's over there talking to is for real. I did some checking before I came over here and she has got it, big time. Her husband's estate won't be settled for quite a while, but she has got millions on her own."

Jamie's face tightened a bit as he responded, "God, I never knew she had that much herself?", pausing, he looked away and then back, adding, "Well I guess she's used to millions, but I am really truly impressed with her compassion for poor kids. I could tell it was real.

And then, I could tell she had a sincere and positive response to Sam. She really dug him."

X Man replied, "Talked to her earlier when she called her accounting and law firms while I was standing there. She told them what she wanted them to do for me and immediately. Man, when she put me on the phone to them, they listened to me like I was the Trump man. Jesus, Jamie, I'll have all that shit, in hours."

Jamie replied, "I am sure now they will be working on setting up some type of structure for what they eventually want to do."

"Oh, yeh, that's what their talking about over there at this very moment, and with this goddamn virus shit coming down the fucking road, they will need to get something in place before everything in this country gets tied down because I hear, we may be fucking shut down by the weekend."

Jamie, looking like something had popped into his mind, which it had, said, "Did Sam get a hold of his attorney Calhoun?"

"Calhoun, Calhoun, and Leibowitz," X Man answered.

"Who's the second Calhoun?"

"His son, Leroy. Fact his granddaughter just started working for him after she graduated from Pitt.

"Who's Leibowitz?"

X Man replied, "A Jewish lady who has a son working for the firm. Old Calhoun is almost as old as me and Sam and has really built himself a big-time law firm. He's on TV all the time like me."

Jamie smiled and said, "It kills me that Sam hired him, what twenty, thirty years ago only because his name was Calhoun, and he was an attorney?"

"Absolutely the truth, my man. You know why he picked him don't you? Zacq asked.

"No idea," Jamie responded.

"Well, when he was a kid, Amos and Andy was Sam's favorite comedy show back in those days of black and white TV. Funny to say that in this day and age, ain't it, but yeh, he loved the Kingfish, but he especially liked his attorney Calhoun, who stuttered all the time. When he was looking for an attorney, he hired Calhoun unseen because he saw this ad in the paper for an attorney named Calhoun. He knew he wouldn't be a black man, but he didn't care, he just wanted to be able to call his attorney Calhoun and when you're with them, it's hilarious, 'cause Sam the Man will say, 'Calhoun, Calhoun, now what 'chu think about that' whenever Calhoun was with him. After a few years, Calhoun, his big white attorney would always come back with 'Kingfish…'" stuttering, 'I'll get right on it, Mr. Kingfish", just the way Calhoun said on that old show. Calhoun's real first name is William; his middle name is Andrew, and last name is MacDonald. What's so funny is that this Calhoun is whiter than snow and Scottish, but when he's with Sam, he's as black as anyone could be. It's hilarious when he's with Sam. You know he'd only been out of Carnegie Tech a couple years when Sam found him. But as usual, Sam was right on. Old Calhoun is not black, but he tries to imitate the TV Calhoun at times when he's around Sam which cracks me up," which caused the X Man to break out into laughter again. "And by the way, Calhoun has been great for Sam over all the years."

For a few seconds it was quiet between them and then Jamie said, "Well, it looks like their coming back this way."

X Man replied, "Yeh, you know Jamie, I got to tell you how much I really appreciate you given that money to Sam. You are the man and," as he pointed to Margaret, "that woman in there is the woman. I cannot believe that woman is going to do what she has said, but I do believe her, a hundred percent. My God, man, our boy Sam might see his life dream come true. Unbelievable, is all I can say."

Jamie watched Sam and Margaret talking like old friends as they walked back to the office. He remembered thinking at the time, all that had happened in just a few days and that Sam, a man who had devoted his life to helping poor kids, mostly black, just might have his dream come true with the help of a rich, white lady who had literally come out of nowhere and if she was to be believed, she too was having a dream come true. 'Life is amazing,' Jamie thought as Sam and Margaret had come back into the office.

Almost immediately as she came into Sam's office, Margaret went to his desk and began to make calls while Sam and the X Man went over some paperwork at a table. Jamie just sat there and watched them in action. In the time Jamie was there, he heard her repeating what she was being told by her sources in D.C. that the country was going to be literally shut down in a week or less. She kept saying to whomever she was talking to, that if that happens, the people who are going to be hurt the most will be the very people, kids and parents of them that she was now forming this business to help. When she was done talking, he listened to her talking to Sam about what she had found out in D.C and they agreed they had to act fast to get their system setup with the X Man listening intently. It was quite a scene and he would always remember the last thing he heard them say was that by the end of the week, they had agreed to come up with a national name and get ready to start working together, virus shut down or not.

As Jamie realized he was getting close to his stop, his thoughts continued back to the day and couldn't believe what he had just experienced. In all his days, he had never seen people of completely different backgrounds, beliefs, colors, and ages, come together on a mission to help the young needy in this country. He was so proud to be a small part in this mission that had come literally out of nowhere and laughed out loud, thinking about Sam's bizarre group of partners. From the Xavier, the X Man, the accountant; to Calhoun, the attorney; and now Margaret, the millionairess; what a group. This experience of pure humor in a time of building turmoil in the country, was a time he wouldn't forget. This day had saved his hope that there could and would-be better days ahead, especially how Sam's band of warriors was reacting so positively in the difficult times they were headed for. He realized his stop was next and that hopefully a restful evening was coming up, because it had been quite a day.

CHAPTER TWENTY

Jamie had a great sleep after the intensity of yesterday with Sam. His schedule for the week was switched around with Margaret in town and with the virus causing so much chaos. Both the library and the transplant clinic may be closed by the end of the week. Margaret was going to be with her lawyers today and possibly tomorrow and he felt he should get to the library early because it might be his last day. He got to the library and put in almost four hours of computer work which got him caught up with all the data that needed to be entered. The supervisor, Lee, told him that he hadn't received official word yet, but all the talk was about closing the library, because the virus epidemic was picking up across the country and in Allegheny County. It was a bit scary. By the time he left the library, it was late in the afternoon, so he decided to head home and get some rest.

As he walked out onto 5th Avenue, Jamie saw that he had two messages on his phone which he checked as he rode home in the declining daylight. The first one was from Rachel who wrote that her father had emailed her after receiving her letter. He said that he wanted her to either fly to Phoenix, which he would pay for or he would come to Pittsburgh. He wanted her to decide and pick the time, then call him, as he had given her his cell phone number, which excited her. He then checked Sandra's message, which stated that she would be performing Saturday night with the Pittsburgh Opera, which announced that it would be the last performance due to the pending closures being discussed in Harrisburg because of the epidemic. As he shut his phone his bus rambled up to his stop and he climb in.

As Jamie sat down, the bus began to roll along towards his neighborhood. Suddenly, he was scared about the quiet atmosphere he had noticed on the streets and now in the bus. He seldom was really scared, but the deadness around him, did just that. He thought back to the night he would never forget over ten years ago when Louise suddenly collapsed and he rode with her unconscious in the ambulance, holding her limp hand. Nothing had ever scared Jamie as much as that night. The mind was like a seesaw going back and forth between fear and joy; back and forth, except recently he hadn't been in the downside of the see-saw because of so many positive events that had occurred.

The bus slowed as it approached the next stop and Jamie realized that the next stop was his. He jumped up, bumping into a woman leading a young boy down the aisle towards the opening front door. "Oh, so sorry, mam," he uttered. She gave him a "yeh, yeh" look and led the tiny kid up to the door. Jamie slowly followed her out the door and headed onto the sidewalk. The lady and her boy were already walking down the street going the opposite way from Jamie. He watched her holding tightly to the boy's hand and was reassured that in a flash of a moment, natural instincts of mother with child were literally in good hands. As he began to head toward his apartment, he thought back to Sam's philosophical discourse when he kept harping on the fact that life, our life, is only a moment in universal time. That within our moment are mini moments even fractionally dividing up our earthly stay, as he remembered Sam's most profoundly, pertinent commentary. "Boom", Jamie quietly said out loud to himself and the squirrels who were sneaking out from under cars and heading for the oak trees by the road. "Boom", he repeated, as he swung his arms in rhythm of his walk. "That's all it takes," he said to his audience, himself. "A flash, a boom, a time so fast we can't even sense the mind reacting to a mental decision we cannot even control," he thought. "Where is this all going?", was his added thought, as Jamie tried to rationalize Sam's philosophy with daily, living moments. He realized that Sam was right; that human life itself is a flash in this universe of ours, but that each moment of our individual lives is even fractionalized into nanoseconds as he had observed when first trying to understand where Sam was coming from. He thought at that moment, as he walked up to his apartment, that he now understood Sam's point. Like a snap of the finger, one's life is begun, goes on; and then disappears. "Just like that", as he snapped his thumb while walking into his apartment.

He sat in the living room with the nightly news muted. He couldn't listen to the usually bombastic announcers talking so loud and so fast, that nary any understanding was possible, as far as this admittedly old listener was concerned. He couldn't quite get it, that young announcers had to talk so fast and usually, in his era observation of young announcers, hadn't a clue what they were talking about. He said out loud, "You are of a different world, so forget Edward R. Murrow and those guys of years gone by, you are gone by, for that matter." He smiled as he realized that being alone had its draw backs, but some good points as he debated back and forth with himself. 'I seem to do it all the time, these days', he thought. Jamie rubbed his face and looked up at the ceiling with the cross beams and said, "Getting old, Jamie boy, getting fuckin old."

The next morning Jamie got to the hospital early and worked non-stop and completed all the new data that had come in, but before he left his desk, he decided to send text messages to Sandra and Rachel. The morning news had been non-stop about the restrictions that were pending for travel in the U.S. Locally, events like the performance Saturday night at the Benedum Theater in downtown was in jeopardy because of the virus. As he was turning off his computer, his phone beeped and it was Barbara Zyzmanski, who wanted him to stop by before he left. He noted when he came into the hospital, a tense atmosphere. Everyone was quiet with some already wearing masks at the entrance. There were a lot of hospital police walking around the lobby and added hospital security people walking around the hallways. He walked down the hallway to Barbara's office.

Barbara Zyzmanski in her fifties, had worked as the supervisor of volunteers for many years. She was a blonde with a bun in the back of her head and was still in good physical condition, with glasses sloping down her cheeky face above a deep blue mask. "Hey, Jamie, I really appreciate you changing your schedule and coming in this morning, I really do. How did it go?"

Jamie replied, "Very well. I got all the new data into the system."

Barbara had hired Jamie as a volunteer which was his first venture into working for no pay but with the satisfaction of helping an organization that simply needed help. He came to love the work and could justify the time by the patient's information he transferred via computer to their doctors, no matter where they were from in the world. A few times he'd met the transplant patients, or their families and he never felt better when they expressed their appreciation of what he had done with getting the data to their doctors after he explained to them what he did. As he sat there, he could tell by Barbara's look that there was a problem and he soon knew what it was. The University transplant department would be shutting down this weekend because of the virus with cases already reported in Western Pennsylvania. She opened a drawer in her desk and pulled out a light blue mask and handed it over to him telling him to put it on while he was in the hospital. Barbara explained that it may be possible for him to work from home on his computer if he was able to get it set up correctly, but that was still in the working stages. When he hugged Barbara as he left, she said to him that he had been a blessing to the department, and as he walked down the hallway to the elevators, he never felt so good about the work he did in the clinic and sad that it was stopping. As he stepped into the elevator, he realized that this may be his last day for a while coming to the hospital, something he was really proud of doing.

As Jamie left the building, his phone buzzed, and he saw that it was Rachel.

"Just leaving the hospital, how are you doing?" he asked. She told him that her Dad was coming in Friday afternoon and wanted to know if he could meet them Saturday for breakfast or just coffee because she wanted Jamie to meet him. Jamie replied that he would love to meet them and for her to pick the time and place. He said for her to keep tabs on the news because so much was changing due to the virus. When the call ended, he thought he'd check in with Sandra to see if the production was still on. He walked down to a bus stop and sat on a bench and called Sandra.

"Oh, Jamie, so glad you called. Yes, as of right now, it is still on, but we're to hear by Friday morning if there is any change," as she paused and added, "I am really down because of all times for this to happen."

Jamie said, "Sandra, dear, you did it. You have been accepted by the Pittsburgh Opera to work in their chorus when needed. That won't change. There will be productions, maybe Saturday, maybe next month, and for sure, next year and you will be on stage. That is really an accomplishment. Don't forget that?"

She was quiet and then he heard her sigh before saying, "You're right, you're right. I have to think that way. I have all these relatives coming in for Saturday dinner and the show, but… we can do it again if it is called off."

"That's the way to look at it," Jamie replied. They talked for another few minutes and then the call ended. Jamie felt good that she understood that she would be on stage with the Opera some time, whether this Saturday night or another time.

He left the bus stop and walked to the corner so he could cross over to get his bus and it was strange seeing some students walking along the street with masks on. According to a news app which just popped up on his phone, there were statements about people having to wear masks outside and getting spray to kill the virus. He would stop at the hardware store near his apartment to see if they had any of these items. 'What is this world coming to,' he thought.

As Jamie waited at the bus stop, he thought he should phone Sam and see how he was doing. He punched in Sam's number. "Sam, it's me. How's it going?"

He heard Sam breathing before he spoke to Jamie, "You know, I was just sitting here thinking about you and you called. Tell me there's no Universal power working. What I was thinking was that ever since you first called me and we met after all these years, my whole life has changed. You know that Margaret of yours ordered a thousand, you hear me, a thousand goddamn computers to be delivered here because she believes that schools are going to close, and our kids will need to do schoolwork from their homes or here. She's already has contractors looking right now at the attached area behind me and has you as the guy to oversee it. She wants it turned into a teaching area that she swears we'll need for this goddamn virus shit we will be or are going through. My Man, where did you find her?"

Jamie paused and said, "In the Universe, my Man, in your Universe and it only took a moment. The key word is moment, right?"

The laugh was loud and raucous, then, "You got me there, but you are right," then Sam paused, and said, "And I have converted my Anglo-Saxon white man to my new philosophy. You have made my day."

Jamie replied, "I may have made your day but you, I think, no I'm sure, have made my life."

Sam laughed and said, "Well, oh converted one, you coming over? Got a couple things I...," he paused, "we want you to do."

"Tell you what, I'm going to stop by the apartment, take a hot shower and I'll be over. Can't stay to long 'cause I'm whipped, but keep the Glenlivet ready, I might need a touch."

"A touch it is, and I'll see you, my Man".

Jamie picked up five light blue masks at a hardware store which was their limit, but they were out of any Clorox or anything to use to spray. After taking a shower, he headed over to Sam's on a bus wearing his mask and most of the passengers also were masked. It was quite a spectacle and the Port Authority had signs up that stated by the coming Friday, all passengers would need masks. 'What a time,' he thought as he got up for his stop.

By the time he got to Sam's it was getting dark and he knew he couldn't stay too long. It was quite a sight when he sat down in front of him as they both had masks over their faces. Then Sam told him he had heard that masks should be worn when your outside and people were supposed to keep six feet away from anyone else, but that they didn't need the mask inside if they stayed separated, so he reached back and took his off, which Jamie did too. Sam added this virus attack on humanity just showed that the Universe is always in charge and this was just another show of force. He switched quickly back to their work and that they had much to talk about, but he was a bit worn out what with all the virus stuff and what they were trying to set up. Sam talked a lot about Margaret, who he called his new lady partner, and how excited his associates were about the potential backing they were going to receive. Sam's group was working late that night, but he candidly told Jamie, that he was really bushed.

Jamie said he had a couple things to go over and then he would be off because he too was very tired. He reiterated the news of the day and that they had to be prepared to change the way things were now operating. Sam dittoed what Jamie said and added they were already preparing online programs from systems they purchased that afternoon with the money Jamie had put in. He went on to explain more plans for in-house school classes for students that did not have computers at home; food supplies normally provided in schools; and college entrance systems for the older ones, would be available. He went on to say he believed, based on what Margaret was working on, that his staff was ready to handle any of the new major changes coming down the line. As he finished, Sam looked at Jamie and said, "Man you look as tired as I feel, lets pick it up tomorrow, Jamie," as he rose from his chair.

Jamie responded, "Okay, I'll be heading out", as he looked at his watch. "There's a bus in five minutes."

Sam said, "You want Marty to give you a life? He's right in there!"

Jamie replied, "Oh, that would be great."

CHAPTER TWENTY-ONE

Margaret Douglas was the only child of Maurice Douglas a contractor in the South Hills of Pittsburgh. He came from a family of seven brothers and sisters whose father himself was involved in building houses in the southern areas of Pittsburgh. Maurice or Maury as he was known was a tough man who played by the rules all his life but when his wife of thirty years, Barbara or "Babe", as she was known, died of cancer a day after her fiftieth birthday, Maury went into a funk for the rest of his life which only went another five years. He drank heavily after she died and was killed in a car crash late one night in a rainstorm. Margaret married the next summer. Maggie, as she was called, was an obstinate child; played tennis on the high school team; sang in school productions but always excelled in the classroom. When her father met Warren a year before the car accident, he did not like him because he was a rich kid's son who was a bullshitter instead of a doer, as her Dad had told her many times. Maggie, underneath her exuberant personality and good looks, was a tigress. All through college at Pitt she worked both during school terms and in the summer, mostly in the library and helping in the medical center doing paperwork. Maggie first met Warren in high school and dated him for a while, but they separated when he graduated and went to Penn. Maggie went to Pitt and dated him again during their summer breaks. She liked him and he was much different than he was in high school. For some reason, he was much more reserved, quieter than he had been in high school and she liked him. Maggie wasn't ready though for any kind of relationship at that time because she really wanted to work in publishing after she graduated from Pitt. She wasn't interested in having a boyfriend and all that went with it. She was certainly not interested or didn't crave a man entering her body. Maggie was much more intrigued by a man or woman, for that matter, entering her mind and making it work. She was always interested in what she knew nothing about; she was a curious sort, so she set her goal to go to New York and get a job in publishing.

When Maggie thought about Warren, she remembered the first time she met him. It was in the high school library where she worked.

She was putting books back on the shelves that had been brought back. She had a stack of them and was trying to reach the fourth shelf which was a bit much for her, even though she was tall. Maggie pulled over a wooden stool that she used to put books back on the high shelves and as she reached to put books on the top shelf, the stool tipped and she fell sideways, grabbing a hold of a guy who was putting a book back in a lower shelf. Her fall was stopped as he held her for a few seconds then let her down to the floor. She would never forget his concerned face in that second and and obviously a student like herself. She sat down at a table and he asked her if she was okay, which she quickly said she was. He stayed standing there, looking down at her as he looked at her name tag on her sweater, he said something like, "Okay, Maggie, I'll let you be. He turned and walked away, then stopped turned back to her and said, "I'm Warren Decker in case we meet again." He walked off and then turned back again to look at her which she always remembered. She also remembers asking herself, 'Who was that nice guy'? She found out he was a Senior and a guy all the girls talked about, so she was surprised a week later when he asked her out. It was quite a big deal for a Junior to be dating this Senior heart throb and they dated into the spring when the terrible event at McConnell's Mill happened which was all the talk in school. The death of the girl was all that was talked about at school. Warren never called her again in high school and she didn't see him again until she had graduated from Pitt and worked in New York for Scribner's Publishing in New York. It was her dream job, which she still looked back on as the most fulfilling time of her life. It was the publishing firm that editor Maxwell Perkins built with the likes of Hemingway, Fitzgerald, Wolfe, and James Jones. He also had great women writers, one of her favorites, the author of "The Yearling", Marjorie Kinnan Rawlings. Margaret worked first as a copy writer and then became an assistant to several editors, and she loved the atmosphere. She was in the most perfect place she could imagine. One morning Warren called her saying a friend had told him she worked at Scribner's and he was often in New York for his job. They went to lunch and then dated every time he came to New York. He had graduated from Penn and gone to the Wharton School, then got a job in Philadelphia.

Margaret immediately noted how different Warren was from the brash heart throb from high school. He was much more serious and frankly, more interesting man. She was twenty-five when she decided to marry him. They had similar tastes in travel, and her love, books. He read almost as much as she did which gave them much to talk about. His interest in politics didn't bother her because she too was concerned about the country. As their married years went on with children growing up in the eighties and nineties, she became concerned about the times they were entering. In those years, America was a radically changing country, which upset her personality need for calmness and solidarity, but she was mostly concerned about their children setting off on their own in those tumultuous times. Warren did very well in his work career and was active in the Republican Party in Pennsylvania, was elected a State Senator when they lived in Bucks County. He was in construction with a large Philadelphia company and throughout their married years, both his business and political interests kept him busy all the time as he moved higher in both aspects of his career. He didn't have much time to spare for family, which bothered her, but she never stopped loving the man because, down deep inside, he was a good person. Politics is a dirty business, and she was always upset by things written and said about Warren when he was elected and became a U.S. Senator from Pennsylvania. But her understanding of him proved correct over almost fifty years of marriage, to a man who externally was an extrovert. Internally, however, he was like a turtle who pulls in its head under its shell. A man nobody really knew, except Maggie, as he always called her.

She knew about the disaster at a creek on a spring day above Pittsburgh because it was in the papers and kids in high school never stopped talking about it. After they were married over the years, he would bear his soul to her about what he hadn't done on that day. The man was big, six two, muscular, but had never learned to swim, in fact when he was ten, his father scared him to death by tossing him in a pool when he couldn't swim to force him to have to swim. He thought he would drown except for a counselor diving in and pulling him out. The fright of it never left him. His father was a tormented man who tormented his children, especially his only son, Warren. One day, years into their marriage, he talked about that day at the creek and how he had cried many times because of what he did not do. She, to this day, still carried heartache about that event which did two things to Warren; it made him understand human fear and weakness which made him also understand why poor people in this country felt helpless causing him to be the strongest advocate for government to assist them. It also strengthened him over the years because he knew how preparation for disaster was critical for human beings. Over his political career he promoted government to be ready for the worst, especially when times were good. She spent her almost fifty years of marriage guiding her children to follow their deep-down desires, "ddd", as she always told them. Follow your dreams and do your best to achieve them, but do not be afraid of failure because humans fail before succeeding. She was the eternal optimist as was Warren, which was the bulwark for his success in business but especially in politics. He might have become President she believed, and he would have been a great one, in her deep down, honest opinion, because of his fairness and intelligence. But life takes unknown, unwanted and unexpected turns which it did in Warren's case.

On this day, after her meeting with her attorneys yesterday, she was going headed back to Homewood to work with Sam after spending hours going over her estate. It was much more than she realized and ironically, as she waited for her car, she was excited about working with this man who was full of genuine goodness and maybe her realization of how much was her financial wealth, might be another irony of fate. This man Sam seemed not to have any pretense; he was the real deal. This ex-Marine had almost single handily helped thousands of black children and their parents since he began his assistance programs almost forty years ago. She did not know why his accomplishments were not public knowledge except for a few articles in the local papers over the years which she had picked up in Google. In the past ten years alone, he had coordinated a program of assisting young black children and their parents, usually mothers, into a blanket assistance program for kids from broken and single parent, some even with some single, unmarried fathers. When he first started, a hundred per cent were African American children up until a few years ago, when his program began to reach out to poor white and Hispanic families and their children. She had the current breakdown downloaded from his website by Boston data technicians she texted who had done campaign work for Warren. She also asked them to track down data online in Pennsylvania and specifically Pittsburgh and Allegheny Country on all verifiable support funds for low-income families. Margaret Decker, a fireball in her own right, was overwhelmed by what was discovered, but so excited to know that she had found at this stage in her life, a life's mission.

Her car pulled up in front of the hotel in downtown Pittsburgh driven by Gizelle. She had been with her for ten years. Gizelle Dupre' was French, who Margaret met in Paris when she was a representative to a UN Conference on aid to families in Africa who were suffering from malnutrition. It was that five-day conference last year that sort of separated her from Warren's political life. The conference gave her an insight first on problems elsewhere in the world, other than in the U.S. and jettisoned her into the world effort to enter into assisting families in places around the world with basic needs of life's support. From that conference to this day, she had been involved and served on UN programs. Last year she was given an actual title and job assignment with an agency based in Geneva. Their primary objective was to help both financially and logistically in providing health and food provisions to families around the world. It was an exciting, rewarding job for Margaret at her age, especially as Senator Decker was moving into the highest echelons of American politics. Her own family was secure and financially stable, while she dealt daily with mothers and fathers with absolutely nothing.

She looked at Gizelle in the driver's seat and smiled, as she was her right-hand woman. During the past ten years, Gizelle was not only her driver, organizer, researcher, and friend, but her life story was an absolute movie plot. She grew up poor in southern France. When she was eighteen, she joined the French Army and for twenty years served her country. She became a guru on the computer and worked in analytics until she left the service. When Margaret met her in Paris, Gizelle was working for a French American non-profit and was assigned to help her during her Paris meetings. From that day on, Gizelle, in her mid-forties, divorced with no children, became Margaret's closest friend and traveled with her around the world. Recently, she had met a restaurant owner in Cape Cod and a relationship seemed to be developing, but Gizelle had reassured Margaret that nothing would interfere with her helping her in her endeavors.

When they were at Sam's, Gizelle had listened to him talk to the staff and when the meeting was over, she took Margaret aside and whispered to her that she believed Margaret had found her Valhalla on Earth with this guy from Pittsburgh. Then she reminded her Pittsburgh was founded by the French in 1756 which caused them both to laugh. Gizelle then added that something had brought her back to her hometown to this small group of "do gooders" that helped disadvantage children and parents. When she told Sam what Gizelle had said something had brought them here to him, she could still see Sam smile and say, "Margaret, the young woman is right on, the Universe is saying to us," "this is our moment." He had smiled when he said that and then added, "Margaret, this is also your moment, I do believe.

Margaret was now headed back to Sam's. She knew that what she was getting involved in with Sam, was totally correct. When she and Sam talked about his current needs and his vision of how the work could be expanded, she waited for quite a while, before she said to him that she could contribute to expanding his work. Briefly, she mentioned she had resources that she might be able to utilize, not explaining openly, that she had inherited both from her family, both mother and father, but would also from Warren at some time. She didn't detail her wealth to him, but she knew with Warren's trust, that would be distributed later in the year, and what she had received from her family, she had access to close to a thirty million dollars, which overwhelmed her when she thought of it. For the weeks since Warren died, she was actually despondent about her wealth and amazed how quickly people hinted to her about donating funds to this and that organization, especially foundations to whom she had given over the years. It actually disgusted her and as she watched the somewhat dismal city blocks go by of a place that really needed her help, she felt an intense peace.

They were driving into East Liberty section of Pittsburgh, which Margaret vaguely remembered from her high school days. As she looked out the window at the traffic and people on the streets, her thoughts were interrupted by a beep on her cell phone with a headline. President Trump was to speak to the country tonight about the virus. Another headline stated that the country may be getting ready for a national shutdown due to the virus spreading across the country. She called the office in Boston and talked with the staff, asking if funds could be transferred from her trust account to the Pittsburgh account if she gave the authorization. They said they would be ready when she was. She wanted them to also check on finding a computer system that was currently used successfully by schools to hold classes online. She insisted that they line one up by tomorrow because she expressed her belief that this was the way classes were going to be taught based on what this virus epidemic might do to the general public, including schools. She ended the call after receiving confirmation that her Boston group would get back to her as soon as they had the answers. Up ahead Margaret could see Sam's building coming into view. She smiled and shook her head slowly, incredulous about how all of this had happened in such a short period of time.

"Just about there, Mademoiselle," Gizelle said in her French accentuated way as the car pulled up to Sam's old building.

Margaret was out of the car and walked down the hallway to Sam's office area. She noticed the staff on their computers with masks covering their faces and realized the virus scare was real. She turned to Gizelle and said, "We need to find some of those and quickly. Any ideas?"

"I'll work on it."

CHAPTER TWENTY-TWO

Jamie was outside the main building of Sam's site looking over three old brick buildings for renovation. He was designing a plan for the brick buildings behind the main office area. Inside the young staff, with their varied colored masks, were working on adjusting the network that was in place and on ways to expand it to accept new locations they were adding. It was quiet back here which he liked because it allowed him to concentrate on a general concept for the three buildings. He had a pretty good idea what he was going to design and as he had always done on any job in his career, he would seek a time to just be at the site and imagine what he was going to design. As he stood there, he drifted to the strange, new pandemic atmosphere that apparently began in China. This could not have happened at a worse time for Sam's expansion, but Jamie realized it would be bad for everyone. This was the news every minute of every day and it looked like it could be a new world of stagnation. Jamie realized even in this new atmosphere, he still had a job to do, because Sam's kids could be the most affected. Trying to find a way to provide for their clients in this sudden catastrophic world, would become even more difficult. Sam needed these old buildings rebuilt and functional as soon as possible which got him back to the drawings in front of him which were on an old music stand he'd found in one of the buildings he was working on. He knew it was imperative, pandemic or no pandemic, with the increased work force and clients being developed, that more workspace was needed. The key was to design it to fit with the new world of telecommunications of these difficult yet changing times.

He looked at the buildings one more time, clustered in a triangle, then closed his notebook as he decided to go back inside and rejoin the group session. When he walked into the workroom he heard back and forth conversations between the staff about coming up with a name for Sam's organization. They seem to want one that would coincide with their new objective of finding more communities with children to help. Various names had been bounced around and Sam, suddenly perked up, with his mask dangling over his lips, and said, "How about UYC, which is an abbreviation for Universal Youth Care. Margaret, sitting off to the side with a pink mask covering her face, asked if she could add something, which Sam waved her to go on. She said she like it but asked if everyone could still try and come up with something maybe more about what they are trying to achieve. Jamie looked at Sam, to see if he was upset. He wasn't and said, "She's right, you know this is a new world out there, so let's keep working on it and come up with a good one."

The group kept going back and forth with names that would be catchy, media-wise, but also be right on as to its objective. Jamie had written down about ten names, then put up his hand like he was a kid in school.

"How about this one," he said, ... "a bridge. Use a bridge as a symbol, a metaphor for supporting children and providing them a way over the abyss of difficult times of one side and providing education, safety, sustenance, and opportunity on the other side."

The Group of Eight, as they had begun calling themselves, was quiet and then Sam said, "Man, that might be it. I mean we live in Pittsburgh, "The "City of Bridges" and it fits right in to our...objectives."

Germaine added, "I like it. I really do. It tells our story."

Margaret was quiet as she was writing something on her pad. She lifted her head and said, "You know, Jamie, I think you got it. A bridge is a transition, in this case, from a young kid without maybe a father or mother figure or one without a computer or is scared of bigger kids, or whatever, but is someone we can help to get across the bridge of problems to the other side for a chance to live a good life. The key is Sam's work and what he's done and what he wants to expand. It could become a bridge for thousands of kids normally left behind, with no hope."

The room was again quiet, then Sam piped up with "I like it, in fact a lot. For now, we'll think of how we can use that as our symbol. Can anyone write that down?"

Marty said, "I got it all on tape, gramps. We can start thinking how we can use it?"

"Super," said Sam, "and cut out that gramps stuff, my little big man. I may be a grand pa, but I ain't no gramps."

The room was filled with laughter and then Sam said in a toned-down serious mode, "Okay, now, we have to contact our brethren in our new affiliates and talk to them. Fill them in about what's been going on about our new partnership with Margaret and our expansion ideas. Oh, and get their reaction to the bridge concept. I also want to prepare them for having to deal with this virus business because they must treat this with only one thing in mind, our kids. We have to all be on the same page as to how we handle the restrictions that will happen, and if it is as bad as the media is saying, we have to be ready. In fact, ask all of our folks, if we can have a zoom meeting tomorrow, say in the afternoon," he paused, "got it?"

"We'll get right on it. Come on Marty, over to my desk, "Germaine said.

Margaret who had been looking at her iPad, looked up and said, "Just got word from D.C. folks. We're going into a national lockdown mode by the weekend"

Sam quietly said, "What's that mean, to us? Any idea?"

"Well, it's going to affect everything we do personally and what we do here. What we got to think about is how we can get your kids and families through the next weeks or so. School, food, all that you do. My source in D.C. said that everything will be shut down, including all the schools."

It became quiet, only Germaine could be heard talking across the way with Marty. Finally, Sam said, "This reminds me of 9/11, when our whole country stopped, but seems to me this is even worse because that virus is probably going to be all over our country."

"Wow, this is good," Margaret said out loud as she looked up from her iPad," and went on, "the funds can be transferred Sam, whenever we want them sent. It just popped up in my system and the X Man should be able to confirm that. Something else, Sam, I've been thinking about, and pardon all my thinking since I'm the new kid in town, but you got me all fired up. We should think about setting up separate responsibilities to take some of the pressure off you, especially if we expand like we've talked about. One thought is that maybe you focus on what you have been doing so well, your basic programs and then any new programs. Now the X man and I can watch over the financials; and Jamie, our architect guy can concentrate on our physical properties here and any new branches."

Sam replied, "Like that, let's start on it right now. Once we get it done here, we'll contact our other sites and help them divide up their responsibilities. As to the financial transfer, you don't know how great that is and I can't thank you enough. I'll have the X Man set up the financial transfers when needed."

Margaret said, "Okay, I'm also going to stay in touch with my sources in D.C. to know how the Feds are going to handle this epidemic situation. I have a hunch it's going to be drastic because according to a doctor friend who works for the CDC, this virus has been hidden by the Chinese since December and it's spread to all parts of the world in just the last month or so. So, we must get ourselves organized right away, because things may change real soon."

Sam, mask drooping low, waved his hands and said, "We are a small group in this room, but we are what we have been and what we are going to become," he paused as he looked tired, but went on, adding, "Okay, we need a break, but I want to work on coordinating all of our volunteers. My God, we have over two hundred folks who can help us in both our new programs and if this virus epidemic hits us, we'll need every one of them," he said in his deep, but slow-paced voice.

The group disbanded with Margaret heading for the restroom and Sam, dropping his head as if nodding off. Jamie walked up to him and said, "Hey, old man, I'll be heading out shortly. He paused, "How are you feeling?"

Sam slowly lifted his head, looked Jamie and said, "Oh, I'm good, just a bit weary. There is so much shit going on, man, so much shit. Down deep," he tapped his chest over his heart, "I'm worried. I gotta feeling this goddamn virus is going to kill a lot of folks and from what I know, this kinda of shit usually hurts us old people more than the young'uns. Now that's okay, from my perspective, but this happened as we were climbing towards our apex with Margaret's help, we could sink back to our nadir really quick."

Jamie came right up to him and took him by both shoulders. "Hey, you have overcome everything a man, especially a black man in this country, could ever do in your lifetime and this virus is not going to do you in. Somehow this was supposed to happen, Sam, and down deep, you know it."

Sam slowly smiled and grasped Jamie's hands. "You're right, Jamie," paused and then said, "for a second there, I was getting a bit despaired, but looking at you right here in front of my black face, a white man I've known, not known, and now know again, deep down I know," as he taps his chest, "this is our moment. That lady did not just happen. She was supposed to be contacted by you as you were supposed to reconnect with me. This time, this moment, this challenge from this virus, was supposed to happen, to prove to us, all of us here that our ultimate mission is just beginning. So many young folks need us, virus or no virus," he paused and said, "here comes a messenger from the universe, my man, "as he looks at Margaret coming back in the room. "That lady over there is the messenger, and we are the receivers of her message." He smiled again, waved his hand at Margaret who was walking up to them and whispers to Jamie, "she is literally a messenger from the Universe that you brought to me."

Margaret, masked up, walks up to them and said, "Well, men, I think we're off to a good start. I'm just so worried about this damn virus stuff because it seems to me Sam, that what you deliver now for your youngsters is going to radically change. There's a chance of no school and many parents won't be working."

Sam replied, "Well, we'll just have to adjust. I think we can, but it won't be easy," …he paused and added, "what bothers me is keeping them kids busy and out of trouble."

Jamie said, "Well, that volunteer group should be a big help, but we can't really plan anything until we know exactly what's going to happen. What's the Fed going do?"

"Well, Trump is speaking again tonight, so maybe we'll have an idea what he's going to do. God only knows with him, but we should get info about what they're going to do," she paused, "No matter what he says, I have to get back to my home and make some plans because depending on what's going to happen, I need to settle things there and then come back here to help out. My kids are all over the place. Even got one in Asia, Japan, to be exact. Don't know what he's going through. The others are Stateside, but who knows what anybody is going to do. So, I'll have to leave now, but I'll be able to be in touch with you Sam on that iPad I left with Germaine. I told her that she is my communicator with you through that iPad. I have a lot to do on my own with this virus thing going on, but I will keep you all informed about what I'm doing and hope to be back, maybe in week, I hope."

Sam got up and went over to Margaret, he put his hands on her shoulders, then hugged her and said, "My dear, you are a Godsend or as my philosophy tells me, a Universal send because you have blended beautifully into my dream of my lifetime. Thank you so much my dear Margaret."

Margaret was taken aback as Jamie could see tears forming in her eyes as she said, "Sam, you don't know how much you have inspired me. I am simply overwhelmed," as she pushed back from Sam, smiled and added, "We are going to do wonders."

Jamie said, "Wonders for sure."

Margaret said, "Okay, Sam I'm on my way. Keep me posted about what's going on here and I'll do the same from my end." She looked over at Jamie and back to Sam, with a wide smile, then waved at Germaine and Marty and the others in the office area, then walked out of the building with Gizelle following.

Sam watched her leave and said to Jamie, "Going to be some difficult times coming up, I fear, but whatever happens, happens. What we must do is stay positive and concentrate on our plans, but first we gotta concentrate on our resources getting to the kids and their parents that we do every day and then figure out how we adjust if things shut down. So, no matter what the circumstances, we have to get ready. We got the folks here and our volunteers, so we'll just adjust as best we can. Can't lose our focus and with that lady who just went out the door, I gotta feeling it's going to just fine."

Jamie piped up, "We won't lose any focus, Sam, I'm sure of that and with this group and yourself, that won't happen. And I want to be a help in any way I can. I'll get that money of mine to the X Man and with Margaret kicking in, my God Sam, you'll for sure have financial stability with more to come, I'm sure."

Sam looked at Jamie and said, "It's my...our moment, masks and all," which brought on his wide smile, "in this Universe."

Jamie quickly replied, "Sam, I need more of that because I think you and I are literally on the same wavelength and as you said earlier, we were supposed to come together again because some...," he paused and then said," some universal force brought us back and I would add, as you intimated earlier, brought Margaret into your life and mine, for that matter."

"Been thinking the same thing and you and me, need to sit down, I'd say in a day or so, and talk more about what you just said."

Jamie replied, "We'll do it. Right now, I have to leave and get my yearly checkup with my doctor, so it will keep me a bit honest about my health at my young age."

Sam laughed, "Man if your young, I'm a kid," as he paused and added, "guess I should be looked at some time. It's been a while. So, go ahead man get your white ass out of here."

Jamie started to walk away then turned, saying to Sam, "The strange thing Sam is what we are doing is actually a perfect time because of what is happening in this pandemic world. Your help will be so needed for your kids and families based on all the news were hearing." As he started to add something his phone buzzed. "Hold it, Sam," and he looked at a message. He kept looking at it and slowly closed his phone and turned to Sam, "I don't believe it, Sam. Jeremy, my sister Becky's son, just died suddenly."

CHAPTER TWENTY-THREE

Jamie left the building in a daze after calling Becky back and listening to her crying profusely. A neighbor got on the phone and told him that apparently Jeremy simply collapsed at a rehearsal, dying in the theater. When Becky was able to get back on the phone, Jamie promised somehow to get out to Denver for whatever services that were to be scheduled. It was ironic that Jeremy's sudden death occurred as Jamie was having his annual physical to monitor his health status. As he sat in the office area, mask up, awaiting his meeting with Dr. Winthrop, after having some blood work and heart monitoring done, his thought was in turmoil because of the call about Jeremy. He hadn't felt better about his own life for quite a while, but Jeremy's sudden death and how his dear sister would be suffering, was a setback, which he realized is just the way life is. He rubbed his eyes under his mask, which felt tired and he closed them, leaning back against the bench. A gentle touch of his shoulder brought him back.

"Doctor can see you now, Mr. Sloan," came the soft, gentle voice of his office manager, Mrs. Dunlap from her pale blue mask.

"Oh, sorry, just drifted off," Jamie said with a smile peeking out from his mask, as he stood up and followed her across the plaid carpeting to the door that went into the doctor's office.

He was there for close to an hour and the bottom line was that Doctor Winthrop was pleased overall with no major medical situations over the past year. He had his blood and heart testing done which he said Jamie was doing extremely well, for a man of his age and physical condition, with the exception his blood pressure was lower than past tests. He wanted Jamie to drink moderately and wanted him to have more extensive blood and heart monitoring tests. Jamie told him he would call to schedule them.

When he left the doctor's office, he had an urge to head for a beer, of all things, especially after what the good doctor had just advised him. For some reason, he felt like one, maybe because of the uneasiness with the virus epidemic and then Jeremy's death which was so different from how calm he had been for weeks now with all his great activity. 'How things in life can change so quickly', he thought as he saw the bus coming down the street.

As Jamie rode along in the rumbling bus, his thoughts kept ricocheting with thoughts of Jeremy's death and his sister to the corona virus literally taking over the country; and finally, he actually took a deep breath and a calmness settled in as he thought of the resurrection of his life working with Sam, which caused him to realize how life is like a road with peaks and valleys; the metaphor caused him to smile.

As his bus stopped and then took off again, he checked his phone and saw there were messages both from the library and the transplant office. He read the messages and felt both relieved and troubled, as he remembered his prior thoughts about how things in life swing back and forth. Both facilities were closing down, and all volunteer personnel were not allowed to come in until the virus situation got clarified which was the way both texts read as if written by the same person. No doubt these important facilities in Pittsburgh deciding to close down, meant to Jamie that this was a serious situation. Riding beside a window in the middle of the bus, loaded with passengers of all ages, colors and life situations, had always been a pensive and usually calming situation for him. But on this ride, as he looked at everyone with their masks on, he thought about what the news media was saying and what everyone may have to do to avoid the virus. Looking around, the faces of the other riders could barely be seen because of their masks, seemed frozen. It was so different when usually he would see a variety of joy, fear, emptiness and even laugh lines, as people thought of joyous or troubling things that either happened to them that day or what they were expecting when they got to their destination. But now, it was like a picture of covered faces up and down the aisle as if everyone was heading for a death camp. No smiles visible, no laughter; just silent, serious, men and women of all ages with a few little ones looking around with tiny masks. 'Where was this bus and this virus leading everyone too', he thought as he rose to get out at the next stop.

The atmosphere did not change when he opened the door and walked into McDonough's Corner Pub. It was as if he was going into a funeral home. The TV was on with the President talking, with people standing behind him who looked to Jamie like doctors. Even Bart, was looking up at the TV with a grim look on his usually smiling Irish mug. He noticed Tommy and Jerome, who he hadn't seen since their encounter, were also looking up at the President, both serious which was totally out of character. Jamie sat down a bit from Tommy and Jerome who never noticed him. He looked up at the big, blonde haired seventy-two-year-old man who was an enigma, not only to Jamie but to the country. It was quiet except for the voice on the screen, then Bart noticed Jamie and walked over.

"Sorry, buddy, listening to the asshole up there. What can I get you?"

"Just a…," Jamie paused, then said, "I want one, just one, mind you, of a shot of Glenlivet."

"Jesus, man, Trump is something else, but you sure you want a scotch old timer?", Bart asked.

"Old timer I am, but I just want a taste of my origin. Just a taste, that's all."

Bart turned and went back to the racks of bottled alcohol against the wall. He reached up to the highest level for bottled whiskey, pulled down a brown bottle and brought it back to Jamie. As he pulled a shot glass out from under the bar, he said, "Here you go, Jamie," he said, pouring the brown liquid into the glass.

"See if those two down the way would like a shot of my heritage? Tell them it's a peace offering. One Protestant Scotsman to two Catholic Micks."

Bart turned and walked down to Tommy and Jerome who were still listening to the President. "Yinz two want a shot?", he said, leaning into them, "from your ex-friend down the way." They both looked up at him like he was crazy, looked at each other and then both looked where Jamie was sitting looking up at the TV. Tommy looked back at Jerome, and then both looked down at Jamie and smiled.

"My God, it's the old fucking Scotchman and he's offering us a shot of his booze," Tommy broke out. "He must be remorseful about what he did, but being a soft-hearted Irishman like myself, go ahead, Bart, pour it."

Bart poured a shot for Tommy and then put another glass down in front of Jerome who was all smiles and yelled at Jamie, "Thanks old buddy. Sorry for the other day." He picked up the glass and downed the scotch, wiped his mouth and said to Jamie, "We should duke it out more often, for Christ's sake," he paused and added, "Wow, that was tasty. I needed that after listening to the big dog up there," he said looking up at the TV screen.

Jamie down at them, took a sip of the brown booze and replied, "No harm done, guys, but what's he talking about, anyway?"

Tommy and Jerome both said at the same time, "The fucking corona virus."

"Guess it's really serious," Jamie responded as he looked up at the TV.

"Going to close down the country," Bart injected. "Gonna have to close down the bar, for Christ's sake, as per our Governor. I'll be out of fuckin business."

It was quiet then Tommy said, "Christ, it's only the fucking flu, for God's sake."

Bart looked at him and said, "It's like the flu, but we got a fucking vaccine for the flu. We ain't got nothing for this one and from what I heard so far, it kills old folks mostly, like what I'm looking at right now," he said angrily as he threw a dish rag down on the bar and walked down towards the door to the kitchen,

"Jesus, what the fuck did I say," Tommy said, first looking at Jerome, then leaning down the bar looking at Jamie.

Jamie sipped his shot glass, then downed it in one sip and motioned with one finger in the air to Bart as he was coming back out of the kitchen. He said Tommy, "I think we are heading into unknown territory, guys. A place none of us have ever been before, so we better get ready for big time changes."

"What's that supposed to mean," Jerome asked.

As Bart poured him another shot, Jamie replied, "I have no idea, but I'm going to my pad, guys," he said as he looked at the shot, realizing he hadn't had two shots of scotch in years, but thought, 'what the fuck', and downed it in a second, before sliding off his stool.

Putting a twenty on the bar, he waved at Bart, then down at Tommy and Jerome adding, "Glad we're back on the same team guys, take care of yourselves, okay?" Jamie heard some type of acknowledgement from the two of them as he headed out the door and the voice of President Trump, who was still at the podium as a smaller, grey haired man with glasses was coming up.

As Jamie's weekend developed, he found out that flights to Denver were cut back and the ones still scheduled were booked. He called Becky's house and another neighbor was at her house. He told him about the flight situation and did not think he could get there any time soon. The neighbor said that any family burial service in these days may be put off until after things returned to normal in a month, two months or whenever, but that a private service and cremation would take place Wednesday for people from the Denver area. Jamie asked him to pass on to Becky, that if there was any way he could get there, he would make it, but that if not, he would come for the family service later on. Afterwards, he felt so very sad. He tried to eat his dinner slowly, but for the first time in a long time, he was so despondent, he could barely finish his meal. He tried to watch some tv but turned it off and played some of his old jazz tapes for a while and read the paper from two days ago. He also checked his phone and had text messages from Rachel and Sandra. Rachel texted him that her dad could not come because of the virus but would as soon as things settled down. She added that they were communicating by text and emails almost daily. She had sent him pictures of her which he said had him crying and she texted him back that she couldn't stop crying herself. She ended her text by typing, "I can't tell you how much I appreciate what you have done for me" which caused Jamie to become a bit teary eyed himself. He then checked the text from Sandra that the program was off for Saturday night, but she was so excited because she got a letter stating that she would become part of the chorus whenever they begin to work on the upcoming programs whenever that would be. As he thought more about all that was happening in these difficult new times of the virus, things were in pretty good shape, especially his work with Sam and Margaret, which was really moving along so well. There was resolution in all of his situations, except Jeremy's sudden death that had put a damper on all the positive things that were going on in his life. .

It was ten, so he turned the news back on. He watched the usual shootings, car crashes and fires when the broadcast was interrupted by a news flash. The CDC announced that national guidelines would be coming this weekend that would literally shut down the country. After listening for a few more minutes about the impact of the virus, he turned off the tv and two thoughts stayed with him; one was fear about what was going to happen to the country, especially after some of the guidelines were proposed, and two, that Sam's organization was really going to be tested during this time. Hundreds upon hundreds of people, young and old, mostly young black children and their families would be without the basics of living, based on what the news anchors were saying might be in government restrictions. Sam's organization may have to expand what they do to help these families during these coming days. His last thought before he headed for his bedroom was that the coming days were going to be a real test for all the tremendous enthusiasm he had felt earlier, plus for the country as a whole.

CHAPTER TWENTY-FOUR

The spring and summer months of 2020 was really were a test for Sam and his crew, as it was for the country and the world. It was like walking through the end of a hallway and opening a door and walking into a completely different living atmosphere. In America alone, there were so many conflicting events in one short quarter of one year; from an epidemic world of Corona Virus with people wearing masks; into a violent pre-election world never before experienced; to the killings of Black Americans by police and then violent protests literally taking over American cities; marches for black Americans that stifled the country for obvious reasons; and natural calamities, of devastating weather of heat and storms. Yet, Sam Wescott's forty-year program of helping struggling American children, succeeded in these extremely difficult times because it reached out to the most vulnerable in need, not only in Pittsburgh, but branching out across the country.

It was well into Spring and for weeks the staff and Sam continued to bounce around names for their group. At one point, they thought Margaret's idea of using a bridge would be a great symbol and Germaine and Marty had come up with several drafts to consider it. Sam, however, held back the final okay, as if there was something else, he wanted to use to both get attention and tell their story. One afternoon, Jamie and Germaine were talking about some new ideas for what they did, and she said to him, "We're sort of a lifeline for them".

Jamie looked at her intensely, then took Germaine by the arm into see Sam, who was sitting at his desk. As they stood in front of him, he asked her to repeat what she had just said, and she did. Then Jamie said to Sam, "Did you hear that Sam, we're a lifeline for these kids, a lifeline. That's a perfect name for what you do."

Sam looked at them, paused and said, "Lifeline, wow, by God, you're right. That hits the nail on the head. It's perfect, my darling Germaine perfect."

So that is how Sam's work got its name, LIFELINE. A lifeline that captured the hearts of America during the pandemic days; racial unrest like never seen before; and an election that divided the country that seemed on the fringe of a revolution. That was America in the first half of the year 2020, yet Sam, Jamie and Margaret, banded together with their crew, to create an American success story with the evolution of Sam and LIFELINE, into an icon of what an American, an African American, can create in one of the most difficult times in American history.

As for Jamie, the old boring, Scotch-Irish White American, his life change dramatically beginning in the winter of one of the most tempestuous years in American history. The pandemic atmosphere that engulfed his life's pursuits was oppressive. He struggled, like everyone else, to alter his life. But as he looked back over his immersion in Sam's work, he discovered phenomenal individual attributes during this difficult time of so many young people he encountered when he looked at the new computerized site that analyzed every child in Sam's new system. There were athletes, of course, who at age twelve, could eventually throw a ball or hit a ball like an older teenager that could get them college scholarships because of that ability. But what amazed Jamie the most, was how many of the youngsters had exceptional mathematical and writing skills, which would be critical in the new programming world that is needed in this day and age. Within their innate capabilities discovered by the data analysis, were vital hints of exceptional interest in medicine, which might lead one to nursing or even to becoming a doctor. Jamie was astounded that so many had interests and skill sets that could lead them to careers in various areas of work, opportunities in the radically new youth-oriented society of the times. Degrees were not necessarily needed or desired; jobs in online companies were paying well and requiring just youthful exuberance and technical abilities. Traditional jobs were not the primary objective in today's world. Sam's own technical crew sought out positions in smaller companies involved in the new technology-oriented work environment. Sam's work force was concentrating on this area in Pittsburgh and in areas around their growing associates or partners.

Another thing that impressed Jamie was how Sam directed many young men and women into the military which could provide a pathway to a career. In some situations, Sam recognized that some boys and girls needed more discipline in their lives, and he led them in his positive way to sign up in the military for a career. He would subtlety not pressure them but would calm their sometimes "abrasive traits", a term he overheard him use when talking to some of them. Jamie had been impressed many times by the insights of the young ones that was instigated and perceived by their parents, who normally, because of costs, could never have directed their children into potential careers. These personal insights relayed into the system by the parent or parents through interviews into Sam's computer system, was incredible. It broadened the potential career paths for some children and in some cases, the troubled ones. But, as importantly, careers and college education were still the majority of career lines developed. It was an incredible time for Jamie; he was so proud and excited to be giving poor kids a chance to succeed.

But because of the covid, another new chapter of Sam's LIFELINE, came into play and it directly involved Jamie's expertise as an architect. Their office center where most of the computer technology was carried out by their staff needed to be redesigned. This necessary change did not stop the young, vibrant work force of not only continuing their work, but expanding it from its Pittsburgh center to additional sites. Jamie and Margaret with the help of their staff in Pittsburgh and Boston, during the initial stages of the pandemic, came up with an assistance program for all the children and their families by providing masks; setting up virus testing schedules; and providing and delivering food supplies. During these traumatic times, it didn't hold back LIFELINE. Their system had become coordinated with similar non-profits in in D.C., Baltimore, and Cleveland that maintained their expenses.

The next fiasco in 2020 occurred in late spring with the killing of George Floyd in Minneapolis, which completely inundated the media and the country already overwhelmed by the virus. Sam, of course, was incensed by what those cops did, but he also recognized how many black brothers had killed white policemen and fellow black policemen. He was in turmoil because he was glad the centuries old issues of brutality of white power was dominating the news. He, however, was a focused person who knew it was not only just white against black; it was also black against black. He knew and he talked about it but was careful what he said or did. His first response was to reach out to the

"Black Lives Matter" leader in Pittsburgh, Billy Thompson, who he knew very well. He had helped Billy and his mother when he was a youngster; then through high school; and with getting Billy into Pitt. He got a hold of Billy and asked him to come to see him in Homewood. Billy Thompson came by himself the next day. Sam had called Jamie and asked him to come by to meet Billy. Jamie, in retrospect, was affected by listening to these two black brothers, one in his mid-eighties and the other his mid-twenties. They talked about what had happened in Minneapolis; in Selma; to Martin Luther King; to Joe Greene; to Wynton Marsalis; to Roberto Clemente; and to hundreds of little black kids trying to survive in the world in this year, 2020. It was something that Jamie, will always remember.

Jamie, his mask draped over his face, sat back next to the wall, while Sam and Billy sat across from each other and covered everything possible about the status of black men and police, especially in Pittsburgh. Billy was wearing a bright red mask when he came in with a narrow goatee below it and he was vocal and angry about what he called "nothing issues" that he had experienced himself with police over the past few years. Then he, his voice rising, talked about others who had been beaten and thrown in jail for what he thought were again "nothing issues".

Sam asked him to describe a "nothing issue". Billy paused and then, looking his mentor directly, laid them out. Painting on walls; rocking cars; throwing objects at windows; and gathering in numbers on streets over some minor event that had caused an outburst of anger with his fellow blacks, men and women. Sam softly asked him did he reject any action against restraint that police might have put on him or his groups over the years. Billy looked at Sam, then away, then back to him saying, "Sam, you are old school, man. Very old school. You accepted what those white motherfuckers did to you and you just go on. We don't and never will."

Jamie looked at Sam digesting what the young, black man, who he had helped over the years, had just said to him. Sam, who had turned away from Billy, his eyes peering over the rim of the lowered mask, looked like he was seeking something far away. After a long pause, he turned back to the dark faced, good looking young man and said, "Son, you are young, and you are wrong. This man you are looking at has fought more fucking battles with white men, black men, yellow men and maybe purple men than you will ever do in your whole life. I have never accepted anything someone did to someone else, let alone to me, black or white, if it was wrong. You're right, I am from the old school, but I do accept the new school, which is what you are part of. You have never faced what we used to call, discrimination, like what I went through from white men. But let me tell you something, boy, which you still are, I have been discriminated against by some black motherfuckers probably as many times as by white ones. It don't take color to make you a motherfucker. But," he paused added, "I admire what you are doing and I hate what was done to that man in Minneapolis by those bad cops, but one day, oh, about five years ago, right down the goddamn street from we are, two young black dudes pushed me into an alley, hit me with a club of some kind, knock the shit out of me and took all of my money." He paused, then went on, "And you know what young man, a white cop came down the alley, picked me up, and carried this big son of a bitch of an old man to the back seat of a police car, then took me to Presbyterian Hospital. That white dude cop saved this black dude's life because I was bleeding pretty bad, black boy, pretty goddamn bad." He paused, then said, "so yes, I hated what happened to that black man in Minneapolis, but it was done by a bad man, a bad white man, but that don't mean all men of white color are bad or that all men of black color are good. It means that we got to stop the bad ones of any color."

Jamie couldn't believe the silence in the room. No one spoke until Sam looked at Billy now with a slight smile and said, "Billy, I am so proud of you. I believe that you are doing what you were created to do in this life, just like I have been. I support you in all that you do and maybe this was the best thing that happened to this country, as sad and bad as it was. Maybe we all can grow out of this hatred spell and work into a giving spell...giving to people of all color and all needs. Boy, this man can use your enthusiasm because I believe in you and what you are fighting for. Let's do it like we've always done it, you and me, together." He paused and looked deeply at a stoic Billy and went on, "Black Lives Do Matter, in fact, all lives do matter, but I have an idea about something that has always bothered me. "Black Lives Matter" can possibly become involved in, as soon as things cool down a bit, something that has bothered me my whole life. I hope you and your group keep up your primary work but expand into into what I have been trying to do by helping me with children of black color have a shot at life. Your "Black Lives Matter" can help this old black man, Billy."

It was quiet as Billy digested what Sam had just said; a man he truly loved as the father he never had, just as Sam had never had. Then they slowly began an interchange that went on for another hour or so. Finally, Sam paused, looked at Billy and said, "What I'm going to say now may set you off again but hear me out." Sam went on to suggest that Billy's group could not only spread the "Black Lives Matter" mantra about black injustice, that he totally supported, but they could help Sam spread the word about other black children's and single mother issues. After going back and forth, Billy finally seemed to get what Sam was driving at; that the publicity in the white dominated press would always cover "Black Lives Matter" for their protests, but they could begin covering ways to help needy black kids and young, single mothers. Billy nodded his understanding.

In a darker tone, Sam brought up the one issue that had bothered him his whole life and that was black men creating babies and then disappearing and not supporting their children and their mothers as he had mentioned earlier to Billy. He turned and looked over at Jamie and added, "And that is with every race there is". He looked back over at Billy and said, "we have to try at least to have these boys, men own up to what they did by creating young ones that our women have to raise". With that, Sam, sat back and looked at Billy, who was silent.

Billy finally straightened up, looked at Sam, and said, "You are right old man, as always, you are absolutely right on. What the cops do to our people has to be our priority, but I realize from what you just said, that we, us, have our own problems that only we can fix. And you know something, it actually would fit right into our beliefs of justice. For our black men who are killed by cops and our black men who run from their babies".

They were quiet for a while and Sam said," Who knows better than you and me about fathers that hit and run, and this is important, son, and not just our folks, but men of all color that have fucked and run since time began, leaving little babies and mothers to simply die or barely exist. But we, you and me, can do something here and maybe other places to help them. As an old preacher of our church used to yell at us from the pulpit, 'Are you listening?'

It was quiet as Billy wiped tears from his face and came over to Sam and hugged him tightly. They stayed entwined.

Then Sam slowly disengaged from the tall, narrow young man and said, "We'll do it, son, we'll do it."

Billy looked at Sam, who was noticeably tired, and then looked down at his watch and said, "Well, Mister Sam, this has been quite a session we've had, and I thank you, as always, for your inspiration. I think, no, I know we got it right and I got some stuff I gotta do, so I'm going to head out."

Sam leaned back, smiled and said, "Billy, you haven't said a word to my good friend over there in the corner. You should because he has been a supporter of mine over the years."

Billy looked over at Jamie, "Sorry, brother, guess I'm allergic to white dudes."

Sam bristled quickly, saying, "You watch your mouth, black boy. That man is a good man, white or fucking black, don't make no difference to me, you hear me?"

Billy was shocked a bit after just hugging this legend who got him to where he was today and then hearing him scold him. He said, leaning towards Jamie, "Sorry, brother, any friend of Sam is one of mine."

Jamie slowly replied, "I don't care son, if you mean it or not, but me, I just want you to work peacefully for what your goals are and by helping Sam's kids, black or white, you will gain my trust and friendship. Simple, eh?"

Sam smiled and said, "That goes for me to, Billy boy. Now get your black ass out of here, me and my old friend have some talking to do."

After Billy left, Sam and Jamie called Margaret at her home. Sam talked to her about some financial transfers that had been completed by the X Man. She said she hoped to be able to come to Pittsburgh next week. They talked for a few more minutes before Margaret told him about being approached by CNN to have a telecom about her major involvement with LIFELINE. Margaret was being interviewed because of the violent protests that were overwhelming the country concerning "Black Lives Matter". Apparently LIFELIFE had gotten some notoriety as a positive program in the negativity news involving police brutality in black neighborhoods. She told Sam she thought it was a perfect time to explain their new relationships with organizations around the country.

As Jamie listened to Sam and Margaret, he thought how unique and purely American, was it, that three completely different human beings from different backgrounds and experiences in the world, had gone against the grain, by blending into a unique relationship to unite their personal skills to literally help other humans without the opportunities to a life of better existence. They were doing it not for their benefit, but for the benefit of others. Jamie sat back as they continued talking and realized it was necessary to reflect how well, during those difficult days that Sam's concept had actually succeeded. As they continued, Jamie sat back and smiled that he was involved in such a unifying concept.

CHAPTER TWENTY-FIVE

Jamie Sloan's life during the months of the corona virus were difficult like everyone else in the country. During this time, Jamie had time to fill, because of the closings of his volunteer work, yet, miraculously, he came through the desolate pandemic days a stronger, more vital person, due to his involvement with Sam's program. When ensconced in his apartment, he spent a lot of time reading and thinking about ways to help Sam's outreach. He made sure he kept in touch with Rachel and Sandra, whose lives he had become emotionally involved with. He didn't see either of them for months. McDonoughs Corner Pub was closed, so Rachel had no job and school was done by computer. Sandra's nursing work at the transplant service finally reopened after a month, but it was limited to only extreme patient situations. Her music career was put in limbo as the Pittsburgh Opera also closed shop and was not sure when they would be reopening. He received texts from both of them and like most everybody, they were going stir-crazy. Gradually the transplant service opened, but volunteers were not being asked to come in, and those over sixty-five would not be allowed back. Jamie thought probably because the virus was more deadly with older people than younger ones. This really upset him as he truly liked working there and felt he was contributing to the transplant group with the work he did. The library remained shut down and was, like every other organization, beginning virtual events which Jamie hated. He was an in-person kind of guy. He started going back to his bookcase where he had hundreds of books; novels, histories, and biographies, collected over the years, picking out ones that he had never read which were many. He made time to read books he had always wanted to read for years and it was a time of relaxation for his mind and body during his increasingly busy days with LIFELINE. What amazed him in these difficult days was that many people were suffering boredom because there weren't able to maintain their normal life, which made him so grateful for his work with Sam and Margaret.

As they worked on providing supplies to the families in their expanding operation, Margaret asked Jamie, via a Zoom meeting with

Sam, if he could assess all the buildings that Sam had purchased and work them into a new home base. He became totally involved in the project like he had years ago when he was a full-fledged architect. Jamie would catch empty buses back and forth with a mask on, to get to Homewood to work on his prime project. The project was to redesign old brick two story buildings and blend them in to the existing structures of Sam's corner, but with them built to fit the needs of the 21St Century. When he completed the work, he was amazed at their absolute functional beauty. There were three classrooms; two large storage areas; three communications rooms where computers were set up; and a small gym where basketball, volleyball and even tennis could be practiced indoors. The glass ceilings sloped and were both functional and he thought, beautiful. He also turned a smaller one-story dilapidated building next to the alley into a dining area for after school and weekend dining that would be available for students and families if necessary, which as it turned out was absolutely necessary. It was a fulfilling task for Jamie, and he was surprised how his skills of architectural planning had not gone away.

By summer, the project was completed, and the dining facility was operating with kids coming in daily with masks. The staff, which had been increased by twenty, many who were volunteers, including two Jamie was thrilled to see, Sandra and Rachel, who helped to serve food to the kids. They also worked on class and work schedules, plus setting up a supply system for deliveries to families in Homewood and to poorer neighborhoods in all parts of Pittsburgh. Sam had hooked up with other services in the City and County to fill in gaps for food and medical supplies when they were not available. Sandra and Rachel were in charge of finding supplies at these various sources, plus with grocery stores. Jamie was excited to see his friends working for Sam and when he talked to them, they seemed thrilled to be helping in coordinating the task of finding food for the kids and their families.

Sam found out, as the pandemic continued to take hold of normal living, that in talking with mothers of the kids, that they were having great trouble finding cabs to take their kids to medical appointments or special needs situations. Because of the pandemic, it was almost impossible for them to see doctors or go to emergency rooms. Sam decided to set up a service like UBER, that mothers could call for rides and he found drivers to be on call. It was similar to UBER, but relied on older drivers, men and women, black or white, to participate, as Sam called it. First Sam thought he would call the service after the name of the only cab service in Pittsburgh owned and operated for blacks in his day, the OWL cab company. But after thinking about it more, he came up with the name AMOS, based on his favorite TV show as a kid, Amos and Andy. Andy was a the driver in the show. Critics were quick to jump on Sam, even teachers complained that it took kids back to the bad old days, but Sam challenged them by saying that you cannot simply ignore the bad days. You must accept them for what they were, terrible, but also recognize the good days that have come since and that he is trying to make permanent in kids' lives. Some understood, but Sam didn't care; he said it was a pure racist reaction but that it emphasizes how far black Americans have come since those days. "Reality" is better than "fantasy", was one of Sam's bylines. "We are living our reality that we are constantly changing for the better", while fantasy of yesteryear is just that, "yesteryear".

When he was interviewed by a local TV Station reporter who was in her twenties and black, who brought up the controversy, he was adamant. "I suffered as a black man sixty, seventy years ago and I know how awful it was. You don't. I am working every day to make these days better for my black brethren. That show was just that; pure fantasy in a TV sense, yet also really funny and sadly, real, as to how the entertainment world treated black actors and black people in general. Even the great singers of the time, Nat King Cole, Sammy Davis, Ella Fitzgerald, Sarah Vaughn, my God the greatest entertainers of the time and in my opinion in American history, couldn't even stay in hotels or eat in restaurants. Fortunately, this country has overcome that and now we are in an opposite scenario, whereas all TV has blacks with blacks and blacks with whites, as if commercials and shows can rearrange reality. Sam believed the media should be concentrating on helping young black children live in stable environment, so those kids can have a chance in life. That's the reality of what we are trying to do." Sam did not stop and was never interrupted by the reporter. The station got hundreds of calls, mostly applauding Sam's comments, but some upset about his old way attitude. For days the interview got a lot of controversial feedback, not just in Pittsburgh, but it went virile and responses came in from around the country. Suddenly new individual support for his programs came from letters, PayPal and from older white people with seemingly more conservative viewpoints. His criticisms came from letters to the editors and even phone calls from what his staff told him. There were liberals complaining he was covering up for the past white treatment of blacks. Some called him an Uncle Tom, which caused him to laugh at first and then react vehemently when approached a second time by the same young black reporter. "Uncle Tom, I was called. Uncle Sam, and a black one I am and always will be," he said and laughed as the reporter didn't seem to know what to make of his sense of humor with such a delicate, controversial stance. In any event, Sam and his work, was now getting national publicity for its service of providing goods and services to people in need. Rough times to have achieved so much in such a short time, yet Sam seemed like he had gotten twenty years younger throughout these days of his lifelong pursuit. He was in touch daily with Margaret in Boston and her folks were now connected online to his Pittsburgh techie crew who were set up in the new computer lab designed by Jamie.

What Jamie had witnessed through these otherwise challenging months, was literally like watching a sci-movie of the Twenty-Fifth Century, of a country stymied by a deadly virus. Even some civil unrest eventually hit close to their headquarters home in Homewood, but things calmed down because Sam's work was well known in the community. The young crew, who all dutifully wore masks and were separated properly, became creative in their covid designer styles which livened up the overall negative atmosphere created by the virus. These folks working for Sam were almost all African American with some white young people and a few Asian students working part-time from their studies at Carnegie-Mellon and Pitt. Jamie was astounded how beautiful the buildings looked, not only from their aesthetic look, but also their practicality, especially when he looked in on the young crew in their workplace.

It was a warm summer day as Jamie and Sam strolled throughout the completed buildings. Sam was ecstatic as he walked, in his slow, deliberate pace, in and out of the buildings, his smile permeating that face of his with a large, blue mask hanging off his neck. For the first time in over forty years, Sam was realizing the dream of his lifetime coming into a reality. Jamie eyes teared up as he watched Sam silently walking within his dream. As they turned to go back to his office area, Sam looked at Jamie and said quietly, "You know it looked like we might get through this catastrophic dilemma until that black man got murdered in Minneapolis. I can't remember as much back-to-back trauma in my lifetime affecting this country." He looked ahead and went on, "You know Jamie, this time that we are in has got me thinking about what I was explaining to you a while back, which seems like years ago and it was only, in what, March? about my life theory that I had finally nailed down."

Jamie stopped as Sam kept walking until he realized Jamie wasn't beside him and he stopped, turned and looked back with a questioning look on his face. "You, okay?" Sam asked.

Jamie looked sad replied, "Yeh, I'm okay, but sometimes I wonder if our country can survive all this turmoil and sickness and just plain hatred towards each other. There seems to be so much separation," he said, as he reached Sam.

Sam responded, as he looked at Jamie, "I know how you feel. I've been excited about all that we have accomplished in these disastrous times, yet I am sad for our young people living through this country's divisiveness. Oh, it's about time or I should say, it's a crying shame that black brothers had to die to cause the country I fought for, to maybe come to grips with the treatment of us black folks by the cops." He paused, then said, "and don't give me that bullshit about it's only a few bad apples, Jamie, because there are many bad apples wearing blue, believe me. Don't get me wrong, they aren't all white, for sure, but I've been stopped a hundred times in my life by some bad ass cop even when I was going to church, for Christ's sake. There are a bunch of underachieving white dudes who take out their insecurities in life on someone they think is lower than them on the totem pole, so they arrest them; harass them; or shoot them, for no fucking reason. I have seen it. I have lived it. I have, unfortunately, really ignored it as that's what it is. You've listened to Billy. He's a fine young man, and although he only has one opinion based on his life, that's what it is. Me, I got me, seventy, eighty years of seeing shit happen. So, Billy and his folks and all of us, are saying, no more. No fucking more," he paused, looking Jamie square in the face and added, "no fucking more, my man." They looked at each other and then Sam turned and started walking back towards the exit that led to his office. Jamie didn't move, he was paralyzed. He waited until Sam was through the door, before he started to walk toward him and stopped. He didn't know if he should go into Sam's office or just leave. Looking at him, Jamie knew something had been boiling in him for days.

Jamie decided to leave. He needed to take a walk. As he looked into Sam's office, he saw him sitting at his desk with his head down and he couldn't just walk out, so he leaned in and said, "Sam, can I do anything for you?"

Sam did not respond, his head stayed down, then slowly he looked up and said quietly, "Jamie, you must forgive me, but this shit has been boiling inside of me for years and I have always tried to keep my calm, knowing it's only a few fucking up the whole world all the time, but it finally got to me," as he paused and then said slowly and calmly, "Just be my friend, that's all."

"Always, Sam, always."

Sam's continued calmly and he said, "You leaving?"

"Need to take a walk and get some quiet time to think."

"You know, as I was sitting here, I remember our talk months ago about my theory on the Universe and for some reason, it came back to me. As I said to you, this world we live in, is such a click of the finger, you know? Snap and we're gone. Snap and this Earth is gone. As I dug into the essence of the Universe I realized, as I told you, that our time is a moment, as is our whole planet. Poof, it's all gone, but you know, Jamie, that's all we got, my man. No matter how short it is in time, it is all you and me and everyone has of this here reality of life," he paused, "Oh, wow, you know, you and me have got to go have a drink and talk about what I just said. I didn't realize what a guru I had become," as he started laughing.

Jamie came into the office and said, "You are my guru, that is for sure, black or white, you are one fucking guru."

Sam burst out laughing in that booming, guttural laugh of his, "Sam the Guru. I like it."

CHAPTER TWENTY-SIX

Margaret was sitting waiting to see the President of the United States. It was noon and a press conference was scheduled in the Rose Garden for one o'clock which had her completely puzzled as to whether she would actually see the President. She was dressed in a white outfit with and a deep blue scarf around her neck that matched the blue mask she wore. Masked staff buzzed around her as she sat by herself in a deep, tan leather chair after being processed through all the security checks. She had known Donald Trump for close to thirty years as her husband was a friend of his from dealings in the nineties. Her opinion of him was always the same; the most ego centric man she had ever met, yet one who possessed a personality that drove him to finish projects once decided upon. That was the one trait she admired, as did Warren. The times they dined with Trump were usually all about him, but several times he would become introspective, talking about his father who was very tough, as he put it, and a brother who died of alcohol abuse, which he subtly put on his father. Apparently, his brother's death had a tremendous impact on him as he never drank alcohol. The thing that really surprised her was that the man was smart and had a phenomenal memory about things that had happened to him as a youth and especially the powerful impact his father had on him. His mother was the one though, that apparently impacted him positively as a young boy. He talked of her with such calmness and great respect, the opposite of his personality in prime time. Margaret shifted in her sofa and looked out of the window at the tree branches that were waving far away from a wind that was expected to bring storms to D.C. later in the afternoon.

Suddenly the door opened and a young lady, smartly dressed said to Margaret, "Mrs. Decker, can you follow me?" Margaret followed the woman into the Oval Office where she talked for close to a half hour with the President and his wife Melania and daughter Ivanka without masks but sitting well apart. They sat the social distancing distance and it was exciting meeting because they all surprised her by knowing a lot about Sam and his business venture in helping young African

American kids and single mothers. Even the President truly seemed interested. He asked if Sam could come to the White House sometime which Margaret said she felt certain could be arranged. After that exchange, the President had to break off. She then spent more time with Melania and Ivanka, who asked how they could help in promoting Sam's program across the country. She left absolutely exhausted and she was totally surprised to see how much the two women and even the President, knew about what Sam had accomplished and how he was expanding across the country. As she left, Ivanka asked if she could come see the facilities which Margaret agreed to.

Her meeting at the White House seemed to be almost a climatic event in her association with Sam and Jamie. She, in retrospect, was amazed that she took the chance on an eighty-four-year-old African American man and a concept that she never knew existed. Her children were astounded, but after looking up Sam and also Jamie online, they too were amazed by their validity and the Google articles about their work, now their own mothers. Her life had felt completely turned around and she felt so fulfilled as she headed for her car with a smile, realizing it was now "their" programs and that Sam was just one incredible being.

After the initial lockdown from the epidemic, Margaret spent the first months in Wellfleet, Massachusetts, in the home purchased thirty years ago by Warren. It was the favorite place of all their homes because it was peaceful, and they loved to walk along the shore at dusk. Since committing to work with Sam, she had it updated with all the new technology so she could keep in touch with Pittsburgh and Boston, as she gradually took over exploring potential new cities and locales for them. The latest was Seattle where they not only treated young black kids and mothers to new Security Blankets, which was the slogan attached to the packages of support they were creating. The mothers loved the Security Blankets because they provided a sense of security, not only for the children, but for them. Another new venture she worked on was designing a job training program for the mothers that allowed them to get part-time jobs in the food delivery business, which was booming in the burgeoning days of covid. Restaurants were closed and food was being delivered either directly to a residence or curbside to drivers. Close to a thousand parents in all the offices had picked up jobs during these days because of the new program. She was so thrilled to see Black Lives Matter, led by Billy, begin a new operation working with Sam in Homewood to see how they could assist in this particular area. Another new job opportunity that was created due to the virus, was creating jobs for single mothers to pack boxes of food at all of Sam's locations. These boxes would go to all low-income families, no matter what their race.

Once she was able to fly from Boston, she went to D.C. several times, and pulled off a real coup' in late May. She met with a group of members of the House of Representatives from both Parties about sponsoring legislation to try and consolidate Federal programs of family support for indigent citizens of all races, creeds, and nationalities who were on American territory. During their meeting, a young representative from North Carolina, referred to research he had done, which listed a pool of over five billion dollars of unused funds already allocated by Congress, that could and should be distributed to local organizations across the country to support children. They vowed to work on a bill to consolidate these programs and begin the process of getting these unused funds transferred to a new program. Margaret was excited and felt great momentum that Congress would come around within the year to support this proposal.

She also met with an organization in the nation's capital, similar to what Sam had been doing, that desperately needed financial help. Because of the funds she had provided LIFELINE, she thought they could become a satellite in D.C. She set up a meeting with Sam, via Zoom and the woman manager of the D.C. operation. After their meeting, it was agreed they would become associated with Sam and LIFELINE. Margaret really felt this was a critical development, especially with her group in Congress trying to consolidate the federal funding programs. But she was not done yet in D.C. She arranged a meeting with three representatives from Microsoft, who agreed to provide the technical equipment necessary and assistance in developing the logistical information to try and create a program to locate potential mothers when job openings were found in each of their locations. This would be a pilot logistical program that would be done first in Pittsburgh. If successful, it would be made available to all of their locations. She felt so good about what she had accomplished and looked forward to some quiet time at home by the sea.

One afternoon, as she was packing her bag in D.C. to fly back to Wellfleet via Boston, Margaret watched her Boston staff being featured on FOX News as a supportive backbone for LIFELINE created by an ex-Marine man in Pittsburgh to help black single mothers and black children. The reporter was explaining that LIFELIE was now expanding across the country as a national phenomenon. As she listened, she felt that this was the coup de gras' for all that had happened to her over this past year since Warren's death. He always told her if anything happened to him, she should keep up her personal work that she did so well. She followed his advice and dug right into projects involving the European Union using her home in Wellfleet as her base which also allowed her to calmly adjust to life without Warren by walking and sailing like she loved to do. Margaret had been stunned by his sudden death and couldn't see what she could ever do that would give her fulfillment; then came the call from Pittsburgh and here she was working to help young people get a chance at life.

During the summer in Wellfleet, Margaret was in daily contact with LIFELINE in Pittsburgh, but was glad when Gizelle found out that they could finally fly again from their small airport instead of having to drive to Boston. She contacted Sam and Jamie, proposing a meeting of the whole crew. It was agreed and weeks later, LIFELINE was to have their really first, what some would call, board meeting to take an accounting of where they were and where they wanted to go next. All were present in Pittsburgh in the expanded complex designed by Jamie. The staff went over all of their current projects and it was decided to gradually add to their operations, of what they had found successful. Margaret talked about her work in D.C. Sam went over briefly the history of his organization and how amazed he was by looking out over the group gathered on this day. He reminded them that no matter how they had grown up, their primary role was to serve those folks who are in need, especially the children. Not only for food and school assistance, but in some cases financial and a growing need transportation during this pandemic time, which brought up his last point. Sam then ended the meeting by talking about the success of AMOS the service that was used to drive mothers and children to appointments. Sam explained to the group, that he knew a couple old friends of his who drove for Uber and they explained to him how that company worked. He went on to explain that he came up with the idea of a new jitney service because mothers mostly, were telling the staff it was hard to pay for rides around town. So, he had idea for a taxi service like Uber in black neighborhoods, that would pick up children, family members and elderly folks to get around for shopping or medical appointments. It was proving a great success and Sam smiled and said he named it after his favorite character of the Amos and Andy Show, AMOS. AMOS was so successful in Pittsburgh, that it was being added to other communities of their associates around the country. When Sam was done and the meeting was over, the group clapped in unison as their first board meeting had ended on such a positive note and Margaret was so pleased that, despite despair in the country, LIFELINE was settling into a positive stage.

It had been an outstanding meeting and Margaret left after it was over to fly back to Wellfleet. As she looked out of the window of the jet, she was pleased to see that her contacts were attracting funding from some very high-end individuals and companies, but not those who had contacted her after Warren died; they were off her list anyway. LIFELINE was expanding into new locations and their bottom line was growing as it was more expensive in this beginning period as they expanded services. Thinking about Sam's life, that began in Homewood and what he had accomplished over the years in the same neighborhood, was the fundamental reason for its growth because his people and all people, trusted him. When he said he would do something, his people knew he would do it and that he hooked up with a couple white people, Jamie and herself, that was okay, because if old Sam trusted them, then they had to be okay. She could not believe the responses she got from black politicians in D.C. when she told them she was working with Sam. His reputation was well known, not just in Homewood, but in the halls of Congress because the black coalition of reps who had heard about his successes, wanted to support this man as he began to get national publicity. Much of what he was doing was slowly getting accepted in the Democrat side of the House, but also on the Republican side, because Sam's history was an American success story, not just some government program that happened to get coverage on CNN and FOX. Sam had been interviewed by networks and highlighted his programs as a real uplift for a suffering country that saw nothing each day but updates of the deaths from the corona virus; protesters taking over the country; and the mindless, idiocy of current politics with a country coming literally apart at the seams.

In Wellfleet during the summer, Margaret had become a bit of a hermit, only going out for medications, food, and occasional meals outside with masks, if one of her children could find a way to Cape Cod. Her work was on the internet with messages back and forth with attorney's; bankers; and with contacts in DC about LIFELINE. The most exciting time for her was when she participated in ZOOM meetings with Sam and the staff. The summer was extremely hot and with the virus seemingly pausing a bit, it looked like things were getting a little back to normal. On her trips to DC or Pittsburgh, via Boston, which were the only ones she had made, she was extremely careful and so far, it had worked. Neither she nor Gizelle had any symptoms. On this early morning, Margaret drank a cup of expresso while turning the pages of the New York Times, a habit going back at least thirty years with Warren.. This morning, all by herself, no phone, no TV, just the Times, and coffee. She looked up at the fog covering the quiet water swell and she was thinking about her life. Here she was, by herself, except for Gizelle, who stayed in a bed and board in Wellfleet. This morning she probably was already at the airfield checking out their plane because Margaret wanted to go to Pittsburgh tomorrow to talk face to face with Sam and Jamie about her recent discussions in D.C.

Thinking of Gizelle, she wondered, what did she get out of their relationship, other than, obviously a well-paid job and traveling about the country and world, when that was possible. She often talked of her childhood and her military service as being separate but critical to her being what she called "a loner". After she had worked for Margaret for a while, she wondered why this beautiful woman was not attached in some way. She knew she dated different men but apparently had never found a man she wanted to only be with. She remembered a day in Paris a few years ago when she had decided to walk to the Eifel Tower by herself and gave Gizelle the afternoon off. Later as she passed a café on the Left Bank, she spotted Gizelle roaring in laughter as a very handsome guy with dark curly hair who was smiling and patting her on the back. It was as if she was with her lover, the warmth expressed by them both. As she stopped laughing, she spotted Margaret and waved her over. It was delightful. So, Margaret knew that she was just an independent lady, who lived her life exactly as she wanted to. She had made Margaret's life a thousand times easier since Warren passed away because she literally watched over her. Even her children were in awe of how lucky their mom was to have her at her side, literally.

But tomorrow she was heading to Pittsburgh to continue her new and exciting life in person which she really enjoyed because she hated living through a screen. She smiled and then laughed as she thought, "Who else in this day, could get excited about jetting to Pittsburgh and driving to Homewood?" "Homewood" sounds like a senior center residence one of her old friends had said to her last week when she was explaining her new venture. The woman, an old friend from D.C., eventually committed ten thousand dollars to LIFELINE, after listening to Margaret simply explaining its function and its growth. To add to everything else that was going on, she had seen Sam interviewed on CBS Sunday Morning last weekend. The interview was so timely, and she came to tears watching him explain the history of what is now called LIFELINE. She thought my God, what a positive story in this day of riots, virus and politics and I am a part of it.

Ironically her day ahead was jammed with an early morning "Zoomer with Sam and Jamie and then she needed to organize an update on her work in D.C. for them in Pittsburgh tomorrow. She paused to think about these two male partners. 'Ah, Jamie, one super nice guy and Sam, is one of the most incredible people I have ever met'. As she continued to think of Sam, she thought that he's one of the most intriguing people, she had ever come across in her life, which covered fifty to sixty years of meeting all kinds; from college to her years with Warren all over the country and the world. He was like some Greek god who sat on a throne and committed life to his followers. She went from a grieving widow, to working with two men, older than her, that she was enthralled by their pure honesty. Maybe it was their ages; nearing the end of their lives, they had absolutely no pretense; no ego trips; no phoniness about them; traits she just wasn't used to in her life. These two, who came to her, many months ago, were the most honest, loving, good people she had ever met. She was devoted to making sure Sam's dream is more than he ever imagined, and it was happening. Jamie was just the kindest, gentlest, honest man with such a solid personality, she could not believe he and Sam had come into her life. She also was grateful for Jamie's honesty about Warren based on what he saw on that spring day fifty years ago when he thought Warren had allowed a woman to drown and die. Anyway, it was cleared up and when she explained how Warren had supported the girl's family over the years, it erased all the negativity he had felt for all these years. How strange life is, she thought, so strange. Yet Warren would be so proud of her and how this had all come together. She polished off her last sip of coffee as a new, heavy wind rippled the waters in front of her. It was time to get moving, Sam would be hooking up pretty soon, it was Zoomin time and then she'd get ready for her trip to Pittsburgh.

CHAPTER TWENTY-SEVEN

Sam's "Zoomer" call was his second in as many days, because he wanted to introduce two officially new cities to his roster, Denver, Colorado and Seattle, Washington. Jamie got there with his mask on like everyone else. The main staff were twelve feet apart and sitting behind plastic shields. He looked up at the large master screen to see Margaret and there were twelve other separate screens online from the Boston group: the new cities of Denver, Seattle, and D.C., and eight other sites around the country, looking down on the assembled group in Pittsburgh. What Margaret had recommended to Sam and Jamie had agreed, was that the country be divided up into areas. So, there was the Northeast, the Southeast, Central, Southwest, and Northwest at this time in anticipation that they would be expanding during the rest of 2020.

The meeting was also designed by Sam to welcome Billy Thompson and two young ladies from Black Lives Matter to everyone. They were sitting at a narrow table set aside from the desk areas for the staff; Billy, Yvonne, and Michelle with black" Pittsburgh with pink and white masks. All three were dressed in Levi's and dark shirts with their logo on the front below their masks. Sam introduced Margaret from Wellfleet on the multi-faced screen and Jamie who was next to Sam. Sam walked over to Billy's table and introduced Billy, then reached down and gave him a ferocious hug, mask and all.

Sam then looked right at Billy's ladies and said with that smile of his, "Man, I'll tell you something, Billy, you can bring them around here every day, you hear me, son?" which made the whole group crack up and seemed to break the ice of this first important meeting.

Sam went on to talk of their plan to implement a portfolio concentrating on registering all single black mothers within the locales of their current system in a national database that would have their basic financial and support data. He said to get it started, it would be set up first in Pittsburgh and then established in their satellite offices around the country. The first goal was a registry and secondly, to create an activity plan for every family. Over the next three hours, there was participation from most of the branch offices. By the Zoom call ended, there was excitement amongst the workers about how to move forward. In the Homewood headquarters, as they were breaking for lunch, Billy asked Sam if he could talk to him privately. Sam waved for him to follow him to his office.

Soon, the staff with their wild variety of masks pulled down, were deep into laughter and conversation as they ate their lunch separated in the new eating area in an outside patio that had a rolled back Plexiglas designed by Jamie. They quieted as Sam and Billy walked back into the area together, with Sam putting up his hand for attention from the work force. Sam said that Billy was extremely enthused about their new relationship, but he and his team had one request for him. Sam explained that the idea of the cabs to take kids and mothers various places was his idea alone, but Billy and his team wanted Sam to consider renaming the system because they felt it was old school, hinting at what white people thought about blacks, referring to the Amos and Andy shows of radio and TV. Sam said, at first, he was taken aback, because, as he expressed to them, it was just tremendous humor; black people who were funny, very funny. Billy, Yvonne and Michelle had disagreed vehemently, so Sam asked them had they ever seen the TV show. They hadn't, so he had Marty find old TV show of Amos and Andy on YouTube. As the show went on, he had laughed his usual roaring laugh at the Kingfish talking to Amos. When he turned to look at Billy, Yvonne and Michelle, their eyes were looking straight ahead. They were not laughing. He waved at Marty to stop the program and asked them, if the three had seen any humor in the program. Billy lowered his mask a bit and was stone-faced as he looked at Sam then vehemently said to him that the program was demeaning to them. Sam said he was shocked, but then looked out at the staff and said, "Okay, so I decided to change the name because this program is working so well, we don't need any conflicts of age, for goddamn sure, so here's what I'm going to do. The cab service has to have a new name, so what do we call it then, if anything? "

The group looked around at each other and then Billy said, "How about Floyd?"

Sam replied with that smile of his, "Done deal, young Billy, done. I understand and from this moment on our cab service is called FLOYD." He turned to the group and said, "So now we got the FLOYD Jitney Service and I like it. Thank you, Billy, Yvonne and Michelle." The group applauded.

Sam asked Billy to come over to him. As they stood there Sam paused and looked out over the mixed group of people who were working day in and day out on expanding the network, they had created, and it made him so proud. He waved his right hand and the group quieted. "I wanted to add that Billy and Yvonne and Michelle also heard me out on a problem that has been with our folks for centuries, here, everywhere where young women are impregnated by young men and then the donor, the male, disappears. He just...," Sam paused and adds, "walks". It was quiet, stone cavern quiet. No one said a word until Sam said, "I did not mean to upset you but each of you know women who have given birth and the man never, ever helped that woman or that child, ever, like my old man, and Billy's for that matter. For us black folks here, we accept all the good we are doing, but we also have to recognize the bad that some folks do. Boys and men bailing out after they get their way with a woman and then never, ever help that woman or child that follows. They must be held accountable. I ask you to please think about what I have just said." He turned to his right and said, "Billy, Yvonne and Michelle heard what I said and have agreed to try and find a new way through our computerized society to track these delinquent men, not just black men, but all men, so they can be approached, in some way, to help the mother and the children they created. I want to say also that what we are considering may need to be cleared legally with the State and the Fed's, because I don't know if we can do this. I know there are systems in place for child support in all States, so maybe we start there, I just don't know," he paused," but maybe we can have some impact on governments to find delinquent fathers to help the mothers and the kids. By the way, I must add, that as we expand our work for white folks and kids, all folks and kids, for that matter, we will insist, lobby, whatever you want to call it, for a system to be created to hold all those studs of any color accountable for the little souls they have created.

These men must be held accountable. I think in this day and age, there is the DNA technology which we can use to find a lot of them."

The room was quiet, and Billy raised his hand, "All you folks know we must still continue the help that LIFELINE now provides, plus our new FLOYD service, but we must recognize what Sam has just said is the truth…not only the African American truth, but American youth and frankly youth around the world. For my people, we have been revolting against lies for centuries by white people, well I think, since Sam brought it up, that we must not allow black men and yes, white dudes, as Sam has so well said, to just do what they do and take off. They all must be held accountable, and we will also help with that project."

There was an explosion of cheering in the room.

Jamie put up his hand, as the noise quieted down, and said, "Okay, we have some more powerful information," as he pointed up to Margaret's face, "coming from Margaret Decker up there in the middle of the screen", he said, pointing to Margaret's face, "who will be working to get bills introduced to mandate a complete overhaul of the Federal system and that has been in places for decades to supply women, all women, across this country with basic family support. In these days of our computer technology advances, we believe the systems can be integrated with the States and the Federal government. In talks with two internet providers, we have been told a system to handle every case of support in our country could be developed, assuming we can get cooperation from these various governmental agencies. That's our goal and as I said, and Margaret has been working with Congressional folks to develop this type of system in the near future." Sam added, "This is just right, folks, for all those mothers left literally holding the bag, an empty one. So, let's look at all that we do with one common denominator; to offer support and hope to our children and the parent, usually a woman, of them. Now I say we get back to business and don't forget, keep these damn masks on."

There was a muttering as the group went into their groupings and the Zoom screen was still on with faces from Sam's new network including a still smiling Margaret who said, "Sam, that was terrific and hopefully I speak for all of us on screen that we'll do all we can to support all of you have so well outlined. That Federal Registry is my pet project and I'll have more to tell you tomorrow when I come to Pittsburgh."

"Can't ask for more than that,

Margaret, and looking forward to seeing you," Sam responded. "So, let's call it a day or I should say a meeting and we'll do this again, maybe Friday unless anything comes up and if it does, any of you on screen, please get in touch. "

Margaret spoke up, "Sam, as I mentioned I have some really important things I want to go over with you and Jamie, that deal directly with what you just outlined, so as I said I'll be coming in tomorrow. Gizelle's got the plane set up, so I should be there around 1 o'clock. Maybe for lunch, what do you think?"

"Sounds great to me. I'm hankering for the place down the street, Café Benny. Maybe I'll get our cohort Jamie to join us."

"Great, you told me about Benny's, count me in. If all goes well, I'll see you there," Margaret said as her screen image disappeared.

The Zoom screen disappeared, and Sam sat back and turned toward Jamie.

"Well, Jamie, that was some meeting."

Jamie replied, "You handled it well Sam, especially with Billy. At first, I was a bit upset that they would object to your name for the cab service, but as I thought about it, Sam, these are young people who have no understanding of anything that went on before the year 2000. We are definitely of the old school and one of the best things about working with these young folks is that is has brought reality to me, Sam. We are from a different time. We were affected by the assassinations of John F. Kennedy and Martin Luther King, the Viet Nam War, the collapse of Russia and even 911. To them that stuff never happened; to them iPhones, Facebook, Barack Obama, Google, and now the corona virus is their past and present. Our stuff never happened."

Sam looked at Jamie and said, "Yeh, you're right. They wouldn't know Sammy Davis, Jr. ever existed and me, he was the best entertainer ever," he paused, "you know, Jamie, saying that really hurts me, but you're right it is the truth of this time, anytime I guess". He paused and looked away from Jamie then turned back and added, "you know, not only is what we are doing phenomenal for our kids, but for you and me, it's added years…, maybe months to our lives," as he smiled.

Jamie laughed and said, "You, me and our favorite lady, Margaret. We're all benefiting from working to help these young and mistreated kids. Just want to add, that was a great session, Sam. You nailed it."

"Thanks, I think so. So glad I got Jimmy working with us. He is one fine young man," he added, "You going to be here for a while?"

Jamie responded, "Well I wanted to doublecheck on a couple things in the new buildings.

Sam replied, "Hey, let me go with you. Haven't taken time to look over everything you been doing, except this place is really looking good, thanks to you Jamie," as he and Jamie walked out of his office.

CHAPTER TWENTY-EIGHT

Jamie and Sam spent the next morning working on an overall resume of all that LIFELINE was currently working on with Margaret coming later with her updates. Sam wanted to have a plan for everything that they were working on because they had taken on so much during this difficult year of transition within the country. By late morning after working non-stop, they paused, Sam said, "Jamie, my man, I need some calm time especially with that Margaret coming in with her fireball approach."

Jamie smiled as he folded up his laptop then said, "Sam, if I thought I would ever hear you talking about someone who had a fireball approach, I'd think you were talking about yourself."

Sam laughed and said, "Got me that time Jamie," as he paused then said, "What say we head over Benny Brown's down the street. Margaret said she would meet us there and I know she'll be on time what with that lady pilot of hers.

"Okay by me," Jamie replied.

"Yeh, I've been itching for my man's tomato rice soup which is his special today." Sam was talking about a new restaurant that opened up by Benny Brown who was a graduate of his program almost twenty years ago. Benny learned how to cook while in the Army and because Sam's business had grown so much, he decided to open up a restaurant down the street from LIFELINE. Benny Brown's, "Café Benny", had been a success from day one, especially since the old man, as Benny called Sam, had been there the first day and almost every day since.

Sam and Jamie left for Café Benny with their masks hiked up on their faces. In minutes, they were seated at a window and Sam was looking at the newspaper style menu.

Jamie said, "Man, you know what you're going to order, why are you looking at that?"

Sam smiled and said, "I just like to see how well my old student is doing when I look at all he has to offer and to think I first saw him with his Mom when he was, I think about five years old and he was skinny as a rail. In six months, he was plump because of me and it makes me feel so good to see this dude succeeding in life."

Jamie replied, "You should, old man, you should. There's thousands today you should feel good about."

They were quiet as a young, chubby waitress came up to their table with a blue mask and said, "Well, Mister Sam, what do you want today as if I didn't know?"

Sam laughed as he said, "Well, Loretta, my dear, we gotta wait for a while because a lovely lady is going to join us, so I'm going to have a Bud and maybe some of those great potato chips the man makes."

Loretta laughed, then looked at Jamie and said, "And you, white man, what you want?"

"How about a Yuengling and double up on the chips," Jamie responded.

"My man it is. You young men want anything else?" she said.

"Not now but with my lunch I'd love one of Bennie's chocolate milkshakes. Best ever made."

"You got it" as Loretta turned to Jamie. "You?"

Jamie replied, "Haven't had a chocolate shake in years so I'll have one too."

They sat quiet for a minute as both looked out of the window at the street that seemed to be bustling a bit with people walking and talking. Then Sam said, "You know Jamie, it's about time we continue our talk about our lives and where the hell we're going to be in a couple years, know what I mean?"

Jamie didn't answer right away because for some reason, deep down, he knew this conversation was long overdue because of all that happened in the past months. Sam was ready to continue his new philosophical belief he touched on before. Jamie thought 'I'll bet that this will be a lunch for me to remember'. It would be.

They sat silent for a few seconds and then Sam said, "You know Jamie, I was watching a show on my TV, Netflix I think, about my man Quincy Jones. He has always been a hero of mine because the man devoted his life to one thing, music. His story of sitting down at a piano, I think it was his uncle or some relative, and he hit the keys and knew right then and there where his life was going. I used to pray for a time like that. You know something that hits you in the head and you knew exactly what you are going to devote your life to. It never happened to me, until I walked into a dirty, filthy room behind a diner just down the street from where we're sitting. I was looking for the men's room and went into this tiny room where a young girl was trying to change diapers on two little black kids who were crying their eyes out. I went up to her, turns out her name, which I will never forget, was Simone Williams. I asked her if I could help her. She was scared of me and shied away, grabbing hold of the little ones like I was going to take them or worse, hit them. As it turned out, after I had calmed her down, Miss Williams had these two little guys, who had to be twins. They lived above a garage in a two room, I guess you'd call it a flat. She worked part-time as a waitress in the diner and also cleaned houses in Squirrel Hill for the rich folks over there. What was Miss Williams doing in a room next to the diner? She had to bring her twins there while she worked, 'cause she was the only who could care for them. She couldn't afford for anyone to watch them. I was so fucking mad, Jamie and when I asked her where the boy's father was, she said, and this is her exact word, 'I ain't never seen him since the night he fucked me'. I was so goddamn mad, Jamie, I would have busted that dude in pieces if I had found him, which I did about a year later. What happened that day got me started and looking back on that day almost forty years ago, it was my Quincy Jones piano event."

Jamie said, "What exactly do you mean, Sam?" he said as Loretta put their beers and a large plate of chips in front of them.

Sam looked up at Loretta and said, "Thanks, Loretta, thanks", and he picked up his glass and took a sip. He put down his glass and looking at Jamie said, "Well, I knew right then and there how I was going to spend my time, which I had plenty of, since I got out of the service. I had a lot of money in the bank and a couple job offers that didn't pay much but would have been okay, but I knew at that moment, that I was going to start helping young black folks, especially young single mothers and their young'uns."

Sam's phone buzzed and he answered, "Sam here". He looked out the window as someone was talking to him. Jamie sipped his beer while watching Sam listen. After a short time, Sam shut the phone and said, "Guess what, Jamie, our partner is on time and will be here within the hour. She's got some important stuff she wants to run by us".

Sam waved Loretta over. He asked her to bring some more chips over and another beer. They sat quietly for a few seconds and then Sam looked at Jamie, smiled and began to talk in quiet, soft voice. "As I talked to you before about what I've come to believe, "we, old friend, are just temporary inhabitants of this temporary miniscule planet in this space with no beginning and no end. Earth is but a grain of sand in the gigantic ocean of the Universe and we are tiny crystals within the sand. Yet, we humans are able to study from our Earth the endless Universe. My God, but what will we be like in just a thousand years?", as Sam took another sip and looked out the window. Jamie didn't say a word as he just looked and listened.

Sam looked back at Jamie and went on, "Jamie, all I know is that we must respect every thought of every moment that enters this brain of ours up here," he said tapping the side of his hear. "Our God, for me, is the Universe. So, we must do all we can to experience every living second we have, of what we call life," he said, as he took a deep breath, then went on slowly, "like I know that we are we are doing," as he paused and said, "this is my moment, Jamie, and your moment and actually the lady coming to see us shortly, it's her moment. This is each of ours's moment, also our moments together and I truly believe it's the most exciting and fulfilling sense any human could have." He sat back and sighed, looking tired from this powerful monologue.

Jamie remained motionless but had tears in his eyes. He reached across the table and took the sweaty hand of this man of the ages. As he looked at Sam, he thought how fickle our own lives are and how miniscule are our real understandings of other people. The man across the table, in Jamie's mind, was from another world and somehow, he had allowed him to join in his life's venture. Neither spoke, finally Jamie said, "Sam, you are special. You are a special human and I know that somehow that special power I feel when I look at you brought us back together and Margaret into our world."

Sam smiled, tightened Jamie's grip as he said, "In our moment, we are going to make a difference for so many young folks who would have never had a chance. Now ain't that worth all that we are doing in our moment, so they can have theirs?"

As Jamie looked across at Sam, his eyes strayed and noted a large blue Cadillac pulled up to the curb. The back door opened, and he could see Margaret stepping out onto the curb. She leaned inside and was saying something to Gizelle, who he recognized through the front window. "Margaret's here, Sam", he said as he watched her back away, turn and look to the restaurant, as she closed the car door. She was dressed in slacks and a light blue blouse under a short tan jacket with her large brown carry-all hung over her left shoulder and her face covered with what looked like a fashion scarf of deep blue acting as a mask. Jamie waved at her through the window as she approached the restaurant and he smiled because he knew she did not usually frequent this type of place usually. Sam was looking out and he waved also and slid his chair back, gentleman that he was to get up for her. She came through the door and headed towards them as the folks in the restaurant stared at this obviously well-off white lady walking into this off the beaten track diner.

"Hey guys," she chirped as she came up to the table while taking off her scarf. She came over to Sam and gave him a big hug and then pushed back and said, "Looking good, old man. So great to see you in person after all those Zoomers." She came around to Jamie and gave him a hug. "You too, Jamie. So great to see you both," and she pulled out the chair that faced the window and sat down.

Sam sat back and said, "Well, I guess the meeting will now come to order," and he gave out one of his booming, hearty laughs, which caused them both to join in.

Jamie said, "Why don't you invite Gizelle in, Margaret?"

"Oh, she's got a beau in Gay Paree she wants to talk to, so she's fine," Margaret replied as she pulled out a chair and sat down. She looked at them and then around the diner then said, "Been looking forward to eating in this establishment ever since you told me about their black bean burger so that's why I was so excited my two cohorts were eating lunch here," she said looking towards the main counter and waving her hand. Loretta waved back and came over to the table.

She ordered and from that moment on they never stopped talking or laughing, but got serious a couple times, especially when Margaret told them about three new cities in the South that they were going to add. Their lunch came and they all ate as if it was their last meal. Then, as they finished up, Margaret tapped on the table and said, "If I may be so bold, as my dear Mother used to say, a board meeting is in order because I really have some new stuff that is incredible. Are you ready?"

Sam looked at Jamie and then at Margaret saying, "You got the floor or table, young lady".

Margaret's began, "Now you two, this may take a while, but listen up. Sam talked about the Federal Registry yesterday that I'm working on so I've got the update on all the current programs in the Federal, State and local governments to help all young children from low-income families or "no income" families, as I call some of these folks. We have to realize that we are trying to do something that is both unifying and disruptive in a Federal system. Unifying for what LIFELINE is attempting to do for all disadvantaged young people and yet facing the monstrosity, called our Federal government's bureaucracy. But I feel strongly that over the next months and years, we can put all children in one unified system and that Federal programs will also become unified. If it is too successful Sam, it will probably replace your years of work, but you will have achieved what you have always wanted, that is no child will be without assistance. So now, as to LIFELINE, in our time frame, now, listen to this. My Boston group has spent weeks going through all these various assistance programs that have funding and are supposed to support poverty-stricken families. There are a variety of them with millions of dollars dispensed through the various states by the Fed's. Some of these states, by the way, are absolutely despicable in how they treat families, especially black ones, even in this day. My staff became so confused by the various Congressional programs that are designed to help families that it took them as I said, weeks to create a one-page outline of them. Millions and millions of dollars allocated and processed through various programs called SSI, SNAP, WIC, and

TANF. Now we cross checked some our family's information in our database and some do get these benefits, but it is a mish mash. All of these programs and the costs associated with just processing them is astronomical. They need to be one, pardon my white lady trash talking mouth, fucking combined plan, which I, we, are going to make a priority. What you do Sam, or we do, is give a direct safety net to families, not only of food, but learning assistance, from birth to graduation and even beyond. Look at the thousands of laptops we provided these young kids who never had one before. The City here is providing some, but we are going to make sure all kids who need them, have them in this town and the others we're involved with. We have supplied some online teaching sites to help kid's use them and even for the mom's, so we are on top of this one. But we also must assess what each of our families is getting from government sources because if they are getting funding, we must know that and how much." Margaret paused looking at Sam then Jamie and said, "Okay, so far any questions or thoughts?"

Sam looked at Jamie, then back to Margaret and said, "No, I'm just a bit overwhelmed how you have really got into this maze which has driven me crazy over the years. No, nothing, just awe in how you have really got into this."

Jamie said, "I have read a bit about this and know that you have really nailed it, so no, just excited about what you're doing."

Margaret went on, "Okay, guy's, we are not going to change our programs, but we are going to work with members of Congress from both parties, who I have spent the last weeks talking with in person, mask and all, in trying to set up a way of coordinating all current government programs, Federal or state. We are also working to include our family assistance above and beyond basic living assistance, I'll call It," she paused and went on, "Next week I have organized a task force meeting in D.C. of friends of Warren who are either in Congress or work for the Feds, to work on coordinating current governmental programs that are to help poverty families, black, white, whatever. My goal, our goal, is that by next year, Congress, will begin to work on creating one Federal plan to cover all aspects of low income, poverty living families. Just throwing this out, but the name I came up with his is Family Care for this new program that should ideally be or should be, folded into a new Medicare/Medicaid combo, so that all support programs are under one program." She then took a deep breath as she looked exhausted, looked at the two of them, who were spellbound.

After a few seconds, Sam said, "Lady, where did you come from. You are worse than me," which then brought on one of his great smiles and uproarious laugh which caused Jamie and Margaret to join in.

"I am not done yet, oh Zen master. Now listen again because I have an answer to something you mentioned a week or so ago on a Zoom meeting in passing and I was impressed immediately, so I have been doing some research in D.C. with the help of our Boston staff."

Jamie asked, "On what?"

"Sam, you made a comment about how Native American kids are being treated in this virus world we live in, but more importantly, or actually to our basic mission, how are they being treated about eating, schooling, and life careers like we do with our African American kids."

Sam straightened up and said with his calm, serious voice, "What did you find out?"

"It's a disaster, gentlemen. The problem is that many leaders of Native Americans very often do not want interference from government unless they control how it is done. Fortunately, one of Warren's closest friends from Arizona is a Navajo and very close to several Nations. After many hours of talking, he found out there may be a way we would be acceptable to the tribes. I will know, maybe in the next couple of days. Anyway, I think we may get somewhere which would really expand our mission where it is needed from what I have found out."

Sam said, "Well done, darling. Wow that is a coup' if you pull that off."

Jamie added, "That would be super."

"Oh, and one more thing you are going big time. LIFELINE will have its Facebook, Twitter and I can't remember the other networks, up and running in the next week. So, the story and your communication with this world of 2020 is just about set."

Sam looked at Margaret and said, "You know young woman, I was just talking with my old buddy here about how critical our moment and I mean our moment is to this world of 2020 you just mentioned. We have got something here that is so important to this critical time in this moment of this country. I think that we are really on to something and so glad you and Jamie are with me because without you two I would be closed down probably with all the riots and virus stifling our country. I'm not now a praying man like my Momma taught me, but if I still was, I'd say my deep-down prayers have been answered by that energy force that is our Universe."

The three were quiet for a few seconds and then spent more time just talking about the times and upcoming work that needed to be done. Finally, Sam smiled and said "You know Margaret, if I was ten years younger," he paused, "I'd asked you if wanted to go dancing somewhere, slow music only, though."

The three laughed as if they were all teen-agers at a high school party until finally Margaret tapped her water glass and said, "Sam, that's about all I could do, the slower the better," which caused them another round of laughter.

Loretta the waitress was coming up to give them their bills when she came upon these three laughing like she hadn't seen for a while. "Wow, it's so good to see people laughing. Ain't seen as much laughter in this place since we opened, except when you're here Sam. Care to let me in on it?"

Sam slowed down, and said, "Loretta, this young lady here just proposed to me. Can you imagine such a high-class babe from back East taking a shot at an old black dude like me?"

Loretta didn't hesitate for a second and replied, "I sure can Sam, but if she don't make the cut, watch out for me," as she looked around at the three of them. This only brought more laughter and people at other tables and from the counter were looking at the three older folks all bent over in laughter with Loretta the waitress doing the same.

CHAPTER TWENTY-NINE

As they worked on their new associations with programs across the country, Sam was approached by a young girl who was a student at Pitt, Sarah Ryder with an idea for a new concept for LIFELINE. Sarah grew up in the Hill District, where she lived with her grandmother who was a friend of Sam's mother from high school. Sam asked her to come to his office and explain her idea to him. Sarah lowered her mask and went on to explain to Sam that she had read in high school about the coffee growers in Kenya and how their product was one of the best in the world. They farmed on their small acreage called estates growing coffee beans that were processed then sold usually to buyers at what's called "farmgates", who sell the final product, green coffee, in what's called the auction system. She read that Kenya coffee was extraordinary and wrote a letter to a man, Daniel Maathai, who apparently was instrumental in helping smaller estate farmers at the base of Mt. Kilimanjaro with growing techniques to improve the quality and amount of coffee beans available for sale. Two months later, she got a wonderful, handwritten letter from him, expressing great enthusiasm in her interest in the farmers and in the package that arrived, was a tightly wrapped bag of green coffee beans. He said he probably should not have done that, but he wanted her to see what the coffee looked and smelled like before it went to buyers for shipment to be made into the final product. Over the next months they had written back and forth and in one letter she said to him, why don't they communicate via email which they began to do. Daniel Maathi wrote of his family and wanted to know what Pittsburgh was like because all he knew about the city was it had a great American football team. In one of her emails, she mentioned how she volunteered at a local organization that helped young African Americans, which she explained was what their race was now called in the United States. Sarah received an email back asking her if she could ask her boss a question. The question was, did he think his young people would be able to process Kenya coffee beans for sale in Pittsburgh? She was astounded by the question and she replied she would go talk to Sam, the man who ran the operation, which was why she was sitting in front of Sam this day.

When Sarah explained to Sam what Daniel had proposed he was so excited that he called in Germaine and Marty in red masks to explain what the man had asked. They didn't stop talking as Sam just sat back and took in their enthusiasm. Sarah then brought out the bag of coffee beans that Daniel had sent her, which made Marty run into the kitchen. In a few seconds he came rushing back with an old coffee grinder someone had found in the debris when clearing out the old rooms in the building. He then took the beans and slowly work the grinder until the whole bag of beans was now a triangle of dark coffee sitting on Sam's desk. Each of them took turns sniffing the dark, but sweet-smelling grounds. Sam got up, his mask drooping on his chest and went over and took up the scooper from his coffee maker. He scooped up eight portions and dumped them into the coffee maker, poured water in and pushed the button. They all just stood there watching the coffee maker works it magic and when the red light came on, Sam looked at the pot of deep, black coffee and asked Marty to video the coffee and him pouring them all cups. It was like waiting for the winner of the Academy Awards for best picture as they all slowly sipped the coffee and then slowly, all that could be heard were "ahh's".

Sam took another sip and turned to Sarah and asked her to email Daniel to see if he had access to Zoom. If not, then could they talk sometime today. Sarah sat down at the front of Sam's desk and tapped out a text on her phone. As she finished, she said to them that there is an 8-hour time difference between Pittsburgh and Kenya, so he might not be available, but that the message was sent. As they finished their coffee, her iPhone buzzed, and she read the text. She A smile came to her face and she said, "He can Zoom in a half hour and he will text me back a code number."

"Make some more Sam, we may need it," chortled Germaine.

Sam laughed as he rescoped portions of the coffee and put it in the maker. They drank the coffee until Sam's PC tinged that a message had come in and Germaine went over to the keyboard, tapping in a message. In a few seconds a picture came up and she tapped in a number which brought in a clear picture of a light brown skinned man, probably in his early twenties staring into the picture.

"Hi, there, Pittsburgh, this is Emmanuel, Daniel's son. My Dad is right behind me and will be sitting here as I move away. We can see you all perfectly."

"I'm Daniel, young lady. Thank you for setting this up and hopefully setting up an in-person meeting with us,' as he paused, adding "Is Mister Sam available?"

"Right here," Sam replied as he sat down in front of the screen and waved at the younger man who had a wide smile with perfect white teeth beaming into the screen.

They talked for close to an hour and by the time they signed off, they had agreed to an exclusive arrangement with the company that handled the purchasing of coffee from farmers that Daniel represented at the auction. They would supply their coffee to Sam directly to increase their net income and would be paid at purchase time with verification of quality by a representative working on Sam's behalf. It would be profitable for the farmer and the coffee would be shipped directly to Sam in Pittsburgh, all being handled by a mid-representative, chosen by Daniel and the farmers and approved by Sam. It would be coffee beans, not generally available directly in the Pittsburgh and most American markets, so that if it works well, Sam could provide coffee for the other programs in other locales. As the conversation ended, Sam and Daniel agreed that they would have to make sure what they were doing was approved by both of their governments. When the meeting ended and the screen emptied, Sam was so excited, and he called Jamie and Margaret. Jamie said he would be glad to coordinate the purchasing as he had spent time in Ghana, advising on one project, just ten years ago and Margaret vowed to help with the governmental data that would be necessary between the two countries.

While they were talking Sam interrupted their three-way conversation by saying to them, "I can't believe what I just remembered. Recently an old friend, Wilson Howard, mentioned to me that there once was a coffee grinder business in Homewood back around the turn of the century which lasted until the depression when it went out of business. Wilson told me it had been a storeroom; a storage facility for a hauling company; and for the last thirty years had been an empty and deteriorating brick building. Within the last months, I thought about converting the old building into a warehouse for all the products we were purchasing but decided not to do anything." He paused and added, "Actually, it was you, Margaret, that said we should put the brakes on any more property until we had a better handle on all that we had added."

Margaret excitedly said, "I remember Sam, but this is incredible that this opportunity has smacked us right in our collective faces. Jesus, Sam, I think we're in the coffee business now and I think we better go look at that old building and see what might be still stored away inside it. Who knows?"

Jamie added, "This really is something unique. We could help those farmers while we help our kids and even the older ones."

Sam listened and said, "Your so right, Jamie. As important as this may be for our children, this could be a good thing, no I know it will be a good thing for those poor farmers in Kenya. Based on what Daniel was telling us, most of the coffee is raised by poor farmers, so we must first help them as best we can by paying more for their coffee, somehow," he paused and then said, "We can't go around the system which apparently is a good one, but we also must find a way to get these folks more than they get now."

Jamie piped up, "Right on, Sam and I'm going to do my best to find some intermediaries in the coffee purchasing system to find a way to do that."

It was quiet for and then Margaret spoke up and said, "I'll work on my government sources to see what they know and if they can help us. One thing though, as you two were talking, I checked out the Kenya coffee system and it is one of the best, but as you said, Sam, the majority of their farmers are small and poor. We must wiggle our way into their system to see how we can help them and create a business venture for our young folks here. As you said before, we can help poor folks in both countries."

They worked trying to set up the coffee program and finally Sam organize a meeting to try and finalize all the details that needed to be done in order for the program to be able to go forward. For days they worked on setting up a coffee network. Margaret had come to Pittsburgh and her prime responsibility was to contact people in D.C.

while Jamie worked on transportation of products. The group was congregated in the main office area when Sam said, "I just thought of something. We need another name. This time for the coffee."

Jamie spoke up, "Kenya Homewood. KenWood…KenHome…. Sam'sJava…..for openers. We have to come up with a name that honors both of us. Kenya coffee farmers and Sam's LIFELINE."

They spent some time going back and forth between them trying to come up with a name that would honor the Kenyan farmers and Sam's LIFELINE. Finally, Germaine yelled out loud "BLACK MAGIC", how's that grab you all".

It was quiet then Sam said, "Man, I like that. It is magic that we are coming together with our brothers and sisters from our homeland and man, it is magic."

Sam asked Germaine to see if she could reconnect a "Zoom" meeting with Daniel and see if he agrees with our name. It took a while but as the day was getting into night and was early in the morning in Kenya, somehow, Daniel came up on the screen.

"Mister Daniel, we were wondering if you would okay us calling our coffee here, "Black Magic?" Sam asked.

There was a pause as they could see that Daniel was thinking about what Sam had said. Then came a smile as he looked into the screen and said, "That is perfect because what we are trying to do for our farmers is just that, magic and we folks over here believe in magic in many ways. Our working with you folks over there is magic and me looking at you in this screen is magic. Our brew is black, and the taste is magic, so Sam, if I may call you Sam, that name is magic. Black Magic it is."

Sam's office was filled with elation with high fives going over the room. Sam then talked a bit with Daniel, and they set up a Zoom meeting next week to confirm the delivery process that would take place over the coming weeks. Sam was overwhelmed for now they had provided direct help for youngsters and their families, but they could now branch out by providing jobs with the coffee business both in Pittsburgh and in their new associates, especially in one of the most difficult times in American history. LIFELINE was quite an accomplishment for the aged Marine veteran.

CHAPTER THIRTY

The United States and the world were literally in limbo as a result of the worst virus epidemic since 1919, yet Sam, Jamie, and Margaret had created a thriving non-profit organization in the historically difficult year of 2020. It became a direct and efficient organization in bringing support initially to young black children and mothers, and then to poor children and family members of all races. They were now providing jobs through the "Black Magic" coffee business that had exploded to all of their subsidiaries around the country. Over a hundred women, primarily, were working in another building, designed and renovated by Jamie, that packaged and shipped the Kenya coffee. It had become a real asset to LIFELINE and to the Kenyan coffee farmers who were making more money from their coffee beans sent to LIFELINE, than they ever had before.

Jamie could not actually believe what had happened to him. Sam was on news shows; the President of the United States had met with Margaret about Sam's program and she had donated millions of dollars for Sam's program. She also was instrumental in working to initiate Congress to unify Federal assistance programs for poor children. Jamie had rebuilt buildings in the middle of one of the poorest areas in Pittsburgh, Sam's home as a kid and now refurbished for his business. Sam, himself, was absolutely living in a dreamworld. His idea of forty years ago was blossoming into a national system. Besides the success of Black Magic, LIFELINE was now supplying work, food, and access to health care and schooling for not only children but their parents in sites across the country. In some areas of the deep South, LIFELINE, was now providing these benefits to poor white children and single mothers. Sam was ecstatic about working with Billy and Black Lives Matters in pushing for States to upgrade their computer systems that would track down fathers of any race to support children they fathered. It was controversial but support for the program from the black communities had been overwhelming, but the surprising thing to Sam was the support from the white suburban communities.

Late one afternoon, after a lunch behind the center, Sam, Jamie and Margaret were having drinks sitting on a patio under an ancient oak tree that had survived the years in Homewood and was now an umbrella over the brick patio. It was a warm for this time of year, but under the oak it was shady and quiet. They were sitting around a round, wooden table, enjoying the end of another profound day. Germaine had just given an email to Sam that he read from their Boston group that LIFELINE was going international after an organization in Manchester, England contacted the website wanting to join their network. Margaret was ecstatic as she said that their website was drawing interest from all over the world and was thrilled that they wanted to join. They tapped their glasses in honor of their first international contact.

For the first time in the day all three were became quiet, as if each was enjoying the solitude in the outside respite which was a rarity in their non-stop, hectic days. Ironically, each of them loathed noise and non-stop people stuff. Jamie loved his walks; Margaret loved her boat; and Sam just loved to sit with a beer and think, by himself, which they all did whenever they had the opportunity in their individual lairs, whether it be the East End of Pittsburgh, Cape Cod or Homewood. Now they sat like folks after a hurricane when the winds have stopped, and only quiet breezes blew through the hanging branches. Well, as they sat quietly, together on this late afternoon, the wind was slightly moving the hanging branches of the oak and several different birds, robins and red birds were chirping from high in the laden branches.

"Man, this is paradise," Sam said in his low, bass voice.

Margaret responded, "I never would have believed it if anyone said to me in Acapulco on the beach that if I chose to relax in one place in this world it wouldn't be there but under an oak tree in Homewood, Pittsburgh, Pa. They, of course, whoever the "they" were, would look befuddled and say to me, 'Where is this Homewood resort? Is it on a beach; is it a ski resort; or is it a new place we'll be in next year?' I would tell them it hasn't been discovered yet, but when it's ready, I'll let you know."

Sam laughed and said, "Lady Margaret, you are a real gasser. You crack me up and your sense of humor is so subtle, which I never realized you had until we started working close together," he paused, "course I didn't really know anything about you or even my old buddy sitting over there, the Anglo-Saxon good boy, Jamie Sloan, until we worked side by side over this past year. But I do now, both of you."

Jamie laughed, took a sip of his beer and said, "I've just been thinking about where in the hell we go from here. I think the complex, as I have labeled it, is done, except a bit of finishing on our communications center."

Sam smiled and said, "Well, as I have preached to you Jamie, what we have done together has been destined by our relationship, by our universal bond, if I may call it that. There is a cosmic bond that brings ideas and people together or people together to bond ideas into a solution to a problem. Make any sense, old boy?"

"Old girl, me, yes, it does," Margaret interjected. "I know and feel exactly what you just said, Sam. I felt that bond, as you call it, the first time we talked and felt a bit of that with Jamie when we worked on our house at Fallingwater and more so when we clarified something in the past about Warren. It's something in this day and age when social media dictates relationships, to look someone in the eyes and know them, believe them and above all trust them. Guys, I trust you so much and for a woman, believe me, that is rare and unusual," as she paused looked away from them and then looked back and said, "There just was something," she paused, "okay, binding us, as if I had been waiting for you two to walk through my door. When you Jamie told me about Sam, for some reason I still can't figure out, I felt that he was something special," as she paused, "unless it was his Universal bond already working," she said with a smile. "Then when we talked or he did, I knew we had a relationship that was meant to be. And wow, look what we three have done and all those great young folks back there," she said waving back towards the central complex. She smiled and added, "And I know Warren is smiling down and saying, "Great job, girl, great job", which caused her to slowly wipe a tear off her cheek.

Jamie smiled, adding, "I know he is, Margaret. I'm sure what we have done is a fulfillment in life we never imagined we could do and wow, have we done it."

"Fulfillment is the word, Jamie," Sam responded. "I have looked at you two separately and together and each time after the day was over, I would be sitting in my chair alone thinking about why you two came into my life. With Jamie, you came back to me and with you, Margaret, it was, literally from out of nowhere But when you walked in that door, that day, I immediately knew, I knew you, Margaret," as he paused then added, "and Jamie knows where I'm going with this, but I knew you were meant to walk through my door." He paused, looked out the new wide windows on the wall that one could look up into the sky, which he did, then looked back at them and said, "That power from up there in that Universe brought you, Jamie back to me and Margaret to me. No fucking doubt about it."

It was a peaceful sight to see these three simply relaxing and enjoying their accomplishment, but more importantly, they could see how America had taken to what they were achieving. Sam's vision, his tenacity over forty years of struggle seemed to catch the imagination of all America, which was in dire need for something positive about what it stood for as a country in the early years of the Twenty-First Century. Of course, Sam would say with his last breath, that we have no idea what century we are in; we are just in these years of humanity's growth on this Earth in this tiny speck of materials that spin within a tiny spot in the Universe. But yet, he would also say, it is the most precious and important time for himself and his work mates and more importantly, for the youngsters, mothers and fathers, who will have a chance to be fulfilled as human beings in the coming times of this Earth in this Universe.

The sun rays poured down on them, deflected by the leaves of the old oaks. For the first time in days, weeks or months, they could actually relax knowing they had really created something important to so many needy people. The week was ending, but tomorrow would be quite a fulfilling day as Sam was headed to Harrisburg, with Billy, Germaine and Marty to meet the Governor of Pennsylvania; Margaret would be flying to Wellfleet; and Jamie was headed to the Laurel Highlands for a weekend in the woods.

CHAPTER THIRTY-ONE

It was into early winter of this incredible year. Margaret was home in Wellfleet and Sam was in Harrisburg with Marty, Germaine and Billy Thompson, plus the X man to handle any financial questions, if they came up. Sam was getting an award from Governor Wolfe for his outstanding work with young African American children and Billy for his work with Black Lives Matter, plus with Sam. Sam wanted Margaret and Jamie to go with him, but they said that no one else deserves this honor, just him. They were adamant and Sam accepted their decisions. As for Jamie, he was southeast of Pittsburgh, in a cabin deep in the Laurel Mountains south of Ligonier. One of the doctors he was close to at the transplant service had told him numerous times he could use it. After checking it was available, he drove deep in the woods to the cabin which was by a roaring creek. There was some remaining snow from a storm days before, but when he got out of his car all he could hear were birds chirping and the creek roaring. It was a place of solitude, which for some reason Jamie felt he really wanted to experience. As he stood in the silence with the remaining birds chirping away and water racing, he thought that his peaceful mind of this moment had come from his indoctrination into Sam's world.

After getting the cabin set up, he went outside with a cup of coffee and found a tree stump and sat down. He sat looking out at nothing but thick woods in an absolutely peaceful setting until his phone pinged. He checked the text message. It was from Cousin Hugh asking how he was and then asking if they could work on a Sloan reunion the fall of 2021 because of this horrific year the world was going through. He believed by next fall things would be back to normal and he would do all he could to help with rounding up as many Sloan's as he could. Jamie replied, tapping out where he was and how great it was to get his message. As he put the phone away an idea hit him. He was going to invite all of Sam's army and Margaret and any of her Boston people to join the Sloan soiree. It would be a magnificent celebration especially if Sam's kids and families could join them. It would have to be held in someplace incredible and maybe right here in the Laurel Highlands, say at Ohiopyle by the river. There were many large, rustic facilities not far from where Jamie was sitting, and he decided to make a tour tomorrow and see if he could find a place to nail down. The Sloan reunion would become a Sam and Sloan event, which made Jamie smile in anticipation. It would be the culmination of pulling together all the facets of his life which had brought incredible fulfillment in these elder years. A smile came to his face as Louise's face came into his mind; he knew she would be so happy for him with what was happening with his life.

Over the next days, Jamie drove around and found a large site alongside the roaring creek that flowed through Ohiopyle, that would be able to handle a large group with picnic tables. Accommodations were nearby for those staying overnight, which he expected many would. He stayed in his secluded cabin for three more days with another brief snowfall that made the trees and vista absolutely beautiful. Jamie even threw snowballs at a pine tree. As he was packing up to leave, he texted Hugh about his idea about having the Sloan reunion at Ohiopyle, inviting his friends from where he was working, LIFELINE and the place he had found along the Lower Youghiogheny River. All packed up, as he drove down the narrow path through the woods his phone pinged, and he stopped. Hugh replied in two words, "Right on". As he left the woods and headed back to Pittsburgh he vowed to come back as often as he could for some peace filled moments.

Jamie turned on the TV when he was back in his apartment as he put his clothes in the washing machine and straightened up his rooms, as he had left in a hurry. The local news channel had headlines of a new outbreak of the virus in the County and that new restrictions may be coming but for now the recent 25% restaurant quota and partial bar sitting would remain. The major headline featured Sam's meeting later that day with the governor. He saved the broadcast so he could watch it later. It took him some time to get settled before he decided to sit down with a yellow pad to plan his next days.

Jamie realized the first and most important thing he had to do was to find out how his sister Becky was doing. He then wanted to check up on Sarah and Rachel and then with the library and the transplant office to whether or not they would begin again. As he sat there, he had an urge for a cold, dark draft at the pub which should have reopened with social distancing which in that place brought a smile to his face. He also thought of his recently rediscovered manuscript he had begun and thought maybe he should start working on it again. He sure had a lot to add to it what with had happened in this crazy year of 2020. He took a big sigh of relief as he realized how relaxed he felt after all he had gone through during this time which for some reason, got him thinking about age and was he okay? His last check-up went well, and he felt strong even going non-stop for the past year. He had to admit that the pressure of the last months had gotten to him a bit as he was tired earlier in the day. He knew that he was trying to go full steam ahead in helping Sam and Margaret as if he was thirty. 'Give me a break,' he thought and smiled, but realized that this weekend alone was just what he needed

As Jamie thought of other things he should do or plan for in the coming days, he decided to have that checkup he'd promised Doctor Winthrop. He went to his computer and set up an appointment. This was a good time to get all this done because the way it looked, work at LIFELINE would continue as they expanded their services. Margaret had asked him if he would do a survey of all the facilities, they were now associated with around the country to make sure they had the logistical help they needed. Many of the employees worked from home in this day and age at all the locations, except in Homewood, where their office setup had worked fine with no corona cases during the year which was incredible. But with the new coffee business expanding they needed more physical space for storing and processing the beans sent from Kenya. Other than these responsibilities, it seemed it was the first time that Jamie had nothing to do for Sam or Margaret and the afternoon was open. He had felt so alive and important doing creative and important work to help Sam create his dream, which had become a national treasure. It was as if Sam's favorite power, the Universe, was looking down from its virtual power station billions of miles away and letting these upstart humans on Earth know who or what is really in charge.

Jamie took a shower, dressed in some old khakis with a blue jersey and his walking shoes. It was hot for a late fall afternoon, so he decided to walk on the shady side of most of the streets he would need to get to McDonoughs, assuming it was open. As Jamie walked, he was deep in thought as he stepped briskly along the irregular segmented sidewalks which he looked at closely, so he didn't trip. His pace was strong, and he felt physically vibrant. The streets were quiet in late afternoon. Cars were parked bumper to bumper along the sidewalks as most people were in their apartments or homes, filling time for whatever they could find to keep from going crazy from the stalemate from the virus. His phone buzzed, and he noted it came from Sam who left a message that they had arrived in Harrisburg and were getting ready to go to the Governor's event. Jamie replied, "have a great time and moment" message, closed his phone, as he saw the sign up ahead for the McDonough's.

Jamie pulled opened the door and walk in not what to expect but he saw what he usually saw at McDonoughs. Tommy and Jerome, with blue face masks, sitting two stools apart in the otherwise empty bar with a few people at a table in the dining area. Tommy was leaning over, trying to say something to Jerome, when he spotted Jamie at the door. As Jamie walked towards him, he saw Rachel at a tap filling a pint glass while trying to adjust her pink mask with her free hand. She didn't see Jamie at first, but then turned towards him and waved with her free hand as the pint's head rose above the top. Jamie walked towards her and said, "Hey, Rachel, nice to see you and what you're doing to that pint."

Rachel looked at him and said "Just thinking about you, Jamie. I was talking to my Dad on the phone, and he asked about you," as she closed the tap.

"That is terrific. So glad you are in contact with him."

"That's because of you, you do realize that don't you?" she paused, then added, "The usual?"

"Well thanks, I'm so happy for you and yes, the usual and those two dudes down there could use another one, I'm sure."

"Will do. By the way, not sure what's going to happen with the bar because there's been a been a big change in cases, so the County may go back to the way it was when this all started with no more drinks at the bar. If they go through with it, we can only have 25% for meals and no bar business, which means we really can't be open, so I don't know how long the boss can hang in there?"

Jamie pulled back a stool with a wooden back and sat down as Rachel was at the tap pouring his beer. He looked down at Tommy and said, "Well, guys, guess this may be the last round up?"

Tommy who was two chairs away, leaned toward Jamie and said, "This is fucking ridiculous, old buddy. Christ, all them kids crowd into bars all over the South Side and we have to pay for it."

"You're probably right. You know kids that age can be one dimensional. Party time is the only time when you're that age, I guess", Jamie replied.

"Yeh, well, how you doing? Seen you and old Sam on the tube, in fact he's supposed to be on the news from Harrisburg with the governor today. He's big time, now, eh?"

"Yeh, I'm waiting for that. So excited for him," Jamie paused, "you sound like a Canadian, Tommy with that "eh"?"

Tommy laughs and replies, "Hell no, I always say that."

"Well, Rachel says the Pub's may close again. Where you two going to drink?"

"Jerome has an old bar in his basement his dad put in fifty years ago. We go there and watch old games on the tube like all of the Super Bowl games going back. Seen all the Steelers Super Bowl wins four times already. Ah, those were the fucking days, Jamie."

"They were, they were, but now these are the fucking days, as you say. We got to do the best we can with what we got, eh?"

Tommy laughed, "Eh, are you a Canuck?"

All three laughed and as they all took sips of their beers and then Tommy yelled, "Hey Jamie, there's Sam and that kid running Black Lives up on the TV," Tommy yelled down the bar.

Jamie looked up at the screen as Governor Wolfe with a mask, was patting Sam on the back, his mask almost coming loose, with Jimmy, black mask, standing beside him. Sam was dressed in a tan sport coat, blue open necked shirt, no tie and a page in one hand. The timing was perfect because Sam was just introduced. Jamie looked at

Sam as he began to speak with his mask lowered, "It is an incredible time for this old black man to be with this young black man on one side of me and with the white Governor of this great State of Pennsylvania on the other. especially in this terrible time of corona virus and social black and white turbulence in our State and our Country. You know I fought for this country and would do it again if called upon, but in a way, I, this black man, am every day fighting for this country with the help of two of my closest friends, both white folks. They are not here by my side, but I want you all to know of Mrs. Margaret Decker, wife of deceased Senator Warren Decker, and my old friend of forty years, Mr. Jamie Sloan. You see, we are all Americans and America, for all its faults going back centuries in how my people have been treated, I know is a place where the vast majority of whites accept us as their equals, as we certainly are," then he paused, looked over at Jimmy and then turned to the Governor, then back and looking right at the TV said clearly, "there is no society on earth that does not have inequality, but this country is in perpetual transition to bring us all together. We all are different. There is not one person, white or black, who are exactly like another. So, let's accept our differences of color, but also are similarities in wanting opportunities in life for everyone. That's all that is necessary in life and we at LIFELINE, black and white, are committed to supporting all young children and young mothers of any race or nationality to have that chance for a fulfilling life. A chance is not too much to give anyone and everyone. What we are striving for is to level the playing field of life; giving every child a chance in life; and to eliminate inequality for all people; inequality must be eliminated." He stopped, looked at the Governor, who gave him a thumbs up.

The screen then showed Sam, Governor Wolfe, and Billy in a triangle, each with different colored masks as the music played God Bless America. Jamie saw tears dripping from the dark eyes of Samuel Wescott, in Jamie's mind, one of America's great patriots. He noticed behind the Governor, a face which caused him immediately to break out laughing. It was the X Man, with his wide, white teeth blaring out, looking as if he was coming out of the screen. He couldn't believe it, but of course he did, because only the X Man could pull this off. As he kept looking at this incredible picture on the screen, the X Man kept staring and waving. Jamie yelled at Rachel who was staring at the screen, "Rachel, can you take a picture of that screen with your iPhone?"

Rachel turned to Jamie and grabbed her phone off the back counter, looked up at the screen and snapped several shots. "Got it Jamie."

"Can you send it to this number," he said writing down Margaret's cell phone number on a page from his notebook.

Rachel came up and took the page. She tapped in her phone again and then looked back at Jamie, "It's on its way, Jamie."

"Thanks so much," he said turning to look back at the screen as the Governor was now talking about what Sam had accomplished

Jamie's eyes turned back down the bar to Tommy and Jerome, his two old Irish compatriots with whom he had vented his anger over comments they had made about Sam. They looked like bandits in an old movie with their masks on, but right now, they were clapping as they looked up at the TV screen. Rachel was also clapping at the screen as Jamie looked up at the remarkable scene on the TV. As he watched, he felt like he was seeing a site for all Americans, especially after the year the country had gone through. No matter our heritage or age, we must all come together as we end this incredibly difficult, yet hopefully, healing year, he thought. As he turned back to the bar he smiled, remembering something verbatim that Sam had said to him the other day, "Jamie, old man, what we have created is that ultimate moment I was preaching about the other day, but what makes this even more important, it's the moment in this Universe for my kids, all of them. It's their moment, Jamie, their moment to live in this Universe."

Jamie smiled and looked back up at the TV screen with Sam raising his fist in victory and behind him the X Man was doing the same thing. It was a sight he would never forget.

THE END

www.ingramcontent.com/pod-product-compliance
Lightning Source LLC
Chambersburg PA
CBHW020630110726
47899CB00002B/726